A Hard Yes

Elena—
I hope you
enjoy my Rohans
enjoy love story.
Sinclair

A Hard Yes

A Misguided Masala Matchmaker Romance

Sinclair Jayne Sawhney

TULE
PUBLISHING

Dedication

There are so many people I want to thank for encouraging me to write my latest series, Misguided Masala Matchmaker, especially friend, writer and Tule Publisher Jane Porter, who has always been a supportive cheerleader and not afraid to dish out a large bowl of tough love. I also want to high-five Lee Hyat, a friend and Tule cover designer and art director, who read the story for cultural sensitivity. And no, I have not forgotten my editor, Kelly Hunter, who shocked me by enthusiastically loving the story as I had no idea if I'd hit my target or not. The story and Kapoor family are so close to my heart, and as I wrote, the stakes felt impossibly high. I've never written anything so personal as *A Hard Yes*.

But this first book—*A Hard Yes* is dedicated to my husband of twenty-five years, Deepak Sawhney, who was the inspiration for Rohan. There are a few shout outs to our love story although I was never as cool or talented as Solei, but if I'm going to write a fantasy, I want it to definitely be a fantasy.

I also want to dedicate this story to my mother-in-law, Swadesh Sawhney, who taught me so much about Indian culture, traditions and cooking and was always, always so very welcoming. She passed this year, which is a tremendous loss to us and our extended family and to so many in the

Charlotte community. She was fun, giving, and loved, loved, loved parties. Smile and dance on, Mummy.

Sinclair Jayne Sawhney

Prologue

ROHAN KAPOOR—MAKE THAT Doctor Rohan Kapoor if his mom were making the introduction—slid out of his Audi S4 and palmed the keys. A piercing wail rent the orange-purple sunset as if someone in the house had vigiled and prayed over the dying and now had the task to prepare the dead for their last trip to the Gurdwara. He hadn't even entered his aunt and uncle's house yet, but he was seriously tempted to get behind the wheel and pedal to the metal it back home to Durham on I85.

Rohan didn't do drama, and it felt like he was about to walk on stage.

Somewhere south of Greensboro, his phone had started blowing up about his cousin Asha's groom walking out two days before the elaborate three-day wedding event kicked off. He'd shut his phone off, wrestling with his desire to turn around and avoid the coming storm. Only his love and loyalty for his jilted cousin Asha had kept him on the road. Although it was likely he'd also been indulging in what his youngest cousin and best friend Rani would call magical thinking, he'd hoped that somehow during the two-plus hour drive from Durham to Charlotte, the crisis would be, if not averted, at least mitigated.

Clearly not.

Another drawn-out wail. Rohan winced. It was a canceled wedding, an inconvenience, a disappointment, not a death. But likely a shock. His aunt Anju was an event planner. She was legend in the southeast and not just for Indian weddings and the festival of India. No. She'd helped plan events at the state level in Raleigh. And hundreds of corporate events. The fact that her own daughter's wedding—finally—wouldn't come off exactly as planned was probably creating cognitive dissonance that would morph into rage and heartache over the next few days, and he hated that he had to be anywhere near when that volcano blew.

The first Kapoor wedding of this generation that had been hastily and yet precisely planned down to how many candied almonds would go in the red net bags. Twenty-six almonds in four hundred seventy-five bags. He knew because Rani had shown up unexpectedly last weekend at his apartment to beg his help in filling and tying them. He'd had to change shifts, give up premium tickets to a Charlotte Hornet's game, buy a gift certificate to a new restaurant in Durham's American Tobacco Historic District and promise to cover an extra weekend shift with two other six-year cardiothoracic residents to get a half a week off for Asha's wedding.

And now he wished he hadn't been such a skilled wheeler-dealer.

But family was family, even when they were inconvenient.

He sucked in a deep breath and walked up the stone steps to the massive wraparound deck of the front porch. He tucked his sunglasses in his pale yellow blazer that was a sample from a designer friend and warily eyed the hand carved double doors that his aunt had had imported from India when she'd designed this castle-size new home on Lake Norman outside Charlotte. His parents' equally massive and impressive house sprawled three floors and eleven thousand square feet and was only somewhat screened by the landscaping next door.

Another bloody sounding wail. His brows drew down. This was excessive. It wasn't even Asha venting her feelings. He'd comforted family members he'd had to give the worst news to at Duke Medical Center who'd shown more emotional restraint.

Ah hell, hard no.

This was stupid. He'd be useless here.

But if there was anything he could do to help Asha or any of his cousins in this moment of crisis short of hiring a hit squad, he'd do it. He heard something shatter and then the explosive rat-tat-tat that sounded like BBs ricocheting but was probably just Louboutin's running across a marble floor.

Sucking in a deep breath of warm, florally fragrant mid-March air, Rohan pushed open the front door feeling like someone should shout out "dead man walking."

Chapter One

"HAVE YOU EATEN?" His mother greeted him in the elegant gold and white massive two-story entryway and pulled him into a tight hug.

It was a little over a two-hour drive from Durham. Hardly required sustenance. Plus, he'd been eating lightly for the past two weeks anticipating the food fest his cousin's wedding promised.

"I'm fine," he said. He always said he was fine, but he'd never been able to avoid a meal when he arrived home.

"You need to eat."

"Later," he said. "How's Asha?"

"Asha as always keeps her own counsel," his mom sighed. "It was not a love match, but still Guneet was a solid choice." His mom's tone was already in Monday morning quarterback mode. "He came from a good family in Atlanta. He was willing to relocate and start his career as an anesthesiologist in Charlotte. Your father had paved the way for him at his hospital to join the anesthesia group." His mom airily waved her hand in a "what can you do" manner, and Rohan's stomach churned, acid rising. "Now, who knows? Ungrateful, stupid man. He didn't even attend an elite medical school. Poor Asha practically scraping the barrel. What prospects will she have now? She's thirty-six."

His mother had been singing Guneet's praises along with her sister-in-law only a couple of months ago when the match was finally agreed upon. But now, the man who'd been about to become family in a few days was stupid and ungrateful and about to have a job offer rescinded. And her eldest niece had been consigned to the dumpster of unmarriageable with one unforeseen act over which she'd had no control.

Rohan could barely swallow the acid that burned at the back of his throat. This always happened when he came home, but he'd forgotten to take a Nexium in anticipation for today, and he couldn't ask him mom for a Tums or anything because the brain-picking one hundred and one questions would begin.

"I thought you liked Guneet." He couldn't help poking his mom a little.

She waved Guneet away, her gold bangles making a musical sound.

"Asha is thirty-six; what could she do?"

The casual dismissal had him balling his fists.

"A hell of a lot better than a man who dumped her days before her wedding," Rohan said, barely swallowing his next thought before he said it. Asha deserved a devoted groom and an aunt who would comfort her, not roll her eyes at her pain, disappointment and humiliation or casually dismiss all that Asha brought to marriage—her sweetness and light, Ivy League education, accomplishments, kindness, family dedication, reputation as a top OB in high-risk pregnancies with a wave of her hand while reducing her to one fact. Asha was too far over the line of thirty.

Had Asha felt like she'd settled, or had she harbored feelings for Guneet? He didn't know shit about her dating life.

Your family doesn't know about yours.

Not that what he did what would be considered dating, exactly. Swiping right when he was in the mood for a casual hookup would leave his family—jaws hanging to the floor—aghast. But while he'd had far too many opportunities to count, he hadn't had a lot of choices because he had a hard rule. Hard no on dating classmates or fellow residents. You couldn't avoid someone after things inevitably went south when you had to round with them each morning, look at them over a patient in the OR during the day or night or sit beside them during the case autopsies every Monday.

"That seems harsh, Mom," Rohan said, again bottling up the rest of his words. He'd never publicly argued with his parents or overtly pushed back on anything. "Asha is kindness personified. She's beautiful, intelligent…"

"Of course, of course, beta," his mom called him "son" far more than she'd ever used his name, and somehow it always made him feel shoved back into his childhood. "Of course." His mom patted his cheek. "But Asha should have snagged her husband after medical school or residency. Definitely before her fellowship. Too dreamy, that one."

He didn't think of Asha as dreamy, but when was the last time they'd had a heart-to-heart? She was more than four years older than him. She'd always been in charge, guiding, inspiring, helping them all.

"I didn't," he said, pissed at the double standard.

Wrong thing to say. The speculative appraisal his mother gave him chilled his bones.

"I know," she said softly.

"I'm going to check on Asha," he said quickly, but his mother took his hand.

"You are such a good son," she said. "Your time will come."

Exactly what he was afraid of. Damn, he should have jumped back in his car and gunned it out of Charlotte. Well, maybe he should have texted Asha to see if she wanted to bust out with him. Rani would be game. Five days off. Road trip. The idea beckoned, tempting. He hadn't had more than an occasional weekend off in nearly six years.

"You should do something for Anju Auntie," his mother spoke in a soft voice as she walked him to the kitchen. As expected, several Le Creuset pots—blue, yellow and red—bubbled on the stove, emitting enticing flavors, and despite his protestations that he wasn't hungry, Rohan's stomach growled.

"Like what?" Relief coursed through him now that his

mother was not currently eyeing him like marriage market meat. "Mummyji," he greeted his grandmother who smiled at him. He dutifully took her hands and bowed his head. She waved her hand over him, murmured a blessing, and he stayed crouching a little so she could kiss his cheek. She then patted both his cheeks like he was still seven and smiled and told him in Punjabi to sit. She would bring him food. She was in the middle of rolling out chapatis with his mom's mother. "Nanima," he said, also taking her hands and bowing his head.

She complained he was too skinny. She would have done that if he didn't run most mornings and hit the gym with his trainer several nights a week. If he came home more, he would likely be too fat. There was no middle ground. Again, she urged him to sit, telling him in Hindi that the food was nearly ready. Clearly, he was expected to eat, not comfort Asha.

"I will, I will," he promised. "I'll eat with everyone."

Not like he had a choice.

But he'd enjoy the meal. He loved his Mummyji and Nanima's cooking. For his entire life, Mummyji had lived with him or his cousins, taking care of them all while his dad, uncle, mom and aunt had built successful careers. He loved them for their care and unconditional love, but they both made it so damn hard to stop eating even when he was full.

"I'm going to see everyone." He pressed his palms together, the silent namaste and a promise he'd be back to eat soon.

Of course his mom blocked him from leaving the kitchen.

"You will help her, won't you?" His mom's voice edged with demand, now that she'd lost his full attention.

"Asha? Of course." But what could he do? Rani, who was writing her dissertation in clinical psychology—last he checked—would be better at soothing any heartbreak than he was.

"No. Anju Auntie, you know just a little…" She mimed giving a shot.

"You want me to drug her?" he asked in disbelief.

"Shshshsh." His mom's beautiful eyes widened innocently.

"You want me to drug Auntie?" he repeated. His mom had made some pretty intense and out-there demands during his thirty-two years. And she thought he was essentially responsible for her personal sun and moon rotation—no pressure there. But this? All kinds of wrong. All sorts of breeched barriers.

Hard no.

"Just a little something." His mom rubbed his arm soothingly, while his nanima returned to the chapatis, chattering away in Punjabi to Mummyji and pretending that they didn't speak or understand English so that he and his mom could pretend that they had privacy. The determined whir of the exhaust fan didn't do much to cut the fragrance of the roasted cumin and cardamon overlaying the scents of the daal, sabazi, and butter chicken—his favorite, that he usually tried to resist.

"Anju Auntie is not a zoo animal I can tranq so that I can clean her teeth," he said firmly because his mom would push. And push. And keep pushing.

"Just a little pop of something to calm her down."

"Like what? No. Forget I asked that. I don't even want to know. I have a little over two months more of my training at Duke, and I'm not pissing it all away prescribing something for a family member. Besides, you're a doctor. You can prescribe something if you want."

"I am a dermatologist," his mother said with dignity. "And your language, Rohan could use some elevation. I am your mother."

Like he could forget.

"All I'm asking my only child, my precious, accomplished, loving son for is a little something for my cherished sister-in-law to take the edge off so I can talk to her more reasonably. There are plans we must make. We need a message. Anju needs to calm a little."

Plans? His aunt was the top event planner in Charlotte. Bigger than that. The wedding for her eldest daughter had been spectacular even for her reputation. Sure, his family was a pillar of Charlotte's large Indian community, starting with his grandparents who had immigrated in the early eighties, and they were fairly wealthy, but they weren't celebrities.

"Surely you have something in your car. Pills? IV?"

"No." What shows had some of her friends been streaming and discussing at the wine and book nights that would give her that idea? Besides, his father was a cardiac surgeon. She would know the lines he wouldn't cross.

He wouldn't, would he?

Worry tugged at him. His mother frowned. She was still so beautiful at sixty. She hated the vertical line that had formed between her brows so much that she'd started using fillers a few years ago, which now gave her the look of a familiar stranger. She could be his older sister, not his mother, and it was disconcerting.

He looked across the elegantly opulent open ground floor of his aunt's lakeside house. Everything was bathed in pink and orange. His father leaned against the balcony railing, whiskey in his hand, watching his twin pace. He should join them. They'd expect it, but he wanted to check in with Asha. Maybe she was taking this better. He could see Asha sitting down on the patio by the dock, staring out at the lake. Her sisters—Rani sat in a chair next to her and Shanti was as always, on her phone, hair obscuring her face, sitting on Asha's other side.

An idea took hold.

"Are you even listening to me?" his mother huffed, crossing her arms across her slim body.

Had she been talking?

"Just be with Anju Auntie," he urged his mom. "Let her cry. It's a huge disappointment and shock and…hurt."

"It's humiliating," his mother cut to the bone. "Asha publicly rejected two days before jai mala. Two. It's the first wedding of the season. The largest. Most anticipated and now it's gone. Poof," his mother made a clicking sound deep in her throat and her hands mimed an explosion. "By tomorrow everyone will know that Asha has been rejected. He changed his mind. What does that mean? How can a groom change his mind at the last minute? He had two meetings with her and the family. He agreed to the marriage. He and Asha even attended two social events together. Changed his mind." She pffted her lips and rolled her eyes. "Everyone will think there's something wrong with Asha, that she's da…"

"Keep it down," he interrupted as his mom's voice rose with each word.

Asha was not damaged goods, and the last thing she needed was to be reminded of the public rejection. God. What was she thinking? Or feeling? He couldn't even imagine, but he could easily imagine a groom getting cold feet. Marriage was forever, or it should be. No Kapoor had divorced. Ever.

"And now it's too late," his mom whispered, her tone heavy with significance.

"She shouldn't take him back if he changes his mind again," Rohan said. "Guneet's a douche."

Rohan had only met him once at an intimate family party—with sixty or seventy-five guests—a meet and greet with the family. He'd seemed like a good guy. Nothing spectacular. But no warning bells. He'd been into college hoops so they'd talked for a few minutes, and then Asha had led him off to meet more people.

But Rohan was loyal and any good qualities Guneet possessed were now consigned to the trash bin.

"Your language. You don't talk to your patients like that, I hope."

Rohan barked a laugh, imagining if he rolled out a few f-bombs during a consultation.

"There's nothing funny here," his mom said. "Asha is ruined."

"Mom cut the drama. It's the twenty-first century. Asha's had a disappointment, but she still has her family and her career. She hardly knew Guneet. A few months and she'll meet…" He broke off at his mother's pitying look. Her lips pressed together tightly.

"No one will agree to match with her now." His mom was adamant, like Krisha had just whispered a secret of the universe.

"You don't know that," he objected.

"I do. Everyone does. Asha knows too. People will talk. They'll think something's wrong with her."

"Asha is a lovely person through and through. No one will think this is her fault."

"Beta, you are so sweet." His mother patted his cheek. "You never see the bad in anyone."

That was patently not true.

"But it's true. Asha's good name is gone. People were already saying she was too old."

"Hell no," he burst out, pissed that Asha, who had done so much for so many people in the community over the years, would be gossiped about negatively and reduced to a number she had no control over.

"You do not know this town like I do. Her age is an issue. Her only hope now is to accept someone far beneath her." His mother shuddered.

"I don't buy it," Rohan shook his head. "Asha is at the top of her field. She's smart. Kind. Generous. Beautiful. She's not doomed. No way."

"You are such a good son," his mom approved. "Loving. Loyal. But we have to plan. We need to deflect this tragedy."

His mom and aunt had epic social skills, but this debacle was far too heavy a lift even for them to spin into something positive.

"We're just going to have to take it on the chin," he said, not really caring what people said about them. He knew who he was. He knew the good his family had done for others and for the community.

"No. We don't go down. We fight back. Anju will try for a match for Shanti next. But I think she should wait. Let the gossip die down. We...you and I can give our friends something much different to talk about."

Again, she looked him up and down like she was at a livestock auction.

Hard no.

Hell no.

"Mom, let's just shelve this. I'm going to check in with Asha. See if there's something I can do." Saliva flooded his mouth even though he hadn't eaten today. He felt like he was going to vomit.

Damn. Just damn. He'd been safe while he'd been training. His parents respected academics and training. But early June he was being cut loose to enter the fully adult world. And he could feel the noose around his neck. His father had already started the push for him to join his cardiac practice. And now his mom had all but said she was on the hunt for his bride.

Nope. Not happening. Not now when freedom was in sight.

He pocketed the boat keys, a loose idea forming. It was a bit early in the season, but unseasonably warm. And maybe getting out of ear- and eyeshot would help all of them. Childish. He'd only arrived but already wanted to flee.

Five days to go.

Rohan walked through the great room and outside onto the covered deck. He waved to his dad and pointed at his three cousins down sitting on the dock as an excuse to escape. He ran down the stairs, past the massive patio, pool,

pool house and tennis court, and for a moment, he had an image of himself as a boy, running across a lawn—maybe at his first house or maybe a park, chasing Asha as she ran ahead of him, laughing and blowing bubbles that drifted over her head and trailed behind her like she was a magical fairy.

He jammed his hands in the pockets of his suit trousers and walked down the dock with purpose. This sucked. His three cousins seemed trapped in a bubble world just out of reach. Asha stared blankly across the lake, her sundress hiked up to mid-thigh and her bare legs dangling in the lake. Shanti stared at her phone, concentration absolute, fingers flying. Rani had a pitcher of something that she stirred frantically as if she were creating a critical, time-sensitive potion.

They'd been holding on to this news for nearly two hours. He felt like his head was going to explode from the pressure. The need to do and say something, to solve this problem was fierce. He strode past them without a word and began to methodically tug off the blue tarp on the boat. He hit the hydraulic lift to lower the boat into the lake. He hopped on board and turned to his cousins.

"Let's get the fuck out of here. Bring the juice."

Chapter Two

ROHAN PUSHED THE throttle hard, skimming along the lake, blind to the many opulent lakefront mansions. His parents' and aunt and uncle's houses had been designed to showcase their wealth, status, achievements and taste. No expense had been spared. The homes were an entertainer's dream, but now, after his mother had all but indicated she thought he should happily jump like a helpless virgin sacrifice into the volcano of matrimony to save the family's face, Rohan wanted to fly across the water. Never look back and escape the next stage of his life that his parents thought they could meticulously plan out just as they had his first thirty-plus years.

You let them.

A wave of self-loathing washed over him. Shanti had always kicked back a bit over parental and social expectations. Not him. He'd loved to shine, to bask in the praise. Only the past year, maybe more, he'd felt trapped and squished in the box he'd let his parents build. Hell, he'd handed them the raw materials and the tools.

Usually the water soothed him, but today his stomach

and head just kept churning, and he was helpless to talk himself down.

He knew why his parents had built what amounted to a second house on the first floor—three en suite bedrooms, an office, great room with designer kitchen and covered outdoor patio. His mom had tried a couple of times to loop him in on the layout, design and amenities. He'd clutched his indifference like a shield. They wanted him home, literally living under them, while his father guided his career. All that was missing was his yet unpicked wife.

THE WIND TORE at his hair, and the boat skimmed along the waves bouncing a little. The orange glow of the sunset imbued the lake with surreal lighting. This filter would be killer for a Zoom meeting. Rohan cut a wide swath with the boat, reality seeping in.

He'd always done the right thing. The expected thing.

Been the dutiful son.

His lip curled.

He slowed the boat to idle near one of the larger coves that had been left as public space.

"More," Rani hooted from her perch in the bow, grinning back at them all like a maniac, her recently bobbed hair a wild mess. "Keep laying on the speed!"

The tension that had choked him since he'd headed

home this afternoon, eased a little.

Rani could always pull him out of his head. She wasn't crazy as he knew more than a handful of people in the community regularly speculated. She was unfiltered. Genuine. No brakes.

He envied and protected her the best he could.

Rani would have said she was his spirit animal. Whatever that meant.

"Need an ocean for that." He stretched, hands linked, arms angled backward, trying to cast off the last of the tension that had gripped him the minute he'd walked into his aunt's house. "I got a double dose of thirst happening," he informed Rani.

When was the last time the four of them had met up for drinks? Hella day for it.

"I got the quencher." Rani held up the glass pitcher with the pale green something—mojito, margarita, mint something? With Rani, you never knew. She eschewed cooking— "I don't want to be stuck in the kitchen every party"—but she was masterful, and it had to be said, often overly creative with the drinks—cocktails and more.

"And cups I hope," Rohan prodded.

Her expression was so comical that he laughed and then the reality had him cursing.

"You're shitting me."

Rani swallowed hard, stood up and placed the pitcher on a small side table that pulled up from a side pocket much like on a plane.

"I made the cocktails," she confessed. "I don't have a name for it, but it's got some mystery ingredients I thought would help with grief. I didn't think of cups."

So Rani. Kind, impulsive action without the practical follow-through.

Rohan shot a quick look at Asha, who hadn't yet spoken. She wore dark Chanel sunglasses and faced away from them. Shanti sat squeezed next to her in the back of the boat, still on her phone. The only change was that she'd tied her thick, silky, mid-length dark hair back in a sleek, low pony.

"Rakesh is such a total asshole," Shanti muttered.

"Total?" Rani questioned.

"Unambiguous."

"What's he done now?" Rohan questioned. He liked Rakesh and even though he didn't see him as much anymore, considered him one of his closest friends. Rakesh was nakedly ambitious. Socially smooth as silk. Wildly smart and cool and convinced he was right even when he was wrong. And then he'd set out to prove that you were wrong, making him right. He didn't let anybody's shit stick to him. And he somehow soared above his mom's expectations and the community's comments, not letting their frequently shot arrows prick or pierce his skin. Or at least he never let anyone see him bleed.

Yeah. Total asshole.

Rohan had been groomed since birth to think he was

exceptional. Rakesh didn't care what anyone thought, he knew he was exceptional. Even though he hadn't once listened to what his mom said he *should* be doing, he proved it with every breath. And action. Harvard undergrad political science and economics. Yale law. Fast rise at the DA's office. State politics or the justice department was next. And that wouldn't be the final stepping-stone of his ambition. Rakesh always kept his plans to himself, but Rohan suspected Rakesh planned a US senate run at some point soon. Rohan had no doubt he'd get there. His competitors never saw or heard or felt him coming. They just waited, trembling, prey to his predator, waiting for him to strike.

Pretty much like Shanti.

Rakesh wouldn't be sweating it if his mom tried to hand him a coveted partnership on a platter in one hand and a bride in the other. Rakesh would flash his charismatic smile and do whatever the fuck he wanted.

Basically, the opposite of me.

"Rani, find the cups," Shanti said, not looking up from her screen. "How else are we going to toast Asha's wonderous escape from the seventh circle of boredom hell?"

Rohan drew in a sharp breath and shot a look at Asha. She didn't move. She sat, cross-legged on the back seat, her hands together on her lap like a well-behaved child hoping to be noticed and given praise or a treat. She looked as elegant and remote as a temple god as she stared out over the expanse of Lake Norman.

Was she thinking about the house in Charlotte's Dilworth neighborhood that she and Guneet had put a down payment on and where they would now never live as husband and wife or raise their children?

The wake from another boat began to rock them, and he picked up the pitcher of cocktails. Glass. Rani had made the drinks in a glass pitcher and climbed into a boat. Typical.

"I made the drinks," Rani sniped. "No one stopped you from thinking about something other than your phone. It's not like you don't hoist a few when the opportunity presents." Rani began looking in all of the cleverly designed storage areas as she spoke, coming up empty. "And I'm the one presenting the opportunity."

"Not this time if we don't have cups," Shanti, as usual, took no blame. "I got a situation going on."

"Unbelievable," Rani sighed. "Of all the people to not have cups on their boat, we would be the last I'd suspect. Kapoors are party central. We make the blast last."

"You should make us T-shirts," Shanti said.

"This blows," Rani said. "I was experimenting with a new recipe. I researched herbs that ease grief and…"

"Grief?" Asha finally spoke, perhaps since the first time she'd heard the news that Guneet was backing out of the wedding. "Grief. Is that what you think?" Her voice was more aggressive than he'd heard from her—ever. "Is that what everyone will think?" Her voice pitched higher and louder. "That I'm grieving?"

Rani's eyes bugged, and her mouth hung open. Shanti stopped texting or whatever she was doing and stared at her sister, her expression alarmed.

"Grief. Everyone will think I'm grieving. Of course they will. They'll expect me to grieve and cry and hide myself away."

Rohan widened his stance as the bigger wake waves hit them. He clutched the handle of the cocktails like it was a lifeline.

"That's what everyone will expect, right? That I'll hide away in shame and sorrow because Guneet left me hanging to get back together with his college girlfriend. College. They fell in love as freshman. Freshman," she spit the word like a curse. "A marketing major on a pole-vaulting scholarship."

Rohan had no idea what to say. Should he try to shut down the tirade or let her get it all out while he stood there useless and mute, clutching a pitcher of cocktails with no way of enjoying them?

"Everyone will tiptoe around me and expect that I will be ashamed and grieving and heartbroken because I was passed over for a true-love perky blonde in Lululemon leggings who's a health and wellness influencer with over eight hundred thousand online followers. Why not, because I always do what's expected, right? The good girl. The suitable wife. The accomplished woman who waited too long past her shelf life." Asha's voice was more like a growl.

They all stared at her like she was an escaped zoo animal.

Frozen. Useless. Confused because Asha had never once made a public scene although she had averted and soothed many.

"Fuck that," Asha cursed. Something he'd never heard her do ever. She marched up to him, grabbed the pitcher of cocktails muttering, "And fuck cups."

She tilted her head back and let some of Rani's latest invention slide icy smooth down the long column of her throat, swallowing like she'd walked across a desert.

Then she smiled at them grimly, hoisting the pitcher high, but by the way her eyes glittered, the pitcher could have been the severed head of her runaway groom. "Who's in?"

LATER, BACK AT the house as the sun began to set, and the four of them sat out on the second-story deck off the great room, Rani brought a plate of food—saag paneer, zucchini sabzi, daal, roti and butter chicken to her sister. "Your favorite." Rani slid her hand over Asha's fat, shiny bun twisted low on her neck.

It was a feast, and an overt reveal into how stressed Nanima and Mummyji were. The stress would triple if clean plates and a request for seconds didn't soon hit the kitchen.

"Thank you," Asha stared blankly at the blue flames of the outdoor firepit.

Was she drunk? Rohan had never seen her drunk. Oh, she drank. Over the past ten years they'd met for cocktails or Bloody Mary brunches without the Ps as Shanti called them. He'd always enjoyed meeting up with his cousins. Asha had sharp insights and an easy humor that complemented Shanti's dead, dry assassin humor. Rani provided the color.

But Asha had definitely drunk deeply from the pitcher. They all had, well, not him so much because he'd been driving. But as he'd tipped back the pitcher of Rani concocted genius, he'd come to four stark conclusions. He was in no way ready to commit to choosing a bride. He needed some time and freedom before committing to a job. As much as he loved his family, he didn't want to live in the same house with them, even on the lake. Oh, and Rani was a cocktail god.

The god of mixology returned with a plate piled high for him.

"What?" He stared at the massive offering a little shocked, and he was accustomed to the expectation of overeating when he came home. "Is this my last meal before I'm locked up for a crime I've yet to think about committing?"

Rani stuck out her tongue. "Nanima dished out. I'm just the messenger."

"She needs to know I am not an elite athlete needing to shovel in eight thousand calories a day."

"Food is love," Shanti said, on her phone again.

"And waste makes Nanima cray," Rani said, nearly dancing off to return with more food.

He'd heard more family arrive—Anju Auntie's two sisters—but not their husbands or kids so likely some sort of intervention or war campaign was being plotted. Count him out.

"I'm never going for the bougie spectacle wedding," he muttered to Rani as she sat beside him with half the amount of food, he noted enviously.

"You'll do what you're told," Shanti said, tearing a hunk of the naan from Asha's plate and dipping it into the saag. "You always do, prince."

Rohan glared, not liking her mocking tone.

"You're the only son and the golden boy of Charlotte," she smirked and stuffed the naan in her mouth. "No way are you allowed to low-key anything."

He rolled his eyes. He hated that nickname. No one else had been rude enough to hit him in the face with it except his friend Dhruv, who was his polar opposite and didn't give a fuck about polite customs. It had started before he got into Duke's medical school. When he continued at Duke in their coveted cardiothoracic combined residency and fellowship program, his mother had openly and unfortunately started calculating his worth on the marriage market in spite of his squirming efforts to shut that shit down.

"The bride's family plans for and pays for the wedding," Rani said folding a hunk of naan over a juicy chunk of butter chicken, swirling it in the curry and popping it into her mouth with an expression of bliss. Skinny Rani had never met a calorie she was afraid of. "The groom just rides up on a horse and we all dance in homage to his fabulousness," she announced around a mouthful of food.

"Perfect. I'm marrying an orphan and eloping to Vegas. I always wanted a picture with a fake Elvis."

"If you Insta that, I'm making a poster and hanging it in the temple," Shanti said, not looking up. "Desi woman all over Charlotte and the southeast will wail and gnash their teeth."

"Auntie will wear white and drift round the house muttering in Punjabi that the family is cursed," Rani grinned, getting into the teasing. "Mummyji will take to her bed."

"I'll finally go back to temple just to draw bunny ears on the picture of you and your lucky bride who stole the golden one from the women of Charlotte," Shanti said, taking the ignored plate off of Asha's lap and digging into dinner.

Rohan laughed, the pressure in his head and on his chest eased a little. It had been too long since he'd hung with his cousins.

He loved his family, but they exhausted him. Medical school and residency had been rigorous, but family life had been even more intense. He'd started picking up extra shifts just so he'd have the excuse not to come home.

Sure, he was seen as ambitious, but working too much wasn't healthy or sustainable. He wanted a life, but he wanted it on his terms, and increasingly, he'd felt trapped. He'd thought once he'd cleared all the hurdles his parents had set up, they'd ease off, and he'd have some freedom, but the demands and expectations kept coming.

He didn't want to jump more parental hurdles; he wanted off the track and out of the race.

The expectation to excel in school had been a given his whole life. When he got the inevitable A, his mom had demanded to know if anyone got an A+. When his SAT scores came back four points from perfect, she'd fretted the child of someone she knew would have a higher score. His college major hadn't been his choice, but he'd enjoyed biochemistry; although it hadn't left time for much else. Medical school had been the next step. Then his residency. And it wasn't as if he didn't enjoy what he did. He did. It was challenging—required finesse, planning, and coordinating with a large team. He loved that.

But now that the finish line was in view, he was wishing he'd taken at least one left or right turn along the way. No scenic route for him like Rani, who had changed her major five or six times and added a second or third before entering grad school.

"I want a vacation," he said to no one.

"Where do you want to go?" Rani asked, always ready to daydream.

Go? Rohan stared at Rani as if the answer would scroll down her forehead. He wanted to escape. He hadn't thought where.

They'd all traveled as a family growing up—London, Paris, Delhi, Rome, Florence, Berlin and more European capitals and countries. The families had rented a large van and driven along the West Coast for two weeks. He'd seen the ruins of Ephesus, Pompei and Machu Picchu. But the parents had picked all those places. They'd traveled as a large family. He'd never once gone anywhere alone except to Austin to interview for a job. He'd stayed for an extra day and night just to take in a few concerts at South by Southwest. It had been too short and too glorious. The taste of freedom had left him hungering for more.

And how stupid that he didn't have one clue as to what *he* wanted. Or where.

"I've got to resubmit my dissertation proposal," Rani said gloomily. "It keeps getting rejected, and my advisory committee is getting ready to abandon me."

"Forget all the academic crap," Rohan said hastily, having a moment of rare clarity. "It's not worth it. Look at us," he urged. "None of us are happy."

Asha looked hollowed out. She'd pursued school and her career and now was afraid she'd missed her window for a family. Shanti never stopped working and looked like she'd been surgically attached to her phone much like a Borg—his favorite villains from *Star Trek: The Next Generation*—thank God for streaming. And Rani stayed in school pursuing things that interested her but never sticking with them because the answers she needed weren't there.

"You should open a bar," he said, insight striking.

"Right," Rani laughed. "Ten years of school to do something I could have done with no college. I lost the grant funding for the homeless teen center and the funding was cut for my job as director of the outreach programs at the college counseling center." Tears filled her eyes, and his heart wrenched to see her misery.

"Rani, I'm sorry," he said helplessly, one arm hugging her, careful to not spill his food. "I didn't know."

"No." Her gaze flicked to Asha, and he understood.

"I have to move home. If I don't get cracking on my dissertation, it's all been for nothing."

"You're almost there." He tried to sound cheerful and encouraging just like one of his favorite attendings always sounded first year during rounds and in the case autopsy meetings where they debriefed weekly. "You'll slay your dissertation. You love research and designing surveys. You kill data analysis. And you're a fantastic writer."

She used to write stories as a kid and read them to him. They'd been wildly inventive, often spot-on parodies and funny as hell. "Once you too are a Dr. Kapoor, you can't flip me any more shit."

Fuck a healthy heart for tonight. He took a bite of the steaming, fragrant, delicious butter chicken.

Rani snorted so hard he was surprised no snot came out. "A doctorate in psychology is never going to cut it with anyone."

"It's a PhD." He could barely swallow the food as he felt gutted seeing the hurt Rani tried to stuff back inside the grab bag of her mind. "And your opinion is the only one that matters."

The sparkle of tears in her midnight eyes became a flood, and he leaned forward to wipe them away with his thumb.

"I wish you believed that for yourself Ro."

Touché.

THE FOUR OF them sat quietly with their thoughts. Only Rani had made progress on her dinner when his mom joined them outside. "Why aren't you eating?" she greeted.

"Let me get you a plate, Priddy Chaachee." Rani jumped up, placing her plate on the fireplace surround. "Do you think my mom would be willing to try a little something?" Rani asked hesitantly.

"No, she is still pacing, cursing that boy."

"I should go to her." Asha roused herself a little. It was the first she'd spoken since the boat.

"No, not now betee," his mom smiled at Asha and waved her to sit again. "She has her sisters. She just needs a little time to rally. She even chased Raj away, much to his relief."

If it hadn't been so sad and so serious, Rohan would have laughed. His Raj cacha was notorious for dodging conflict or uncomfortable social situations—likely why he became an anesthesiologist, his twin liked to tease him—his patients were quiet, asleep.

"Shanti, have the men eaten?" his mom asked.

"No idea, Priddy Auntie."

"They said they would later," Rani said quickly as his mom frowned at Shanti. "Dad and Uncle are enjoying the twilight and the view and the quiet and the whiskey far too much to eat."

His mother looked down her nose disdainfully and her lip curled, clearly not interested in anyone else's enjoyment. "Tell them to come now," she imperiously waved at Rani. "We need to plan to mitigate this…"—she paused dramatically, and her beautiful features twisted in pain or distaste because she hated, absolutely hated to fail at anything or be less than perfect and perfectly admired—"disastrous news."

Rohan still didn't have a read on how Asha was feeling. He considered Asha, Shanti and Rani more like sisters than cousins. They'd all grown up together, either in the same large house or next door, depending. But yet, once they'd headed off to college, they hadn't done much more than casually socialize. No heart-to-hearts or anything like that except with Rani, although she'd been the prolific over-sharer. He'd never told her about his doubts or how he felt smothered.

"We have hundreds of phone calls we need to make. We can divide the list depending on the guest's importance to the family."

"What?" He looked at his mom.

"Their relationship to us," his mom soothed. "You know what I mean."

Unfortunately, he did.

"Phone calls," Shanti didn't look up from her phone and she still typed furiously. Her normally husky voice held a professional edge. "That's a waste of time and emotional energy. Just do a group email," she said decisively, finally looking up and staring his mom down. Rohan had a sudden vision of Shanti in a courtroom intimidating a witness and wowing a jury, although he was pretty sure that as an intellectual property attorney, she rarely if ever entered a courtroom. Her work was more in international conference rooms and penthouse office suites.

"We cannot send a group email for something of this magnitude." His mother was scandalized.

"Less hassle and drama and schadenfreude. With an email, we don't have to hear their smirks."

"Impossible." His mother looked rattled.

"Fine. I'll do it." Shanti stood up. "Asha does not need to go through that. It's not worth her time."

His mother gasped. Shanti raised a perfectly threaded eyebrow in challenge. Even Rohan who wasn't on the receiving end of her scorn felt singed. Then his mom leaped up and called for his dad and uncle. She clapped her hands as if she were trying to motivate them to join in a family bonding activity.

Arguing ensued. He and Shanti encouraging a group email. Rani trying to keep the peace, her palms out like she was trying to time out the dialog. Then, flanked by her two sisters who lived in Florida, but were staying with her to help with the wedding prep, his aunt regally descended the marble stairs, looking pale and grim but put-together beautiful like she was heading out to a party instead of reeling from her eldest daughter's canceled wedding.

His father and uncle who had leaped into the discussion, went silent. Nanima, who'd finally left the kitchen to join in the drama brewing on the deck, smoothed Asha's hair like she was a child. Mummyji had also joined them, carrying a plate of food and sitting at the large outdoor table. She saw her daughter-in-law and jumped up, likely intending to dish her out some dinner, but Asha's mom smiled tragically and shook her head, indicating for Mummyji to sit. Instead, Mummyji joined Nanima and stood behind Asha, resting her chin on the top of her head. Asha covered her mummyji's weathered hands.

"Asha shouldn't have to go through any of that," Shanti was fierce, always wanting the last word.

"Agreed," he chimed in.

"Asha must take part, right, Anju?" his mom appealed to her sister-in-law. "Of course she is not at fault. She is a good girl. Smart and accomplished, but she has been thrust into this unfortunate role, and she must hold her head high along with all of us."

"We must all of us hold our heads high and weather this controversy together," his aunt said. Her face was swollen from tears, but she clearly intended to rally. She'd changed into a vibrant royal blue dress and had reapplied her makeup. Gold bangles, earrings and a necklace with pearls gleamed in the lights on the deck.

His mom joined her sister-in-law and put her arm around her, showing solidarity and, Rohan couldn't help but feel, ownership. His mom, a top-rated dermatologist, had always had a flair for the dramatic.

"Shanti, we will need your help crafting a message to the community. The language is crucial," Anju Auntie said.

"We must all be on the same page. Think of it as a script," his mom added. "We must all learn our lines. Stick to the message."

Asha stood up. "Thank you for your support," she said formally, facing the women in her family. First, she kissed her mother, Nanima and Mummyji and then hugged each of her visiting aunts.

"There is no message to finesse," she said. "It is a simple fact. My wedding is canceled. Guneet contacted his college girlfriend to let her know he was marrying, realized he had unresolved feelings for her so he respectfully backed out of our agreement to honorably pursue love and happiness."

Dead silence to this pronouncement except from his mom, who gasped at Asha's bluntness and held her hand to her heart.

Probably why I don't tell her anything.

Fresh tears filled his Anju Auntie's eyes. "There is nothing honorable about backing out of a commitment."

"There is nothing dishonorable about pursuing love," Asha answered quietly, and awe filled him at Asha's strength.

"I will take Shanti's draft of the email and add a few personal touches and send it out early tomorrow morning. I will also call the families that you think I should personally call. If there is someone that you feel the need to call instead, then of course, you must do so. Tomorrow, Shanti has agreed to help me notify all of the companies involved in my wedding. We should have the cancelations all in hand well before ten."

"You were such an organized bride," her mother teared up again.

"Father, I fear that we will not receive any money back at this late date, but I can..."

His aunt burst into another torrent of recriminations about that "faithless boy."

"It was my idea to hire a matchmaker," Asha said quietly, but her voice was laced with steel. "Guneet was my choice. I will reimburse..."

"No," her father growled. "I saved for all of my daughters' weddings. It is a father's responsibility to care for his children. A few emails informing everyone what an idiot, unfaithful groom we chose for our eldest daughter and let it be done." His uncle stalked back to the house to pour another whiskey for himself. His twin and two visiting brothers-in-law, who had arrived a few minutes ago, likely deeming it safe enough to venture into the house to miss the explosive drama followed.

Raj Chacha looked at Rohan through the open slider doors and raised his eyebrows, holding the crystal whiskey decanter. Rohan shook his head, but his uncle poured him a healthy dose anyway. "I got cigars," he called out. "Cubans. Let's put them to good use. We are in the eye of the hurricane. Celebrate the peace before the backside of this storm hits."

"Rohan." His father tapped his hand on the glass indicating that he wanted him to join them. "Come."

"Before you go, Rohan." His mother seized his arm and all but dragged him inside but away from the cigar room off his uncle's study.

"I know. I know. Of course I will help Asha with anything she needs." How could she think otherwise?

He had the next five days off. He wouldn't be selfish and head back to his apartment in Durham, even though the temptation rode him hard. When was the last time he'd had so much time off? He hadn't hiked or run any trails in weeks. He could kayak.

"I am not talking about Asha. I am talking about you."

"What?"

"The best way for us to divert the gossip about Asha's failure…"

"She didn't fail."

"Yes, yes, I know. Of course not. But there will be much talk. You know how everyone is."

"They are your friends," he emphasized the last word. "They should support you and Asha."

His mother's eyes sparked. "You are no longer a child. Some of them will rejoice. Want to eat us alive."

"Then they aren't your friends."

"Don't be naive," his mom ordered sternly. "In another couple of months you will be back in Charlotte living here and working in Papa's practice, and people's opinions will definitely matter," she said. "Papa has been maneuvering you to be in position on a hospital leadership committee and of course at the temple." She may have kept talking. Rohan wasn't sure. He couldn't breathe.

"We need to play this correctly. I know Anju will marry Shanti off next. Asha is crushed, of course and trying not to show it, but really she did leave it too late."

"Mom," he held his hand up like a stop sign. "Asha is your niece, and she's hurting. I am not talking to you about anything except supporting Asha."

"Yes, yes, of course," his mother soothed. "I am here for her and Anju. Always. I will sit with her and make some phone calls. I know what to say. I know how to deal with these people."

He stared at her. "*These people* are your friends, or they should be," but he knew what she meant. Many were also her competitors. His mother viewed the world as predators or prey, and she would never submit to become prey.

"The best defense is a good offense. The best way to divert the negative talk and attention and to re-cement our place—all of our places—in the community is to find you a suitable bride fast."

Chapter Three

I T WAS WELL after two in the morning. Rohan couldn't sleep so he was sitting down by the lake, barely smoked cigar in his hand, glass of whiskey that he hadn't touched on the stones of the firepit.

He wasn't surprised when Rani in an oversize Fordham sweatshirt and matching sweats curled up in the chair next to him. She notoriously had trouble sleeping and could unerringly sense when family and friends were upset. She knew their emotional triggers and seemed to feel a compulsion to help—not always appreciated in their family.

She held a bottle in her hand, and a cigar.

"You're not really going to smoke that thing?" He'd brushed his teeth twice, and he still felt the wet, smoky leaves taste in his mouth. His stomach felt unsettled, like he might puke. His dad and two of his uncles were doctors. They should know better.

Hell, I know better.

"I might try."

"Why?"

"Do you have to ask?" She waggled it like a pixie version

of Groucho Marx.

"Do the unexpected," he said, even surprising himself with his bitter tone. He'd never done the unexpected thing in his life. "Do you actively try to be unexpected?" he asked, genuinely curious. Rani danced to a tune no one else heard.

"I just do me," Rani said, flicking the lighter on and off, her face glowing in the flame. "And that seems to always be wrong."

"Not wrong."

"Just unexpected," she smirked. "And our family isn't comfortable with unexpected." She looked at him closely, and he found himself fighting the urge to squirm under her piercingly direct gaze. If she ever did become a full-fledged clinical psychologist or professor, she definitely had the "I'm peeling open your brain to take a peek" look nailed. "You included."

He flinched.

"Speaking of expected, has Priddy Auntie announced that the only way to save face for all of us is to hire a top matchmaker and marry you off to the highest bidder?"

"What the fuck? You would have been burned as a witch a few centuries ago."

"It's not too late," Rani said, a fey smile curling her lips, and she propped her bare feet up on the fire surround. She flicked the lighter on and off again. "Rohan, you should slip your leash every now and then."

He raked a hand through his hair. "I know," he said

bleakly, "but it's too late."

He was like one of those animals in a Skinner box—wasn't that right? He'd had his only AP psych class in high school, but even then, he'd felt sympathy for the caged animals that were shocked into submission to the point where even when the door was open, they didn't try to leave. He hadn't realized he was at risk of becoming one of them.

Funny how Rani had fallen in love with the head, and he dealt with matters of the heart. That, right there was probably the definition of irony.

"It's only too late when you're dead."

"That looks like the only time I will actually be free."

"Rohan," her voice was urgent. "I have an idea—one that could really save us both initially, and then Asha and Shanti too."

Hope and enthusiasm drenched her features and her body jangled with excitement. Rani with an idea that lit her imagination always spelled doom. She stuck the cigar in her mouth and brought the lighter close to the tip.

"Whatever it is, and I definitely don't want to know, hard no," he said firmly, swiping the lighter and pocketing it.

FRIDAY LATE IN the afternoon Shanti slipped her arm around Asha's waist and leaned her head on her shoulder. Asha stared at her carefully toted up life and furniture neatly arranged in the climate-controlled storage unit after Shanti, Rani and he had spent the afternoon helping her to move out of her southend townhouse. For a woman who'd been out of her parents' home, either in school, training or working for as long as she'd lived with her parents—eighteen years—it was not a lot of stuff, Rohan noted. Initially he'd been relieved, but now looking at the meticulously labeled totes, he felt sad.

What would my life look like stacked in totes?

Asha held herself rigidly in Shanti's embrace, two rolling suitcases by her side.

"She's always like tungsten," Rani whispered. "She was so composed this morning calling people to tell them the wedding was canceled."

"I'm not sure if it's better if she cries or not," he said helplessly.

"Better," Rani said. "But later. When she's on her own. I mean, it would be better for her to be with us so we could support her, but Asha's identity is wrapped up in her being the eldest. She takes care of us. She's going to want to hold it together so that we don't worry."

He was worried. Asha had always been there for him—for all of them—and he intended to do what he could to help, but he felt out of his depth emotionally. He spent his energy avoiding exploring his or anyone's feelings. He also didn't feel he excelled as a handyman, but his cousins had hooked him into disassembling the antique cherry four-poster bed. He'd been as meticulous as he was in surgery because he was going to have to put the bed back together again today in Shanti's empty spare bedroom. Shanti had insisted Asha move in with her until she and Guneet settled what to do with the house in Dilworth that they had made an offer on, which had been accepted. The house had closed, but they hadn't settled who would take the house—and who would buy out the other's portion of the substantial down payment. Asha's townhouse was due to close in three weeks so there was no going back. Only forward.

He wanted to wring Guneet's neck—realizing he was still in love with his college girlfriend, years later. The fact that he would contact her two weeks before he was due to marry and had no doubt stepped out on Asha to euphemistically "test the waters," infuriated Rohan.

"Thank you, everyone," Asha said. The words seemed to take a big effort. "I need to go back and clean the townhouse so that it's ready for the new owners."

"I hired a cleaning crew to come in tomorrow," Shanti said. "We're heading back to my condo. Rani will play bartender. Rohan will set up your bed. We'll order you a new set of sheets and comforter from West Elm or Williams-Sonoma and get someone to deliver it and order Uber Eats. Let's get this party started, roomie." She hip-checked Asha, who clearly hadn't been expecting it because his graceful cousin, the one who had studied several styles of Shastriya Devesh at the top studio in Charlotte for ten years, stumbled.

He caught her.

"Thanks, Rohan," she said softly, avoiding eye contact.

"Hey." He pulled her into a hug. "It will be okay, Ash. It will. Not now. But later."

She had no recourse but to look at him, and he nearly stumbled himself at the pain he saw in her large, dark eyes.

"Don't be nice," she whispered.

"Don't know how. I'm the arrogant prick of the family," he joked, hoping to make her smile.

"Keep your prickness engaged and no hugging allowed," Shanti said side-eying him before she rolled down the door to the storage unit with a satisfying bang. She locked it and worked the key onto Asha's key ring. "We're Kapoors. Badass to the bone. Tough love only."

"DO YOU THINK that she was in love with Guneet?" Rohan asked later at Shanti's as he put the bed together and Rani sat beside him trying to help but getting in his way.

Shanti had ended up ordering Asha a dragon-patterned comforter and sheet set with a black background online as Asha had seemed utterly uninterested. She and Asha were returning the rental truck and picking up the bedding while he and Rani set up the bed.

"I don't know," Rani said, her pause longer than he

would have liked. "Maybe. He was really good-looking. Quiet. Smart. Introverted. An anesthesiologist. She liked that he wasn't younger than her. Other matches had been up to four or five years younger. The matchmaker kept jawing at Mom that she should have started the search years ago."

Rohan hated that. Age. It had become such a defining element for Asha like milk gone bad.

"Indian women hit twenty-five and it's a full court press 'when are you getting married?'" Rani mimicked ruthlessly accurate.

"She didn't know him that long," Rohan said tightening the last of the hardware.

"Sometimes you meet someone and whoosh"—she blew on her fingertips and then made an exploding sound—"you just know. Magic. Soul mate."

"Right." Rohan rolled over onto his back and stared at the pale blue ceiling with the white crown molding all around. "Magic."

"It happens, Rohan."

"Has it happened to you?" He turned his head to look at her.

Rani shook her head and then laid down beside him. "But that doesn't mean it won't or that it's not real."

"Magic is really lust."

"That too, but I think souls can recognize each other."

He barely—barely—managed not to roll his eyes. He'd grown up regularly attending the temple that his grandparents had spear-headed the fundraising campaign and plans for, but he believed that you had one life and when the heart struggled through its last beat, lights out. Party over. No second or third spin on the karma wheel.

"Have you ever been in love?" Rani asked curiously.

"Not even close." He stood up, not wanting to talk about this, especially today.

"What do you think it would take?"

"No idea."

"Don't you think you should start thinking about it?"

He laughed darkly. "Do something useful, grab the edge of the box spring."

"Your life has been so scripted," Rani said, helping him manhandle the box spring into place on the bed.

He waited a moment, hoping screws and bolts held—he'd managed not to strip anything, probably as close to a miracle as he'd get today.

"A plan for everything. No time or activity wasted."

"That was my mother," he said. "And father. Not me."

And wasn't that the weakest, most pathetic argument a man could make.

"But it's your life," Rani said, wrestling to get a hold of the mattress. "Are you really going to let Priddy Auntie and a matchmaker take total control and choose a wife for you?"

"Got the other side?" Rohan seized his side of the mattress and lifted it. Rani staggered. Maybe she'd switch topics.

"Honestly Ro, you are a total ostrich. Do you even know

your love language? Oh. That is definitely something I need to include—an exploration of love languages."

Hard no. She'd better not be referring to her little brainstorm tease last night that he'd shut down.

This morning he'd been thrilled to escape the growing crowd at the house after the phone calls and mass email had hit. Friends brought food, sympathy and gossip, and Rohan had been happy to have the excuse of helping Asha move, especially when a few people had brazenly speculated that it would be his turn to find a bride.

The mattress settled like an exhaled breath. Rani, eyes shining like new pennies, stared at him with an expectant look that he knew meant trouble. And then she bounced on her toes.

"No," he said firmly. "Whatever you're thinking, hard no."

"You don't know what I'm thinking," she said. "This is a really good idea. I want to run it past you before Shanti and Asha show up—fine tune it a little."

This was going to be bad.

"It will definitely work," she doomed the idea, seized his arm and squeaked in excitement. "I finally figured out my dissertation topic, Ro! Finding your match. Or maybe something catchier. Masala match. Too limiting? I'll work on it, but it's all there—history, psychology, culture, sociology, creating a methodology and then test subjects. My family. And a career in finding true love. Oh, maybe masala marriage matches! You can be my first test subject for the questionnaire I'm going to develop."

"Hard no," he said, not even feeling a twinge of guilt for shutting her down so fast. He already had his mom rubbing her palms together and looking at him like he was a thoroughbred racehorse at a stock auction. He did not need Rani on his other side scheming to control his future. With her flights of imagination and lack of impulse control, who knew who she'd pull out of the eligible Desi pool?

He'd find his own bride on his own timeline. He'd barely had a chance to live yet. And he'd hardly dated. Hook ups? Probably too many. But he wanted a companion, a friend as well as a lover in his wife. A woman who had her own goals and dreams and opinions. He didn't want to be anyone's everything. It was exhausting.

"Hard yes," Rani said. "This is so totally going to work for all of us. But I shouldn't limit it to the Desi community. Hmmmm…masterful…no…mischievous, definitely no…magnificent…no, too arrogant. Marvelous? Hmmm…I need another M word and then Masala Matchmaker. I'll be M3. I'll make a website. Write a blog about relationships. I need to get to work. The Kapoors are back on top."

As if to both punctuate Rani's delusion and rescue him from tossing Rani's skinny ass over Shanti's expansive balcony, Shanti arrived home, Asha in tow, banging open the front door and shouting.

"Let's get the party started! To new adventures!" Rohan

heard the pop of a champagne cork.

"To new adventures," Rani echoed and raced around him to run downstairs.

Chapter Four

"I THINK SOMEBODY drank one too many cups of ambition when you were planning this Art-Word-Dance-Music Smash Up," English teacher Tula Reese greeted Solei as she bounded up the steps to their multi-media interactive art exhibit space at the Charlotte Arts in the Park event. She'd watched as Solei, a pink drill in her back pocket, and clipboard in one hand, tablet in the other, had calmly and efficiently run through last-minute instructions with the team of volunteers and student artists before dashing off across the downtown Charlotte park to check that her high school studio arts students' exhibition was properly installed in the juried portion of the show.

"We planned it," she reminded Tula. "So make that two too many cups of ambition." She was embarrassingly out of breath from her sprint across the park. "I'm happy I got an exhibit space for fifteen of my studio arts students in the juried show in the pavilion as well, but doing double duty is harder than I'd imagined."

"What, you can't manifest in two places at once? Or fly? Solei Beals, I'm crushed."

"You are not as funny as you think you are," Solei countered.

"I totally am," Tula said.

Solei had been hired to teach at a prestigious science and arts academy on a year-long contract as a visiting artist. Tula was one of many reasons Solei had applied to stay on as a teacher. She still felt a little shell-shocked at her decision. She'd recently earned her teaching certificate, but it had been more of a safety measure—in case her commissions ran dry. She'd been a working artist, supporting herself and building her reputation since her second year of college.

But lately, she'd tired of being alone, traveling so much. She'd wanted to try to stay in one place and had been shocked at how much she enjoyed teaching high school kids, how much she enjoyed being part of a team. The school staff and volunteer artists and teachers at the Youth Urban Artists after-school and evening program had cemented her desire to stay. She felt a part of something larger than herself and her vision for the first time in her life. And Charlotte as a city—while not a boom town for artists—had a lot to offer.

She'd had her home base in LA since receiving her MFA at UCLA. She'd kept her studio and apartment in the Highland Park area of the city, but she hadn't stayed in one place for an entire year ever since college and felt more relaxed but at the same time energized.

"Have you heard yet?" Tula, who excelled at mind reading as much as she did at teaching poetry and creative writing, demanded.

"No," Solei admitted, finding a little of her buzz fizzling. "Maybe the school's principal and board of directors are waiting to see how the show goes since the school hasn't participated before in the arts festival. Also, since I roped in eight kids from the school to join the Youth Urban Artist program—one of them gave up varsity lacrosse this spring— a lot is riding on this."

"Then let's wow their socks off." Tula was always the calm in the storm. So was Solei, but she'd mostly worked alone, hiring assistants only for her bigger street art projects. This booth today involved so many moving pieces—four teachers from the program and over thirty artists who would be creating live—studio arts, music, poetry, short one acts. The schedule was tight, and while Solei was highly orga- nized, she'd never attempted anything this involved. Her biggest genius move had been to lure Tula to volunteer at the Youth Urban Arts program. She not only brought brilliant teaching and energy, but also her musician husband, Rand.

All of them had arrived at dawn along with a handful of parents and student volunteers to set up the small stage and ensure that everything was in place.

And now it was time to, as Rand said, "rock and roll."

Solei found her Hydro Flask of ice water and took a deep swig while she surveyed the booth that had been divided into several arts sections: street art—her specialty—ceramics with several potter's wheels, charcoal and pastel quick sketching and then the front area for the student musicians, who were going to perform one to two original works at different times throughout the afternoon. Rand, who'd been working this past academic year with kids who wanted to lay down their own beats and mix music to learn to DJ, had built a raised area at the back of the stage for kids to DJ while other kids could dance up front.

The first round of studio artists arrived, and Solei and Tula commandeered them to help mount the several drywall sheets to the posts that Rand and some parents had built to enclose the booth on two sides. Kids could create while the audience could watch from the front and the back and hopefully lure some bystanders up on stage to join in the fun.

Solei blew out a nervous breath. She was used to being watched while she painted. Most of her work was commissioned on city buildings, landmarks or infrastructure so it was public. Gone were the late nights in high school when she and a few artist friends would sneak out and artistically tag abandoned buildings or bridge supports.

She looked at her watch and then at the first group of kids taking their places. She smiled at them, determined to quell her unexpected nerves. What was wrong with her? This was supposed to be fun. To make art accessible. Why did she feel like so much was on the line? Sure, it would sting her pride if she wasn't offered a teaching contract. But there were other jobs. She had plenty of bank and over a dozen commission asks in her inbox.

Plus, Frida.

Her safe port in any storm. She never had to worry about being homeless.

She'd made good friends in Charlotte. If she had to leave, she'd make friends again.

Solei twisted her probably messy hair up in an equally messy bun and stalked over to the section for graffiti where she'd be working with two of her younger, middle school-aged artists, gently reminding them about the rules of engagement and appropriateness, earning herself an eye roll. She checked the fastenings of the drywall to the posts, tightening one with her pink drill. Her penchant for carrying around tools while she worked had earned her the name Rosie for Rosie the Riveter at both the high school and the after-school arts program.

"Four hours of art, music, dancing and poetry," Solei called out as she sorted through her stacked bins of spray paint colors. "What's better than that?"

"Nothing," the students choraled back at her.

"You look like a weird blend of handy man, artist and cowgirl gunslinger," Tula mused as Solei held the drill and her first can of spray paint. "But you've got the wrong style of boots."

Solei looked down at her white Devon Heart Buckle Platform Doc Martens boots. She was—full disclosure—obsessed with the brand. She had twelve pairs.

"Hey, Ms. Sunshine," Eden, the first student DJ called out—his trademark moniker for her since he'd learned that her name in French meant sun. "Ready to kick it?"

Solei tucked the drill again in her back pocket and picked up a second can of spray paint and shook it in his direction. "Always," she said.

"Let's make some noise," Eden said and kicked off his first mix while the six studio artists who were up working in the first thirty-minute spot shouted out, "Let's make some art."

Eden's set was upbeat and festive. He mixed the music, while his sister read some poetry or sometimes sang for the first half hour. A few people in the crowd tried the potter's wheels while students helped them throw clay, and more than a few kids had joined the others at the graffiti and paint sections of the booth. The quick sketch section was busy as one of the program's dancers struck various poses, giving them only a minute to try to capture it. A few poems were read or rapped before another DJ stepped in to mix beats in with some famous opera arias, which worked so well Solei wanted to cry. The multimedia live art exhibit was diverse and beautiful—even more fantastic than she'd imagined and worth the weeks and weeks of organization and long hours. Her students encouraged kids to come up and join them, and it was so sweet, that her heart welled with joy.

The last of her tension dissipated.

The day could not be going any better. She and Tula

hung a new section of clean drywall, displaying the two that were full of art on a rack that she and Tula's husband had built.

Solei bounded back up to the graffiti area, kicked off her boots and impulsively spray-painted a mermaid and wrote "swims with sharks," as she grooved to the dance mix. She added an Om for the mermaid's face and then looked into the crowd, hoping to lure someone to join her.

And then she saw him.

The most beautiful man she'd ever laid eyes on. He didn't even look real—more like a man she would have dreamed up one night when sketching on her iPad Pro.

Her vision tunneled, and the music sounded muffled. There was only this man in the crowd, a few feet from the steps to the stage they'd built for the booth, and when he turned as if sensing her obsession, his obsidian gaze reminded her of the night sky filled with stars. She felt like she was falling.

Forward.

Off-balance.

Was she even breathing?

Without meaning to, she walked toward the edge of the makeshift stage and held out her hand toward him.

"Hello."

Again.

"I'M SORRY, I'm sorry, I'm sorry," Rani sang out as she negotiated Charlotte traffic.

"Not a sitz so stop apologizing."

He'd been so relieved to have an excuse to get out of the house Saturday morning, which would have been Asha's wedding day, he'd jumped at the chance to help Rani deliver coolers of ice, yogurt, milk and fresh fruit to her friends who had a smoothie food cart at some art festival in a downtown Charlotte park. He was the muscle. Rani promised him lunch after they delivered the goods.

He'd made her promise that she wouldn't ask him questions about his love language, deepest fears, superpower or whatever flitted through her agile brain. Rani was *not* going to search for a bride for him!

Of course she'd promised him nothing. Instead, she had given him her "pleeeeease" look that had done him in since she'd been two and had latched all her attention onto him and had learned to speak in disconcertingly long but random sentences.

"It's for research," she'd wheedled. "I'm finally feeling inspired by a dissertation topic."

"As long as it's not about my love life or finding me a wife," he'd insisted.

Actually, "hiring" Rani to be his matchmaker would ensure that he'd be single forever. Not that he wanted that exactly. He just wanted time to himself, to have fun, to do things he wanted to do, not had to do and socialize with people he wanted to be with, not had to be because they were his family's friends and important in the community.

It was a beautiful spring day with a few fluffy white clouds chasing across the Carolina blue sky. He cranked the seat back as far as it would go and savored the sun's rays through the sunroof of Rani's blue BMW X3. He'd changed—casual maroon trousers, white tee and dark pink blazer with a stamped pattern of paisley...or fishtails. He'd never been quite sure, but he loved the brightness of the blazer, and the feel of the fabric against his skin. And the cut. Supreme. Tailored for him. The jacket had been an off the rack sample. He received it instead of payment for modeling for a friend's sister's photo shoot for her senior collection at Parsons. He received more than a few fashion pieces through modeling for design students over the years. He loved clothes, especially vivid colors, textures and patterns. And his sneaker collection had its own closet.

"This does not suck," he murmured, eyes closed.

"You look like a sated lion all sprawled out."

"Not a panther?"

"Ummmmm. Why panther?"

"Dark. Stalking through this jungle called life."

"No," Rani huffed at him. "You are golden. The golden boy and the fairest of all of us," she trilled which jolted him out of his chill.

"Am I supposed to flex?" he mocked.

"At every party," she shot back. "It's really going to crank up the party scene when you move back home to Charlotte. 'Rohan is a very beautiful boy,'" she mocked in a British-Indian accent that had him opening one eye and looking at her. Yup. She was doing the full bobblehead, and Rohan laughed. Rani should have gone into the arts instead of head shrinking. She'd always been an excellent mimic and was funny as hell. "Rohan is such a catch. A golden boy," she exaggerated the accent. "He is so very fair. Very light-skinned. And from such a good family. A doctor you know. A girl will be so lucky, a very lucky girl to have Rohan as her husband."

"Remind me why I wasted fourteen years in higher education if I just had to show up, crunch down a few appetizers and impress everyone with my fairness?"

Rani stuck her tongue out. "I know, right? And here I am the darkest of all of us constantly urged to roll around in sunscreen each time I leave the house. If Mom and Dad had been so worried that I would ruin my marriage chances with a few afternoons of forgetting to slather myself in sunscreen, they should have moved to Forks. Maybe a vampire would have been dazzled by my wit and charms, and I could have become sparkly."

"Truly a missed opportunity."

"About that," Rani inserted casually…way too casually, and he could feel his neck tighten along with his jaw and something start to pulse at the base of his skull. "I did some research last night about dating site questions and matchmakers and refreshed my mind on relationship articles and blogs…"

"Don't," Rohan said. "Hard no to the matchmaking. I told you that."

"Rohan, Auntie's really set on the idea. With me you'd get more of a say, and I'd get a fantastic new sister I could love…"

"And torture," he interrupted.

"And a dissertation topic."

He sat upright, relaxed mood shot. "I'll find my own bride when I'm good and ready."

The skeptical look she slanted at him was as irritating as it was dismaying.

"And what are you waiting for? Love at first sight?"

"Hard no," he laughed. "That's not real. That's hormones. But by all means, tell me a gem you gleaned from your research. Should we be locked in an escape room and filmed to see how we work together as a team?"

"Rohan, that's a brilliant idea."

"Maybe I should have majored in psych," he muttered under his breath and then pointed out an unexpected parking spot. Rani skillfully parallel parked and popped the hatch.

"You aren't nosy enough," Rani said. "Or rebel enough to horrify your family, but maybe we could develop a matchmaking approach together, and you could be my research assistant and guinea pig."

"Let's focus on the Sister Queen Smoothie rescue and then grab something to eat," Rohan said. "Food will inspire me to think of more ridiculous ways for you to match Kapoors who don't want to be matched. Shanti can be your guinea pig."

"Shanti's going to marry Rakesh," Rani announced, pulling out one of the massive coolers filled with ice.

"More like castrate him," Rohan noted, sliding two more of the coolers out of the hatchback. "And he's one of my best friends so please don't shove her into a room with him."

"Rakesh knows how to take care of himself," Rani said, wheeling two of the coolers and struggling to keep up with Rohan once they'd navigated the curb and were on the thick grass. "Shanti just won't accept fate. Mom thinks they're perfect for each other," Rani panted.

"Fate," he laughed. "As if. Trying to match those two together would be so unfair to Rakesh. Shanti would chuck him off her balcony if he ever showed up to ask for a cup of lemon sugar or a bottle of Topo Chico."

"Why did you choose those items?" Rani had that look— the intensely curious one when she wanted to swan dive into his brain.

"Top of my head," he said quickly, not sure why he'd chosen those or what he was revealing with the choice, but he definitely felt uneasy. Rani could be a little witchy at times, and he didn't want to give her any ammo for her new matchmaker whim. She jumped into new passions and while she always took the unconventional route, she was smart and persistent—like a rat in a maze. Or were crows the clever ones?

"No, really, Rohan. Lemon sugar and a specific brand of sparkling water—plain or flavored?"

"Speaking of brands," he interrupted though they really hadn't been. "Have you thought of your third M for Masala Matchmaker brand—maddening? Meddlesome? Manic, Maniac?"

He was forced to stop where he reached the festival as he had no idea where Rani's friends' smoothie truck was.

"I'll think of it," Rani said, and he relaxed thinking he'd distracted her. "But let's return to those two items on your list. They are indicative of…"

"Two things do not comprise a list, and I just spoke off the top of my head." He surveyed the park, now impatient to get away—from this conversation at least. Wandering around looking at art seemed appealing. He hadn't done anything so…so…frivolous or impulsive since…maybe ever.

"But that is when you are the most psychologically re-vealing."

"Thank you, not. Hard no on being your test subject."

"Rohan"—Rani covered his hand with her small slim one, her dark eyes serious, sympathetic—"I can help you. Your mom and the matchmaker are going to ambitiously pick a woman for them, a match that will make the family look good and show how accomplished you are, what a great match you are to get this prize of a woman. I will help you find a woman that you can become good friends with and build a happy life with."

Happy life. The two words hit him like a stone to his chest. Happy life. What did that even mean? What would that look like? Rohan stared over the sea of tents, food carts, stages, and humanity swimming through it all. What would make him happy? What woman would make him happy? What would their happy life together look like?

He'd just turned thirty-two, and he was coming up empty.

"Rohan, we can do this together. Give me a chance."

It was a cry from her heart, and Rani had had so many crushing disappointments, he couldn't ignore her even though everything inside of him urged him to run.

"Rani." An uncharacteristic wave of something heavy and dark swept through him leaving his lungs feeling wet and compressed. "I don't know how to help you. I don't know what I want in a wife. I don't even want a wife right now. I've spent my whole life focused on achieving success by…" He couldn't even utter his next thought: "someone else's yardstick." It sounded so pathetic. "And now when I finally feel like I'm coming to a fork in the road where I will be able to choose my own path and take some time to…I don't know breathe, explore, just be, Mom and Dad want me to take the job they want me to have and live in the house they designed and now they want me to take a wife they choose."

Rani's eyes were round and damp with sympathy. "Rohan, I want to help," she whispered.

He so wasn't in the mood for this. "Forget it. Let's get the ice and fruit to your friends," he said forcefully and resumed walking across the grass, anything to escape his thoughts.

"Rohan," Rani hurried beside him. She'd never learned the art of letting go. "We'll find your perfect match together. Just us looking. It will be fun. I created a couple of surveys last night on Survey Monkey," Rani said. "I thought at lunch we could…"

"No," Rohan said firmly. "Hard no."

"What would be a hard yes?" Rani demanded, not ruffled by his pointed shutdown.

"Giving me some breathing room."

Rani found her friends, and he helped unload the coolers. She'd known the two sisters since high school so Rani's attention was blissfully diverted, leaving Rohan able to absorb the energy of the festival, the music, the bright colors while Rani chatted. One of the sisters made him a smoothie, while Rani connected the two extra blenders she'd brought to their power chord.

"Do you mind if I help them for a little while?" Rani asked, eyeing the long line of people.

"No problem." And it wasn't. He'd take the free afternoon, no agenda, and no hassles or weird, personal questions for the gift it was. "Text when you're ready. No rush," he said, meaning it. Already the day felt brighter, spooling out in front of him.

He wandered down an aisle full of jewelry, searching for the music mix that had captured his attention. It now sounded like a techno beat pulsing under "Con Te Partiro" with tenor Andrea Bocelli slaying it vocally as always. He rounded a corner and that's when he saw her—bright as the sun, bare foot and dancing. Her honey-blond hair spilled out of a messy bun as she swayed and spun and raised her hands high as if in supplication to the sky god or the sun god. She held two cans of spray paint in her hands and shook them occasionally and then painted some sort of an ocean scene with a rose-pink and metallic-gold mermaid rising out of waves of teal, deep blue and silver.

Rohan stood, stupidly staring up at her. She was on some kind of a stage strewn with woven carpets with vivid patterns. A very young-looking DJ bobbed to his music mix— listening in as he cued up the next song, and a wave of something Rohan barely recognized crashed through him.

Longing.

Sorrow.

Emptiness.

Lord Krishna, she was spectacularly and unexpectedly beautiful in a totally organic way, but she was so much more than beautiful.

Some sort of charisma or magic that made her seemed bathed in light that snapped and pulsed around her to the beat of the music.

And then she turned and looked at him.

Green eyes like the forest where he liked to trail run on the weekends when he wasn't on call.

She stopped dancing and her gaze held his. Then she smiled like she knew him. Rohan felt as if lightning jolted him finally to life.

"Hello," her voice sounded familiar.

She reached out a hand toward him, and Rohan wasn't even aware of moving, or ditching his smoothie, but then his hand was in hers, and she pulled him up on stage with her, and he felt like he'd just entered the wardrobe of a book Rani had loved so long ago, begging him to read to her over and over again.

"Welcome," she said.

Back?

It was disorienting. Life mocking him because Rohan, who didn't believe in any of it—karma, numerology, astrology, palm reading, reincarnation, love at first sight—felt inexplicably that he was finally home.

Chapter Five

"**I** DON'T KNOW what I'm doing here."

He had the most beautiful eyes she'd ever seen. Liquid night. A myriad of expressions—fascination, trepidation, curiosity, heat, fear, awe, embarrassment—scrolled through them so quickly that Solei felt she must be staring. She wanted him to stand still, so she could sketch the almost painfully beautiful symmetry of his face—capture each expression, but she knew she didn't possess that much talent.

Say something, idiot!

"What do you want to do?"

"Not sure I can answer that."

Eden swung seamlessly into his next beat, and Solei could feel the rhythm through the soles of her bare feet. On top Eden layered another bhangra song from a movie she must have seen because it sounded familiar, and then he added in a sample of BB King from "How Blue Can You Get."

"DJ's got mad skills," the beautiful stranger seemed captivated, barely holding himself back from dancing. "And balls to showcase such opposite genres."

So much beauty.

Unreal. Like a Michelangelo come to life.

And I have to stop using the B word.

He seemed to hold himself on a tight leash. What would it take to get him to slip it?

You volunteering to help him try?

Seriously she was the one who needed a leash. She'd had three relationships—all of which had ended badly—the last one with Zach had ended two years ago and been the most crushing—not as much from heartbreak but from humiliation. She'd let him, over time, rob her confidence and nearly derail her career. Never again. Caution was her new mantra or at least she wanted it to be.

Time to cease speculating about guests.

"This is an interactive multimedia art exhibit," Solei told him, standing on her tiptoes so that he could hear her without her having to shout.

"Not sure what that means."

He seemed so serious, and yet he had faint lines feathering from his eyes as if he smiled and laughed a lot.

"It can mean pretty much whatever you want it to mean," she told him, this time her lips brushing his ear. She wasn't usually so flirty as she didn't date casually, although she'd told herself she should learn how to when she'd moved to Charlotte "There's not a correct way of proceeding. No right or wrong."

"You've lost me there."

"I see," she teased. "A science guy."

"Guilty."

"But you like music." It wasn't a question. He was subtly grooving to the beat. His body seemed rhythmic, and he had a natural fluid grace. "We can start with that," she said. "Dancing is very interactive."

Solei loved to dance. She'd never had the chance to take lessons growing up, but in college she'd taken Zumba classes, and dancing still was her favorite form of exercise. She began to dance, moving around him, and he followed suit—cutting loose and moving in a style that clearly came naturally and brought him joy.

Solei wasn't sure how many songs they danced to, but they moved together, played off of each other's moves, and closed the space between them as if magnetized. They never once broke eye contact, and yet it didn't feel awkward.

"Tell me about the spray cans?" he finally asked.

Solei had forgotten that she was supposed to be painting. She'd been in the middle of creating a scene. That had never, ever happened to her. Not once.

"Join me?" she asked.

"I've never painted in my life," he said.

"Today's a perfect time to try, but…" She bit her lip and looked at the way he was dressed—like he was on set for a men's mag shoot. Perfectly styled hair—thick, shiny, inky black and blown back from his square forehead and high cheekbones to perfection. His entire appearance and vibe spoke of a man in control of his life. He didn't fly by the seat of his pants or indulge impulse. No mistakes tripped him up. But what was unexpected, a personality tease was his pink sportscoat with the embossed… "Are these fishtails?" She felt stunned.

"I'm not sure. Paisley pattern or fishtails. I just received the jacket last week as part of a…" He hesitated. "Fashion show thing. A friend of mine has a sister finishing up at Parsons and I've…helped her out with…you know…"

A faint blush hit his cheekbones. Solei was fascinated. He was a little shy and not comfortable with the role of hottie, model. She could totally imagine him smoldering into a camera or strutting down a runway.

"I'm not a model," he said quickly sounding mortified.

"You've been her muse." Solei could totally understand and felt a stab of envy—obviously, but jealousy as well, which was totally unexpected and inappropriate.

"That sounds arrogant and creepy since she's only twenty-one, and I've known her since she was a kid."

"Every artist needs a muse," Solei said. God. If he were hers, what artistic avenues would she explore? "Artists also need to protect special clothing. May I?"

"Yes."

Solei used one of the many wipes she'd placed around the booth to clean her hands and then slipped the jacket from his shoulders. She carefully folded it and placed it behind the DJ booth for safety.

He laughed. "I had no idea what you were asking. I just went with it."

"Do you do that often?"

"Never."

"So today's your day." She looked at him a moment trying to get a feel for him and not get so sucked into the perfect symmetry of his features or gorgeous eyes that held sway over her with the gravitational pull of a black hole, and then his body…wow…even better without the jacket—wide shoulders, firm chest, cut arms, and the most beautiful, well-shaped and well-cared for hands—long, graceful fingers with each cuticle pushed back to reveal a half-moon—she'd ever seen on a man. He made her hungry.

She handed him a can of gold spray paint. He looked at it and laughed.

"This color needs to stay between us."

"Okay." The thrill that shot through her at the thought of sharing a secret should have scared her. It was like she was flipping to the back of the book, and they were only on the first page.

"What happens next?" he asked.

"Whatever we want."

HER ANSWERS AND questions floored him—whatever he wanted. When had that happened? Never. And when he'd admitted not knowing how to do something, there'd been no smugness or judgment. No bossing. She had an inner light. She glowed. Warm. Inviting. And she was the most beautiful woman he'd seen in his life. No filters or photoshopping or professional lighting. She was so refreshingly natural and confident and radiating kindness. Rohan felt an odd mix of fascination, exhilaration and doubt.

What was he doing here?

He was so far out of his lane he was on a highway in a different state driving in the wrong direction.

And he didn't care.

Her eyes were deep green with gold flecks. And her mouth was a sexy dream—bow-shaped with no gloss or lipstick to make kissing messy or plastic tasting. When they'd been dancing, he hadn't even bothered to try to look away. He didn't want to miss a moment. The longer they'd danced, the closer they got—hands brushing, shoulders touching, her hips to his, her hair that smelled like jasmine soft against his cheek. She had a beautiful smile that lit her up.

Rohan considered himself to have reasonable game, but she was a different league.

When the music had stopped, he would have done almost anything to keep the moment unspooling, but painting?

He stared at the gold spray paint. No irony there. And as if the gods wanted to mock him further for his irreverence about their power, his phone buzzed with a text and then another. Probably Rani. Only she and his mother fired off text after text as if he had no life until they animated him with contact.

Rohan had no intention of being a slave to his phone today. Not now.

"I'm Rohan," he introduced himself. Probably should have done that earlier, but the music had been killer, and he'd been way into the woman, enthralled by the warmth in her green eyes and smile and the graceful, sexy sway of her body.

"Ascending," she said.

"You know Hindi?"

"A tiny bit. I spent one August in Mahabalipuram through a college art exchange program studying the Shore Temple and a few smaller ones."

"Hot as hell."

"Melty," she agreed, and a song from an '80s band— thanks to Rani's favorite satellite station obsession—now played in his head. He did feel like the world had stopped with this chance encounter.

Maybe it's not so chance.

Where did that come from? He'd been spending too much time with Rani. His phone buzzed again. Too bad. She'd had her chance. Now he was very, very busy.

"I'm Solei."

"So you're used to the heat. Wait. Stop. Pretend I didn't

say something that cliché and stupid."

She laughed. "Sorry. It's out in the universe. No taking it back. Do you want to paint with me?"

"Paint! I was not lying when I said I have no idea how."

"That doesn't matter. Let your inner artist loose." She shook both of the spray cans she'd picked up again, and it was one of the sexiest things he'd ever seen.

"Yes," he said, feeling more than a little like an actor in the wrong play but jumping into an unfamiliar role. "But be warned. I don't have an artist hiding, lurking, or crouching in one cell of my body."

She raised her brows. "Is that a challenge or a promise?"

"It's a fact." He'd never even held a can of spray paint, but he could watch her paint all damn day.

"And you claim to be a man of science—just the facts, Solei."

"Yes," he said unsure if she were teasing him or about to shut him down and kick her out of his orbit.

"Mmmmmmm," she drawled out the letter, and he could not keep his fascinated gaze off her lips. What would she taste like? How would her lips feel against his? Were they as soft as they looked? Would she be shy or bold?

"Okay, Rohan," she propelled him toward one of the boards where no one was yet working. There was a work in progress—the one he'd first seen, a mermaid jumping out of silver- and white-capped waves with an OM for a face and surprisingly detailed fish scales—wow, they looked like the ones on his jacket. "Prepare to be wrong."

"I'm not claiming perfection."

"Perfect is a moving target and takes many forms. Add something here. Anything you want," she encouraged.

All the spit dried in his mouth. "I can't ruin your painting. That should be framed, not defaced."

"But that is what today is all about—art in collaboration. It's a multimedia, experiential art exhibit with students and teachers and hopefully visitors watching, joining us on stage, and coming together to express themselves—a free exchange of ideas. Sharing. Creating. No right or wrong."

He couldn't fathom the concept of creating something publicly and letting someone join in and do whatever they wanted. True he often performed surgery with med students or residents watching to learn, but none of them jumped out of their seats to put their stamp on it.

"I don't know what to do," he admitted. "I don't think I've had an art class since elementary school."

"Make a mark," she suggested, and her smile made him feel like something cut loose inside of him. She smelled hedonistically sexy—a hint of jasmine or was it orange blossoms and then there was an earthy spice. Her scent and presence intoxicated him. He felt dizzy.

"Any mark?"

"Just aim and press the nozzle. Move your hand around and something will happen."

"Yeah, a splodge—a mess."

"No judging our collaboration," she said. "Make a mark and I'll add on to it. We'll take turns."

Hadn't he spent his whole time at Davidson undergrad wanting to try other classes or activities—even if he only briefly strayed from the rigid, well-worn path he'd been obediently trudging down his whole life?

"I really haven't had any art," he reiterated. "Just science."

"There's no test, Rohan. Scientists have incredible imaginations. They are always asking why or what if or how? They see questions and problems and search for solutions and possibilities."

"I hadn't thought about it like that," he admitted.

"Rohan," she breathed his name like a prayer. "Make your mark."

"Solei," he tasted her name, and a sense of déjà vu he'd never yet experienced but Rani had often talked about swept over him like a wave, washing him clean, and pushing him to shore when he hadn't even realized he was drowning.

Take a risk.

Was that him or her speaking?

He pointed the spray can toward a blank section of drywall.

"No rules," her breath was warm against his ear. "No expectations. Just freedom."

He closed his eyes. Freedom. As if such a thing existed.

"It does."

Had he said that aloud? How idiotically uncool. He was making an utter fool of himself. But he couldn't leave. Her pull was too strong.

"We'll jump together," she said. Her hand covered his, her forefinger over his and she pressed down on the trigger.

"I SLAYED THE challenge," she announced ten minutes later after she and Rohan had covered one half of the drywall surrounding her mermaid. Rohan had started with words, then phrases as they'd talked. She'd added on to those, creating a freestyle poem and had painted a few visuals to accompany their words. Inspired, Rohan had enclosed some of the words in geometric shapes, already working out how to create a shadowing effect by pressing more lightly and farther away or layering color.

She stepped back to look at what they'd done. "Art," she swept her hand out.

"That was a blast." Rohan's eyes shone, and she finally saw why he had faint lines feathering from his eyes—he had a wide-open smile. And perfect white teeth. "I'm not sure I'd call it art."

"What then?"

"Fun."

"Just what the doctor prescribed."

"None that I've worked…met," he said quickly.

She noticed the stumble. Was he a doctor? That would explain the insistence that he'd only taken science classes. But most doctors she'd met in LA had an innate arrogance and sense of intellectual superiority that set her teeth on edge. Still, she'd insisted the art collaboration was a no judgment zone so she could hardly judge the artist's true profession. But the fact that he didn't want her to know he was a doctor raised her suspicions. Did he think she'd be interested in him because he was a doctor?

Who cared? His life and money were his. She paid her own way always.

"It was fun." She cut him a break. "I haven't worked with words much," she admitted thoughtfully. "I like it. It felt different. Two halves of my brain working in coordination."

She handed Rohan a wipe. A new group of artists arrived with their parents and teachers and a new group of scheduled volunteers.

"I have an hour break before I have to supervise the booth again," she said, wiping her hands and face. A spurt of nerves assailed her, but she swallowed them down. "Do you want to walk and get something to eat? Full disclosure. I will also need to check on a different group of students who are having an art showing in the juried section of the art festival."

Rohan turned around, picked up a black can of spray paint and toward the top of the drywall in block letters painted *YES*.

Solei grabbed the gold that she and Rohan had started with and looped out: The Power of above it.

She quickly checked in with the new teachers and Tula and then she and Rohan walked into the crowd. She hadn't had a chance to look around the festival yet, but for the first time, the craftmanship and artistry didn't grab her attention. It was the man who walked beside her, wearing his distinctive jacket despite the warmth of the spring day. Solei rarely asked herself what she was doing. She just did it. She wasn't irresponsible or out of control ever. But she did follow her instincts.

My hormones.

Those bitches had caused her trouble more than once and especially with Zach. Looked like they were meddling again.

But with Rohan she felt like she was going to be in a whole different heap of Trouble with a capital T because he was different. Refined. He oozed confidence and money and had an air of professionalism that probably meant he was a suit. Or a doctor. In Solei's experience, men who wore blazers always thought artists were cute. Sexually adventurous. Playthings.

And yet, the three relationships she'd had—one with a writer, the other two with working artists, they hadn't taken her or her art seriously. Their careers and needs and wants held precedence. And for an embarrassingly long time, she'd let them drive.

She'd promised herself she was done with putting herself and her career second.

At least with a suit they wouldn't be in competition.

Think much?

They'd just met, but she already had them in a toxic relationship where she would give and give and give, and he would take and then she would pack her things and jump into Frida and leave.

"Want a chai?" she asked, seeing a cart that bragged of over fifty varietals of loose-leaf tea.

"Sounds great," Rohan said, but when he reached for his wallet, she stilled his hand and paid.

Chais in hand, they browsed one of the long rows of the artists slowly making her way to the pavilion where the local student art was. It was a beautiful day with a beautiful man. She didn't want to think of hurts of the past.

"What did you think really of your impromptu art experience?" she asked as they paused at one exhibit of photography. His phone buzzed. It was the second time it had done that since they'd left the art booth. But he didn't reach for it to check the text. Respectful? Into her? Or girlfriend. She needed to shut her brain off once in a while. They were strangers at an art fair.

He laughed and then sipped his chai as if wanting to give himself time to think of the right word.

"Wait, what is this?" He turned toward her, his dark eyes

flashing dismay and his mouth working.

"Chai. Oh. Oat milk. Sorry. I asked and you said sure." Guilt pinged through her. She hadn't had dairy in years because it upset her stomach. "We can get you something else," she said cautiously, curious as to how he'd react to disappointment.

His thick, dark brows descended, and his eyes narrowed as if he were deep in thought solving a calculus problem in his brain. He took another sip, swished it around his mouth and swallowed.

"That's oat milk?"

"With spicy chai." She waited.

He shook his head and laughed. "It's damn good, but," he pointed a finger at her and then drew it across his firm, well-formed lips that she couldn't stop wanting to draw, "that information is top secret. My mom and Nanima and Mummyji and none of my aunties can ever learn that I drank a chai with oat milk ever."

She pretended to lock her lips but couldn't stop the escape of an embarrassing girlish giggle.

He was such a contradiction. So handsome that women stared when they walked by, but he seemed oblivious of the women's attention. Yet he was stylish and groomed. He oozed confidence but had shown vulnerability when she'd encouraged him to paint with her. His clothes, sunglasses and watch spoke of wealth, and he had a touch of swagger, but he'd let her pay for the chais with a smile and a thank you and had pushed his wallet back in his pocket without any masculine posturing.

She was a little thrown by the flurry of messages or alerts he received, but he continued to ignore his phone.

"So oat milk is a serious offense?" she asked. "Booted out of the family serious?"

"Never that lucky," he laughed. "More like a family intervention with two dozen aunties and uncles weighing in. And the guilt." He pretended to stagger.

"You have a big family?" she asked wistfully, which was ridiculous. Her parents' lifestyle and dreams would never have worked with a handful of kids tumbling around. One had been plausible, and her early absorption with art, reading and journaling had made her an easy kid to explore the world with.

"I have a huge extended family—and three cousins who are more like siblings, but I'm an only." He sipped his chai. "You can imagine how much privacy, freedom and independence I got."

"I am too."

"Sweet. We have that in common. Are you from Charlotte?"

How to answer that? "I've been here a year," she said cautiously because most people found her background odd. "I went to high school in Newport Beach, California, and college at UCLA. I'm teaching art at the Queen City Arts and Science Academy this year, but I'm not sure if the school will have enough interest or money to fund my position so I can stay on."

Why was she confessing that?

"I'll be looking for a job soon as well," he startled her. He seemed so settled. "Or at least I should be. Where will you go if your position loses funding? Back to California?"

Would she? Solei realized in that moment that she really didn't have any desire to go back to LA—at least not right away.

"I don't know. I could go anywhere." It had been her truth for so long, but the concept had steadily been losing its appeal.

He choked on his chai. "Anywhere?" he repeated his eyes goggled at her. "Literally anywhere?"

"Sure. Anywhere I want."

"How is that possible?" He stared at her like she'd told him she could fly.

With a mixture of pride and a weird sense of sorrow she shot back, "How is it not?"

ROHAN WATCHED SOLEI as she spoke to some of the kids about their artwork. She was so enthusiastic. She glowed with an etherealness like her mermaid in the painting she'd encouraged him to join. Pressing his finger down and hearing the soft hiss of the aerosol and seeing the vivid color stream out had been heady. Watching words flow with the sweep of his arm and press of his finger had felt freeing. Creating with Solei had felt more intimate than any sex he'd ever had.

He wanted to paint again.

He wanted to understand how Solei could create such a detailed picture and then risk it all by inviting a stranger to join her.

He wanted to spend time alone with her. Do things she enjoyed. Share his love of water and hiking. He wanted to hear about her dreams. Learn of her fears.

He wanted what he'd never wanted before.

And he didn't want to ask why.

Solei took time with each student and family. She fascinated him with the way she leaned into each conversation, including everyone. She let the student lead but subtly helped guide them. No blanket praise, more of a "tell me about…" Who was the idiot running a school that would consider letting her go?

Rani texted again. He knew he wasn't being fair not answering, but they were both adults, and he had so little free time. He'd already texted her a general message that he'd met up with a friend and would make his own way home. That had only caused Rani to blow up his phone calling. And now another text. She'd been as dogged as a toddler. Rohan sighed and stepped a little away from the student exhibit.

Is it a woman?

Why did she twig on that? He didn't want to lie, but he

didn't want to open himself to a barrage of questions. Rani was nosy. And protective. And she had an ability to track him down and find out what he was doing or had done with the drive and unerring skill of a bloodhound.

Yes.

Friend?

I just met her.

Dancing dots. Unusual. Rani was a speedy texter firing off questions and opinions like a Glock P80.

I want to meet her.

I'll... He stopped, his attention still on Solei. He wanted to spend time with her during the art fair, but also after— take her for a drink or dinner. Walk around the city and watch the lights come on. Was she free?

...give you a full report later, Mom.

Solei chatted a few more minutes and took a few pictures of the students and their artwork. She looked at her Apple Watch, and his heart clenched, hoping this wasn't when she would heave ho him overboard.

"Hey." She joined him. "Thanks for waiting. Did you get everything resolved with whoever was texting you? Was it work-related?"

Her voice was casual, but he felt guilty that she'd noticed.

"I'm not on call this weekend." He gave up on hiding his profession, ironic as his cardiothoracic surgeon status was the first thing his mom and dad trumpeted. "That was my cousin, Rani."

"Does she want to join us at the art booth?" Solei asked as they headed back out into the sun and crowds.

He was ridiculously pleased with the word "us."

"No," that came out a little stronger than he'd intended. "She's got her own thing going on. I helped her bring fruit and ice to some friends of hers who run a smoothie truck. Mission accomplished so I'm free."

"I have another shift at the booth." Solei paused and turned and looked up at him. "I'd love it if you'd join me. I'm free after that. We can't dismantle the booth until tomorrow morning before the art fair starts up again."

One hour. She wanted to spend time with him. A potential night of freedom—no family, no demands, no work—unfurled between them.

"You're not working the booth tomorrow?" he asked already wanting more.

He'd been planning to leave early Sunday to return home to Durham claiming work. Shanti and Asha had retreated to the relative peace and privacy of Shanti's uptown condo. His parents were still playing co-hosts to friends and family who kept dropping by to "commiserate and comfort," while they leached every juicy gossip morsel. He'd felt that the sooner he left, the better, hoping to avoid attention and the overt speculation that drifted his way like a bad odor.

But he didn't have to leave Charlotte, just the house.

"No. The booth was more of a chance for the kids at the Urban Youth Artists program where I volunteer to have a chance to participate as working artists. I was hoping also that the booth would raise the center's profile and some donations, but two days would be too expensive and too exhausting. We have a small pool of volunteers."

He watched transfixed as she took a soft pink scrunchy out of her hair, quickly ran her fingers through the long, wavy strands, making all that honey silk fly, and then spiraled her hair back into a messy bun and secured it with the scrunchy.

He didn't blink. He had it bad. She smiled, and it felt like a burst of heat.

"I've seen my cousins do that hundreds of times, but it never had quite the same impact," he admitted, mocking his utter absorption with the mundane task.

She laughed. "I'm in the same boat," she said softly, stopping by a dogwood tree. She looked up. "If this were a movie, the tree would be in full bloom when I make my confession."

"A confession sounds promising," he said lightly, although it made him nervous. What if she were married or…she must have a boyfriend. How could anyone this beautiful and talented and easy to talk to be single? "We'd have to come back in a few weeks for a full bloom effect."

He was so aware of her—the way the sun made her hair shine. The vivid green of her eyes, and the way they were almond shaped and tilted up at the corners giving her an unusual, almost exotic look. Her lashes were thick and pale brown, same as her brows.

"I like that you're tall," he said stepping closer, but not yet touching. He didn't want to freak her out, but the connection he felt had been instant—something he'd never felt before, and, not to be a jerk, he knew when a woman was into him. "It can make certain things easier," he said conversationally.

"Like what?" she asked closing the space between them even more. "Like this?" Her breath mingled with his. He thought she was going to kiss him, but instead she laid her cheek against his. "Or this," her lips traced one of his eyebrows.

He trembled. And hardened. He quickly shifted his stance so he wasn't so obvious. This close her scent and promised warmth and softness of her skin was heady. He was hungry on a...a...

Soul level.

Wouldn't Rani squeal if he ever said something like that?

"You never told me your confession," he breathed, millimeters from her lips that he'd been fantasizing about since he'd first seen her dancing. Unfortunately, his stomach chose that moment to get in on the action, complaining with a loud growl.

She laughed. "Oops! Guess you'll have to wait for my confession." Her hand cupped his cheek and her thumb feathered once across his mouth. He lightly bit her. Her smile was brighter than the sun. "Let's get you fed."

"I'm not a wild animal," he objected, although he was starting to feel feral. "But Solei," he kept a hold of her hand and brought it back to his mouth so that he could kiss the pad of her index finger, touch it with his tongue, and then nibble on it—he'd always been so oral, "I'm not just hungry for food."

Chapter Six

THEY CHOSE TO his dismay and pleasure and relief a South Indian food truck.

"You're not choosing Indian food for me," he felt compelled to ask.

"What? No. Why?" There were only two people in front of them, and she scanned the menu with interest. Her profile was just as beautiful as her face head-on. Her nose was a perfect size and shape, whereas his cousins always complained that theirs were slightly too big. Her eyes were wide-set and tipped up at the corners as did her mouth so that she looked, even when her face was in repose like she was about to smile. Her features were delicate, though her chin was strong.

"I love Goan Chana Masala. Well, anything with coconut, really."

"Noted."

"Do you like South Indian food, or do you prefer...Punjabi?"

Just the fact that she knew there were different states and foods in the different states pleased him, though if asked, he would have said it didn't matter.

"I love South and North Indian food." Although standing in line at a South Indian food truck offered a much smaller chance that the family owners would know him. "I love food. All kinds of food," he added not wanting her to think that he would only want Indian food. Even his many relatives still living in India were eager to try different cuisines when they visited.

She laughed. "Do you cook a lot of Indian food?"

"Hard no, unfortunately," he said. "I grew up with both my grandmothers taking care of me and my cousins, and I would have been tossed ass over head out of the kitchen if I even tried to enter."

"So no cooking lesson for me?"

"Not true," he jumped feet first into the opening she gave him. "I can google. And I have numerous lifelines I can call."

She smiled at him over her shoulder as she stepped up to order, and he could barely breathe. It was on the tip of his tongue to tell her to forget the food. They could go to an Indian grocery store and stock up, head to his apartment in Durham and figure out how to cook whatever she wanted for the rest of the weekend.

And then it hit him. Solei taught art at a high school in Charlotte. She volunteered with an inner-city arts program in Charlotte. He was in Durham, a two-hour drive at best but had a job offer that wasn't his dream one in Charlotte.

Jump ahead much?

He was so consumed with his racing thoughts that when Solei asked what he felt like eating, he almost said "you."

Noob move. He'd been attracted before and had hooked up with more than his share of appealing and interesting women. Solei made him feel like he had the proverbial two left feet and a clumsy tongue.

They shared one Goan Chana along with saag, with Solei only taking a few bites. Rani was texting again. Or maybe his mom. He'd check later. He didn't want to miss a moment with Solei.

"Are you going to indulge me as a painting partner again?" she asked as they neared the booth.

Indulge. He liked that word, a lot. He'd pretty much indulge her any way she wanted, and he was confident Solei had a vivid imagination.

"That can be arranged in exchange for the confession you teased earlier."

"I *believe* I said I'd tell you later."

"How much later?"

Wait. Did she have a dimple? She did, or was it called something different when it was in a woman's chin? It was adorable and begged for exploration.

"Maybe over a drink or dinner?"

"Both," Rohan tested his negotiation skills.

"Hmmmm," she leaned in toward him. "We'll see." She bounced up the stairs and immediately took charge of a new group of students and volunteers.

"LOOK AT YOU getting your flirt on," Tula teased her later as the afternoon shift began to wind down.

"It's fun," Solei said.

"A little fast. He just appeared out of thin air, right?"

Solei paused. She was feeling really good, like champagne bubbles in her bloodstream good, and she didn't want Tula or anyone else to harsh her buzz.

"It was pretty magic." She didn't want to sound defensive, but Tula had Rand—the most supportive husband ever. Solei had been on her own for a long time, and over the past couple of years she'd had to accept that even when she'd been in a relationship, she'd still been for the most part, alone.

She wanted to stand on her own two feet, but she also wanted a partner.

"I'm sorry, Solei. I worry. You just seem…" Tula broke off. "I just don't want to see some flashy, hot guy take advantage of your sweet and giving nature."

The artists who were doing the street art section had been busy, with more and more people from the crowd joining in—thrillingly successful, but it had sidelined her and Rohan's fun.

You could bring him home.

The impulsive thought shocked her. It was way too soon for that, wasn't it?

It was time to install another section of clean drywall. Solei stepped up to one corner of the fully painted drywall, careful of the wet paint and pulled the ever-present drill from her pocket.

"Can I help?" Rohan was there before she had time to ask some students. "I wondered what the deal was with the drill in your back pocket. Maybe I need to start carrying around some tools of my own. Could prove useful." His smile was so wide and open and his gaze admiring that the attraction sizzled and popped. She also loved the way he flirted, just a little bit of an edge that belied his handsome and sophisticated appearance.

She had a feeling Rohan could definitely get down and dirty, and that just kept flashing heat through her like a blowtorch.

"Depends on how you handle your tools." Solei centered the drill and pushed the reverse button to pull out the two drywall screws while Rohan and two teens held on. She tucked the screws in her pocket and blew on the tip of the drill. "Perhaps another challenge later if you're up for it."

Omg she was being way too obvious, but he thrilled her so much she just kept tossing away any sort of caution. She smiled, feeling bolder than she ever had. She wasn't going to live her life ruled by fear. That was probably the biggest gift from her parents—a sense of adventure and self-reliance.

"I am ready for any type of challenge," he said, his gaze steadily holding hers, and she felt like they were having two conversations.

"Good to know."

"And I love to play with tools."

NEARLY AN HOUR later, Rohan was still thinking about his overtly flirty double entendre. He was so attracted to her—physically but also mentally—and yet, he stupidly felt guilty. He wasn't doing anything wrong, but because his mom had mentioned a matchmaker, he had this slimy feeling that he was cheating on Solei. They weren't even dating. And he didn't want to be matched. Still, he'd spent his whole life trying to do the right thing—be the son his parents wanted him to be, and yet there always seemed to be this invisible bar that kept getting notched higher.

The fact that he was so fascinated by a woman he'd just met proved he wasn't ready to commit to marriage. And he had *just* met Solei. She couldn't expect him to disembowel his life for her perusal immediately.

The conflict between what he wanted and what he knew was expected, gnawed at the pleasure of the day. He'd always known the expectation was that he'd marry a highly educated Punjabi woman from a good family—meaning a family of means like his parents. She'd likely be American born like him, but a few of his older cousins had married women still living in India, who'd then immigrated. But marriage had always bobbed on the faraway horizon. Out of sight and easily ignored. He'd hooked up with women from a variety of races and cultural backgrounds over the years but focused on academics his whole life. Now he wanted time for himself before taking on the responsibility of a wife and family.

But how to explain that to his mother when she didn't listen.

It was time for Solei's exhibition. Rohan moved closer to the edge of the booth so he could watch without blocking her. A young Indian girl named Geeta had taken over the DJ booth. She had a shock of blue hair and an extreme undercut and several piercings on her face—lip, nose and eyebrow. His aunts and uncles would have sent any of his cousins back to India if they'd pulled a look like that. As the music kicked on, Solei rapidly picked her colors—various shades of pink— light to dark, and then black and white. She shook the cans and flipped it a little, playing to the crowd of kids, some of whom were now seated in the booth like it was a show, and he guessed it was—an artist at work.

He wished he'd asked her more about her art when they'd had their snack instead of just lusting after her.

Why pink? Solei didn't seem that girlie—she wore a washed-out, ripped pair of paint-splattered jeans, a thin, olive-colored tank, and she'd put on a soft, creamy-colored cashmere cardigan when they'd been walking around the festival greeting parents. But she did have a drill in her back pocket—something that he'd been obsessing over. And it was pink.

"You will often take your inspiration as you look around," she told the kids sitting around her. The audience moved closer. "Or from what you read or talk about or experience."

She shook the two different tones of pink and flipped them a couple of times earning an "ooooh," from the kids.

She winked at him.

'Inspiration,' she mouthed.

The kids looked at him, and he realized she'd chosen the colors because of his jacket. It was a rush, but also embarrassing. He smiled, ordering himself to keep his shit together.

Solei spray-painted a large outline of a pink rose—her movements were graceful and easy, and yet the image was controlled. Slicing through the middle with a maroon color she wrote, *"That which we call a rose..."* She sprayed another outline of the basics of the rose, just a little off-kilter from the original one. The line was darker but thinner. And then she misted over the rose and her dangling question with red.

Rohan watched as Solei again traced over her staggered pink rose outlines lightly with black, keeping the thin, astonishingly controlled line off-center from the other two. His mouth dropped open. The pink now looked like it was glowing, with the mist of red and black shadowing the letters making them look 3D. Even the letters had dimension. So cool.

"I found you."

Rohan jumped at Rani's triumphant voice. He nearly tumbled off the stage.

"Shshshsh," he hissed not wanting to miss anything. Solei chose another darker pink and layered it, and a lighter pink, and then she put a thin white line of paint through each curlicue making up the rose and the letters.

"What are you doing?" Rani hopped up next to him. "You haven't been to an art fair since you were a kid if ever."

"I've been missing out."

"Seriously, Rohan, what are you doing here?" Rani's way too perceptive gaze lit on Solei who was making a few adjustments to her work. "You're so not into art."

"I haven't had the chance to be," he defended.

Rani watched the rose take form. "That's incredible. It looks like neon."

"I know," he breathed.

"Are you captivated by the art or the woman?"

"Find your own fun."

"Rohan," Rani said, and her voice had a warning in it, much like his mother's often held.

"I am thirty-two years old. Perfectly capable of taking care of myself."

"I'm not worried about you," Rani grumbled. "I'm worried about whoever she is. That rose she painted is the same color as your jacket, and you have no idea how...how everything you are."

"What the hell does that mean?"

He should ignore her, which was of course impossible. Say what you wanted about Rani, and lots of people rudely did, she was never ignored.

"I turn my back for five minutes and you wander off and find a golden goddess."

"I thought I was the golden one," he mocked, not wanting Solei to overhear although DJ G only seemed to think the volume control went in one direction—up.

"You are. That's the problem. You're both golden. It will never work. Not to mention your mom will stroke out if you bring a gori girl home."

"Totally rude, Rani." He was a bit shocked at Rani referring to Solei's race. "I've never brought anyone home for a reason."

"It's time to stop playing games, Rohan. This is serious. I can find you the perfect match."

"I'm fine navigating my own love life."

"Love?"

Shit.

"Figure of speech."

"Rohan. Stop right now." She turned away from Solei's painting and made a time-out sign, dramatically. "This is going to be a train wreck."

"Chill," he objected, rare temper stirring. "I just met her, and I'm allowed to make my own friends. I don't need my mummy's approval nor yours."

"I'm staving off the inevitable heartache. You're totally going to cave to Auntie. I know it. At least I can find you someone..." Rani paused, and he didn't like the lightbulb look in her eyes at all. Rani looked at Solei's now finished neon rose that was next to the other painting of the mermaid, golden sun and freestyle poem they'd done together.

Rani crossed her arms and frowned, her winged brows scrunched.

Shit.

"This is for your own good, Rohan. And hers—whoever she is. I'll prove to you that she's all wrong, and I'm right."

Rani marched toward Solei, purpose in her steps.

SOLEI ACKNOWLEDGED THE crowd's applause and answered a few of the kids' questions. She stepped back to gain a better perspective on her rose. It was luminous. And maybe too revealing, but if she didn't put herself out there, she'd lose out. There were ten easy reasons to walk away, and only two to stay—desire and curiosity, but Solei didn't care. She was going to ask him out.

She didn't know much about him, but what she did know, she liked. Sure, he was vaporizingly hot, but he had a curiosity about life and was willing to take risks and put himself out there that called to her. She took another step back ran into what felt like a brick wall warmed by the sun. Two caramel hands covered her bare arms, and she turned happily. Rohan didn't feel new at all. She felt like she was home.

"Watching you paint was the most fucking awesome thing I've ever seen in my life." His face was tense, his expression serious but warm with admiration.

Solei was stunned into silence. She'd received many accolades over her short career. She was offered commissions from more cities, corporations and wealthy people and celebrities than she could accept, but somehow, Rohan's stark, raw admission, curled up warm and purring in her tummy.

She wasn't sure what to say and nervously moistened her lips.

"Truly incredible, Solei," his voice sounded pressured, his inky, liquid gaze heated. "And not in the way 'incredible' and 'awesome' are usually bandied about. I just lack the vocabulary to effectively express how I feel."

Her lips tried to form a word, but the intensity with which he spoke muted her.

"I feel jolted to life."

"By a rose?" she whispered, and for some stupid reason, a memory surfaced of her last boyfriend Zachary Dean's cutting voice and dismissive shrug of his shoulders as he pushed past her, backpack stuffed with clothes she'd laundered, and jumped on his bike. Just before peeling out of her life and leaving three months of unpaid rent behind, he'd sneered that her art was 'amateur and would never hang in a gallery or museum.'

Rohan touched the cleft in her chin that she hated. "By a woman," he whispered.

"Hi," a young woman with dark eyes wide with curiosity and enthusiasm bounced between them before Solei could fully process Rohan's proclamation. "I'm Rani Kapoor, Rohan's top favorite cousin."

"Oh hello," she moved, making room for Rani, who stared at her with a searching intensity that was disconcerting. Was this the cousin who'd been texting so much earlier? Was she why Rohan seemed suddenly tense?

"Solei Beals." She was determined to be friendly, but careful.

"Solei, of course," Rani said, her dark eyes sweeping over her rather clinically like a doctor's exam. "Solei," Rani repeated, her eyes shifted to Rohan. "That's not some kind of sign."

Solei's smile faded. She was confused and uncomfortable.

Rani smiled. "Inside joke. I am after all, Rohan's favorite, beloved cousin."

"And the one most prone to interfere and interrupt," Rohan said, his voice cooler than Solei had heard it.

Rani looked up at Rohan, clearly startled.

"I can play nice," Rani said quickly.

"I'd rather you not play at all."

Rani swallowed, then turned her attention back to Solei.

She smiled. "Let's start over. I'm Rani." She motioned for Solei to speak. Maybe something was different about her—like she was on the spectrum. Sympathy bloomed.

"Solei," she played along.

"What's your greatest fear?"

"What?" she stammered and nearly choked on her own spit.

"Don't think. Just answer. Instinct."

"Having nothing to say," Solei said, waving at the rose and then the drywall that she and Rohan had done. "No images to express my thoughts and feelings."

"Wow," Rani gaped at her.

"What's yours?"

Rani looked at Rohan, ignoring Solei's question. "I get it, but..." She couldn't see the expression Rani leveled at Rohan.

"Not your call," Rohan said, his voice a low, pleasant, sexy growl. "I'm taking Solei out for drinks and dinner."

"I'll come too," Rani said.

Solei fought to maintain a neutral expression. She'd always longed for a big family—the noisy, fun, busy, supportive crush of it all. Others having her back and more people for her to love and be loved by. She hadn't thought about the potentially inconvenient part.

"Please, Solei," Rani looked up at her. She was much shorter and looked like a manic pixie—huge dark eyes, and small, heart-shaped features, and a jagged shag bob. "Just a drink," Rani held her hands and then made a heart shape on her chest.

Rohan snorted like a horse, and Solei wasn't sure if she should laugh or grab Rohan and run.

"I need help. I'm working on something for my doctorate dissertation," Rani's eyes glowed with sincerity and pleading. "It's about attraction and love at first sight."

"Hard no, Rani."

"It is," Rani tossed her head and looked at Rohan. "Just a few questions for a survey I'm building. It will be a little like a game, and then I will go home...alone," she said dramatically. "Interesting, right? Who's in?"

"No one," Rohan smoothed a few strands of Rani's black bob out of her overly sparkly lip gloss.

"Not like you don't always rise to a challenge. I dare you," she taunted Rohan and turned to Solei. "Aren't you more than a little curious? Don't answer that if the answer is no."

"Behave," Rohan said.

Solei laughed. The affection and exasperation between them was entertaining, and it made Rohan even more appealing if that were possible. Ok maybe she still wanted a large, loud, loving and interfering family.

"Okay, a drink and a game of questions," Solei said. Rani jumped up and down and clapped. She hopped off the edge of the booth. "Is she going to pick our brains?" she asked

Rohan, and loved how his eyes warmed, and his tension eased.

"Highly probable," he said and held on to her as she slipped her feet into her Docs. "How fast are you in those things?"

"Super-fast when I'm running," she teased. "But why would I do that?"

Chapter Seven

H E'D WANTED TO go to Seven, the newest rooftop bar in Charlotte, named because it was the seventh one in the city. He hadn't yet been, but Solei had suggested Skyline. Her green eyes had shone like leaves in the sun, and he'd forgotten why he wasn't really fond of the old-fashioned rooftop jazz bar that was styled like something out of the twenties.

Rani had stared at Solei as if she was a sculpture in an art gallery. "Why Skyline?" Rani had asked.

"I love it. It's got such a relaxed, go with the flow vibe."

Rani had shot him the look. The "see I was right" look.

"It's a jazz club," Solei had enthused. "I love jazz—the liberating rhythms, the way the musicians collaborate in real time, the way the same song can sound and feel different on a different night." She'd smiled dreamily.

"That sounds fantastic. Brilliant." He defended Solei's choice. Apparently too enthusiastically because Rani had then given him another look—her "liar, but I'll back your play for now" look.

He didn't really want her to back his play. And he definitely didn't want to answer any of Rani's off-kilter, disconcerting questions. He wanted her to go home. And he wanted time alone with Solei. Damn it. He'd graduated top of his class in fucking everything. He'd had no trouble ever getting research grants and opportunities. He'd had his choice of schools and programs and now had no difficulty lining up interviews—and none of them had been in Charlotte.

Was it too much to ask to be alone with a beautiful woman without his family weighing in?

Rani had linked arms with Solei, like they were suddenly besties, and set off across the park just as the sun started to dip and turn that deeper orange color while the sky purpled. Solei had stopped at the end of the park and tilted her head back toward the sun like she was a pagan offering. He'd snapped a picture with his phone, wishing he could draw or paint or do something she'd admire and relate to.

Totally unlike him.

And now as they sat outside on the rooftop patio on low white couches grouped around a terrazzo rectangular gas firepit, he had to squash an unaccustomed barely banked irritation. How was he supposed to get to know Solei with Rani dominating the...well, he couldn't even call it a conversation. Rani was channeling Oprah and asking Solei about her drink and menu preferences like they were hugely symbolic and mysterious keys to the universe.

"It's one drink," he said. "Not lifetime commitment."

"Says you." Rani shot him a hard to interpret look, which pissed him off more.

Solei's cardigan dipped off her slim shoulders, exposing her toned, creamy skin that had just a bit of a golden kiss of sun. He was as irritated with himself as Rani. She was being Rani. He was acting like a petulant kid with a new toy he didn't want to share.

"What's your most embarrassing moment?" Rani probed.

Solei perused the drink menu briefly and then handed it to him with a smile.

"I'm not easily embarrassed," Solei mused. "My art is so public so I'm scrutinized when I create and screw up and have to figure out a save so..." She shrugged. "How about you?"

"I'm running the game," Rani said. "And taking notes."

"Hardly fair," he pointed out.

"I'm an objective researcher," Rani lied. "Think of your last kiss," Rani started, and then she flinched when Solei looked at him and smiled rather wickedly.

"Okay," Solei said.

"Ummmm," Rani shot him a WTF look that made him laugh. Solei could make even an interrupted date fun. He leaned back on the couch and sprawled a little, knowing his "manspreading" would irritate Rani. Also, more than a few dates had told him over the years that he looked sexy AF when he did it or "like a hungry lion," one woman had purred a few months ago.

"What color do you associate with that kiss?" Rani asked primly.

"Shimmering gold with metallic flecks and a deep olive undertone."

"Huh?"

"Olive is my favorite color," she said. "And my favorite thing to eat. And my favorite tree. Someday I'm going to have an olive grove."

Solei took her scrunchie out, eyes on his and then she let her gaze shift lower.

Rohan felt like she'd lit a match. He wasn't sure if he'd ever eaten an olive, but he was on board with making an immediate Costco trip to stock up.

"Why olives?" Rani asked.

"I love the climate the trees grow in—warm and sunny and dry. The shape of the branches, the silver tones of the leaves. They are strong, hearty, long-lived. And then the olives make you work for them. You need to brine them. Wait to consume them." The way she said consume nearly jacked him off the couch. Rani stared, as fascinated as he was by the monologue. "Van Gogh painted a series of at least fifteen paintings depicting olive trees in Saint-Remy-de-Provence while he was in an asylum there. The shape of the trunks can be as evocative as the taste. There are so many varietals and colors and sizes. They are fleshy and earthy, and feel decadent, and yet you must be careful and eat around the pit, as if it is a dangerous prize."

Rani blinked. Rohan had never seen anyone derail Rani when she was on a mission. Or shut her speechless. He jerked his head at Solei a little and tapped the couch. She rose like a goddess and came to him.

"And there are many uses and healing properties of olive oils," Solei added just as the server bore down on them with three glasses of water and a bowl of mixed olives.

"Only one of the many reasons I love coming here," Solei said, plucking a large green olive from the small ceramic bowl and holding it to his lips. "Careful," she whispered.

"Not in my nature."

Before today that was not remotely true, but Rohan liked this new version of himself, and he had no intention of backing up—at least retreat had never been in his nature when he wanted something.

He took a bite.

SOLEI LEANED AGAINST Rohan, absorbing his warmth. She sipped at her Sazerac, savoring the bitterness of the drink, the sweetness of the three orange slices and the texture and bite of the olive that had been brined with red chili pepper flakes.

The jazz band, The Blue Fins were in fine form but missing their singer. She felt like the notes and the company soaked into her pores leaving her contented and boneless.

"Why do you like jazz?" Rani asked. Solei didn't like

jazz. She loved it. "Rohan hates it."

"I don't," he objected. "I don't know much about it."

"It used to be called devil music," Rani said, googling.

"That's only one of the things I love about jazz," Solei enthused. "It was considered unsavory and immoral because the Black musicians weren't allowed to play in many of the sanctioned or proper clubs where only whites could go, so jazz musicians had to be more underground and perform in brothels or less reputable places. The establishment tried to shut the music down, but it thrived. The musicians and the fans found a way and people from so many different backgrounds and with different lives and experiences came together to listen."

"So you're a rebel? You root for the underdog," Rani said, shooting Rohan another fraught look. He ignored Rani and toyed with Solei's hair, until she worried she'd start to purr.

"I don't think I'm a rebel." Solei thought about it. "It might seem like that with me being a street artist, but I've worked since I was fifteen. I pay my bills and taxes on time. I have money in the bank. A career I love with room to grow."

"And you love jazz," Rani repeated almost triumphantly. "It says here that people who don't understand jazz are music novices who don't understand the complex chord progressions or the freestyle nature of jazz."

"Ouch," Rohan nuzzled her neck. "True, but I can learn."

"It also says," Rani focused on her phone, "that jazz lovers are intelligent, creative, confident, comfortable with themselves, and extroverts."

"Bingo," Rohan said.

Rani crossed her eyes.

Solei laughed. "What's your next question, gamer?"

"You don't have to play," Rohan murmured. "I can toss her over the balcony."

"Not unless she can fly. I don't want to bail you out of jail."

"You're so sweet. As for flying, Rani might pull it off. She has a bit of the mystic witch in her. It's uncanny and inconvenient."

And interesting. Solei could definitely see it. Rani, went back to her phone. Clearly she had some sort of file she'd started. She was really taking this seriously, and Solei felt a little guilty for messing with her and flirting with Rohan when Rani was so clearly protective of him.

Rani looked up and frowned.

"Do you know that guy with the big whatever, or is he just trying to get a date in the rudest, most public way?" Rani demanded. "You're all but sitting on Rohan's lap waving a flag saying taken."

Odd. Solei got the feeling Rani didn't want her to be with Rohan, but now she was defending his...

Ugh, I am not territory!

"I know him. He volunteers one evening a week giving

lessons and workshops to bass players at the Youth Urban Arts Center. The one that sponsored the arts booth today. I'll go see what he needs."

She reluctantly stood up, hating to leave Rohan. She suspected she knew what David wanted.

"Tessa's running late. Downtown traffic. Late babysitter. Can you sing a couple of songs with us until she gets here?"

"I'm on a date," Solei objected. She loved singing. Loved it. But being in a band usually meant traveling around to gigs. Jazz bands didn't make bank, and she'd had her fill of worrying about money and cramming her life into a backpack and being on the road all the time. That's what this year in Charlotte had been about, trying to put down roots, although she still could fit her life conveniently into Frida.

"With which one?" David looked over with interest, his nimble fingers not missing a note or a beat on his upright bass. "Man or woman?"

"The man."

"He's way too slick and pretty. Sure he's not gay?"

Very sure. She still felt the imprint of his arousal from when they'd danced.

"Just because he's wearing a pink designer blazer," Solei scolded. Then she realized David was teasing her—maybe.

"He asked me out," she amended. She heard the excitement in her voice and tried to tamp it down. "So it's a date. I feel like his cousin is trying to put a return to sender stamp on me. I don't think she approves."

"There's nothing to disapprove of," David never missed a note, "but Indians don't often marry outside of their...you know."

Solei felt a jolt of something. "That's a pretty broad stereotype you got going there, and I just met him."

"Still, not wrong," he said. "And I married a Black woman. You don't think her family gave her a truckload of shit about her marrying me? And my family has deep roots in the Midwest. I had to amputate myself to get free. They weren't exactly throwing around the pom-poms and cheering when I brought Rae home for Christmas four years ago."

It was on the tip of her tongue to say love was colorblind, but she bit back the words.

"I just met Rohan," Solei said as much a reminder to herself as an explanation to David. "It's a little early to be thinking about bringing him home to meet my family."

Her parents would be happy if she was happy and her grandparents would love him if he was good to her. And if he played tennis or golf or loved boating, he'd be golden and enthusiastically welcomed on board.

"Stop stalling. Sing a couple of songs with us. I want to keep the audience and the drinks and the tips flowing. Tess should be here soon."

"Okay, let me check," Solei looked down at her work clothes—the boots, the ripped, nearly white Levi's with paint spatters and smudges, and her olive tank and cropped cardigan. Not exactly a China Forbes look.

As if.

"Did he ask you out?" Rani demanded when she returned. Rohan's curious gaze slid to David.

"What? No. He's married. He's a friend," she objected, perching next to Rohan.

How would he take her singing? Would he feel upstaged and walk out like Zach had done a couple of times when she'd filled in for friends in LA? It would only be a couple of songs, but if he did pout or walk, it was better to know now.

No more jumping into relationships.

"David plays with The Blue Fins. This is one of their regular gigs, and I've filled in a couple of times when their singer Tess is ill or has something with her kids come up," she said, feeling oddly self-conscious.

"He asked me to sing a couple of songs until their singer arrives. She's on her way."

"You're going to sing with the band?" Rohan's eyes widened. "Now."

"Just a couple of songs," she said, and why was she apologizing?

"So you're an artist and musician—multi-talented," Rohan gazed at her in total awe that warmed her entire body.

"You haven't heard me sing yet."

"Get up there," he urged. "I'm about to fall in love with the intricate rhythms and chord changes in jazz."

Fall. In. Love.

With jazz. Not you.

It was just an expression. But try as hard as she could to blow it off as a figure of speech, Solei felt like the sun had just risen in her chest. She could barely break away from the stare fest she had going on with Rohan. The band had stopped playing. David introduced her, but she still felt glued to the couch.

Rohan smiled. God, he had a beautiful smile. He held her hand and stood up, and she rose automatically with him. So polite. So different from the times in college. And later with Zach.

"I'm not really dressed for it," she said quietly.

"I like to wear this blazer when I'm feeling a little swagger," Rohan slipped off his pink blazer that looked as if it had been designed and tailored for him. "You can borrow it if you need a little mojo."

It was silly how much the gesture meant to her. And the blazer would be the most badass thing she'd ever worn in her life.

"Yes." She peeled off her cardigan.

"Is that a hard yes?" He leaned into her, his lips almost brushing her cheek.

She pressed her lips together to keep from giggling like an idiot. He helped her on with his blazer and her eyes closed as she felt his warmth and scent envelop her.

"Break a leg, I think is the phrase, but not literally because I'm not an orthopedic surgeon."

Solei laughed at that. "What kind are you in case I need

to break something?"

He touched his chest, his face serious. "Hearts. But I don't break them."

She swallowed hard, knowing that she should make light of this moment, but completely unable to dredge up anything witty.

"Have fun," Rohan whispered in her ear. She felt the touch of his lips and then he walked her toward the stage.

"DON'T EVEN THINK it," Rani told him in Hindi.

"You're not really a mind reader," he said though sometimes it felt like that.

He didn't bother to look at Rani. Yeah. He was staring. He was a guy. Solei was beautiful. And she was wearing his jacket. Around her body. Her scent and his mingling.

Stop. We're not animals.

Only they were.

He was never going to dry-clean that sports jacket again.

"Stop acting so caveman," Rani said.

Out of the corner of his eye he saw her steal his drink. She tasted it, her expression burst with surprised pleasure.

"You are not going to get Solei on your karaoke team for parties," Rani objected.

Solei was singing what even he recognized as a Nina Simone song. And yes, he was definitely feeling good.

"We haven't even had an official date yet because you interrupted, but you have us teaming up at parties."

"I'm a matchmaker," Rani said smugly. She took another sip of his drink, but he swiped it back. Solei had looked so sexy eating her orange slice, and he had every intention of offering her his. Sharing olives earlier still had him envisioning them both horizontal, which was too pervy because Rani was still here.

"Then your work here is done." He didn't break eye contact with Solei.

"Wait. No. Rohan," In his peripheral vision he saw her eyes bug. "No way. You can't be thinking...I didn't match you. Just the way she talked about spirit animals and..."

"Rani. I'm not proposing. I just met her. I want to get to know her better."

"No. You're going to get fascinated. She's already fascinated. And she's all wrong for you."

"You can't know that from lobbing a bunch of random questions."

"Psych doctoral candidate. Right here. I can prove to you after I finish the first round of questions tonight."

"Hard no. Your data's skewed because you're not objective, and this is not a controlled setting." He smirked. "Find your own date." He toasted Solei with his cocktail as she held out the final note of her third song.

"Solei is fan-fucking-tastic. She's talented. She's beautiful. She has a gorgeous voice and she's a lot of fun. She's everything I never knew I wanted, and I want time to get to know her better. And you," he said plucking the orange slice back that she tried to steal, "are either going to help me run interference with the p's or get out of my way. Decide, Rani. Us or them? In or out?"

Rani threw him one last emotive look and then she hurried up to Solei who was returning to the table. Rani spoke quickly and then she hugged Solei and left.

"Finally, we can be alone," Rohan rose to greet Solei. He liked his jacket on her. A lot.

"She's very sweet," Solei said. "Unusual. And she cares for you so much."

"We're best friends," Rohan said. "Rani's got some...I don't know how to say it. She's quirky, but brilliant. She's loyal and loving but needs a leash. Dance with me? I want to hold you."

The music had slowed, and Rohan didn't care that no one else was dancing. He and Solei walked toward the small stage where the trio played, and he danced with Solei, grateful for the ballroom dancing lessons his mom had insisted on before his first prom and later the group lessons his fraternity had shelled out for when they'd participated in a charity danceathon years ago.

"You and Rani are so in sync," Solei mused, looking up at him steadily. "She said she had to go somewhere, but the next word association game she wanted me to play was with L words."

"Told you. She has a bit of witch in her."

"Or gypsy."

"That suits. Lucky," he breathed.

"Liberated."

"Luscious."

"Laughter."

"Languid."

"Laudable."

"Lavish."

Solei's smile widened as they played the game. He pulled her closer, enjoying the moment, the music and most definitely the woman.

"Luminous," he murmured, kissing her hair.

Chapter Eight

"ARE YOU GOING to see her again?"

Rani didn't bother to knock on his bedroom door. Of course not. Boundaries were never her forte. Not that his mother had any boundaries either.

"I'm not dressed," he objected. Rani leaned against the doorjamb, phone up, smirk on.

"This is a money shot if I ever saw one. Wonder what Clarissa would be inspired to design for you if I sent her a pic of you in your fifty dollar a pair boxer briefs?"

"I don't know why underwear is called a pair. And they weren't fifty dollars. Get out."

"Ooooh, got them on sale, did you?" Rani took a picture and then laughed. He shooed her away with his hand. "No big deal," Rani feigned a yawn. "I used to see you naked all the time."

"When you were two or three." Rohan gave up and grabbed a pair of jeans he'd just folded. He'd been hoping to make a quick getaway and spend more time with Solei before heading back to Durham. Last night had not been nearly enough. His parents and grandparents wouldn't complain too vociferously if he made work the excuse with his serious, slightly regretful look that he had perfected in high school when he wanted to escape.

But Rani could out him and his excuse. She hadn't committed to helping him keep Solei under wraps.

"Whatever," she rolled her expressive eyes. "I bet you sniffed your jacket last night when she gave it back."

Rohan's phone buzzed. Solei? Heart in his throat—physically impossible, but still—one-handed he buttoned the first button of his jeans and reached for his phone. Rani's alarmed expression synchronized with voices coming down the hall.

"And this is my son, Rohan, the cardiothoracic surgeon's room." His mother hip checked Rani so that she stumbled fully into his room with a murmured "betee," and then swept into his spacious bedroom. "We built this entire first floor suite for Rohan and his future family. Thirty-one hundred square feet. Three en suite bedrooms..."

"Mom," he yelped, devoid of dignity, as another woman he'd never seen before followed his mother into his room and instead of looking around at the master suite as his mother was, the woman's full and frank appraisal instead rested on him. Shirtless. Jeans unbuttoned and low, very low on his hips.

"What are you doing in here?" He abandoned his phone and yanked the denim higher and buttoned.

"I live here."

So typical. It was his home until it was still hers. Anger and humiliation warred.

"I'm not dressed yet."

"It is nearly ten in the morning. What healthy, young man is not dressed at ten in the morning? Not my son."

Facts proved her wrong.

"Besides," his mom patted his cheek. "You always liked to show off your body. Always naked in the yard."

He could hear Rani choking.

"I was a toddler."

He yanked his T-shirt—a white one—over his head and jerked his arms through.

"Much later than that I think—always an exhibitionist." His mom moved over to what she called the wall of windows. "Look at the view. The master has a private patio from the rest of the downstairs dwelling and separate from the upper house," she continued, clearly giving the other woman a tour of the house, but why his bedroom was fair game was bewildering, as was the time. It was too early to entertain and tour a house. "Rohan, beta, this is Mrs. Bukar."

The only view Mrs. Bukar was looking at was of him. Head-to-toe. It wasn't creepy, more clinical, like a doctor looking to make a tricky diagnosis.

"Very nice," she murmured in a cultured, British-Indian accent.

"Welcome. Nice to meet you," Rohan said stiffly, not liking the way she kept eying him like he was a product on a shelf she was considering buying. "Excuse me, Mom, I'd like to finish getting dressed."

"Dressed." His mom shrugged and stated the obvious. "You're now dressed."

He wasn't. He hadn't blown his hair dry. Or packed. Or decided if he wanted to go with a button-down shirt or another blazer. Clarissa had mailed him a damn cool ombre blue to purple blazer last week and asked him to take some selfies wearing it in different locals. He'd thought Solei would like it since it did look almost neon vibrant like the spray-painted rose she'd demonstrated yesterday. He'd love to buy that picture. Mount it on his...his apartment wall wouldn't be his in another couple of months.

He looked around at the cool taupe and gray tones of the master suite that he'd had no say over. The walls already featured art—art his mother's designer had chosen.

Would she even let him hang something he wanted in here—something Solei had created? He didn't think street art would impress his mom or her decorator. One more reason to say no—no to the house, no to the job, not to the...holy cow. Was Mrs. Bukar...no...he didn't even want to think about that. She'd seen him half naked. And the thought of her cool appraisal made his balls shrink. But no one ever said his mother was slow to act or miss an opportunity.

"Rohan, put something on better than a T-shirt." His mother finally turned away from the window and faced him.

"Mrs. Bukar has come at great inconvenience to herself for a visit. We are going to have chai. Join us when you have something more appropriate on. That shirt is too plain. Anyone can wear a white shirt. No distinction."

"I would be wearing something else if you hadn't barged into my room without knocking."

"Barged. Who uses the word barged with their mother? Besides Rani was already here, following you around, like a devoted puppy," she smiled at Rani as if the words weren't a dig, and who knew, from his mother, they might not be. She'd always been bemused by his closeness to Rani. "Why should I knock in my own house? Besides, you work so hard on your fitness Rohan. What for if not to show it off? Five minutes. Mrs. Bukar is very busy, and we have a lot to discuss this first meeting."

"Wwww…pardon?" he corrected himself.

"Your matchmaker. I told her you had to return to Durham today to finish your combined cardiothoracic residency at Duke University." His mother sounded like she was pitching a really high-end product to a roomful of stupid people who'd just improbably won the lottery. "We talked on the phone for two hours yesterday. She already feels that she knows your heart. She is a skilled palm reader. She can tell…"

"Mom, I have to get back to Durham," he kept his voice level, reasonable, when his heart felt like it was going to catapult out of his chest and start beating holes in the freshly

126

painted drywall. "I am needed as a consult on a case with the surgical team for tomorrow."

It disturbed him that he lied so well.

It bothered him even more that Rani watched him steadily, not moving, or giving anything away, because she knew he was lying. Knew it. But she was backing his play like he'd asked. Like she always did. Relief warred with guilt. He'd been so resentful of her presence last night. And now he'd made plans with Solei except he was going to have to *American Ninja Warrior* it through a gauntlet of obstacles with the matchmaker and his family first.

"On a Sunday?" his mother queried coolly.

She should know better. She was married to a cardiac surgeon. His father often worked long hours—late nights and weekends. He took a lot of call, but even when he wasn't on call, he would often get called in to consult.

Rohan's brain hit a full stop, and he nearly sat down on his bed. Had his father been lying some of those times, like he was lying now? Had his father wanted to get away from his family and the heavy burden of responsibility? Escape his mom? Him?

"It is good that he is so conscientious," Mrs. Bukar said softly, still watching him so intently that he felt unnerved. "That he has so much responsibility when he is so young and has not yet finished his training, and yet his opinion is necessary to the team to save a life."

He was such a dick.

"Yes," his mom smiled. "Rohan has always been so studious and responsible. He always helps when needed. He's a good boy. A very good boy. Rohan is a constant source of strength to me and his family. Right, Rani?"

Some families would discuss their dogs in such terms.

"Rohan is my best friend," Rani said. "I would do anything for him."

"Such loyalty. A loving family," Mrs. Bukar said. "You are very blessed."

To have an utterly selfish asshole.

"I look forward to meeting you upstairs for chai," Mrs. Bukar put her hands together and slightly bowed her head. "I have a little time," she said. "And am looking forward to arranging a suitable match."

"My beautiful son." His mother—getting her way like always, like she knew she would—was all charm and smiles now, touching both his cheeks.

Rohan namasted back.

"Pussy," Rani said when they were alone again.

"Shouldn't you as a woman consider that a misogynistic, archaic and totally inappropriate taunt?"

Rani laughed. "True. But you don't see me getting trussed up and shown off before slaughter."

Rohan winced.

"Seriously, Ro, you aren't going to try to see Solei again, are you?"

"You seemed to like her."

"Oh, I totally did. She's awesome. Smart and funny and so beautiful she made my eyes hurt. I should have hated her on sight just because of all the check marks she made on my Things to Envy chart. But she was so cool. Not a stuck-up bone in her body. But she's a free spirit, Ro. An artist. She gets commissions all over the US and travels a lot. You need someone to ground you."

"I've been grounded my entire life."

He left the white shirt on. It was bamboo with a bit of stretch and reached for the ombre blazer. The pink blazer hung in his closet. He resisted the urge to touch the material that had touched Solei's silky skin that was so creamy with a hint of gold. He wanted to inhale her scent but didn't because Rani was most definitely watching him.

He ran his hands through his hair and then added a touch of product. Moisturized. That would have to do.

"You look pretty," Rani said. "But you shouldn't see Solei again."

"I can do what I want."

Rani huffed.

"I don't need you approving or not approving my dates," Rohan said, shrugging into the ombre blazer. He hadn't taken her advice when he was in high school, and he wasn't starting now.

"You're right. Your mom and Nanima will," she smirked and then as he walked upstairs, Rani behind him, she hummed the theme of doom "dum, dum, dum, dum," under her breath.

Thirty minutes later, as Mrs. Bukar studied his hands—first his right for a long time then his left, without speaking—Rohan imagined himself rising up from the white velvet chair in the massive living room and floating out through the open, accordion-style floor-to-ceiling glass doors and across the lake.

"You are a fire element," Mrs. Bukar pronounced.

"No, no, are you sure? Rohan is the most grounded and reliable person," his mother objected. "Cool under pressure."

Mrs. Bukar's statement popped the cork off of the conversation.

Comments, memories, and differing opinions flowed around the room. Rani reminded everyone that he'd been a swimmer in high school so he must be a water element. Mrs. Bukar shook her head. "Earth. Definitely earth," Nanima nodded her head.

More than twenty people had arrived at ten on a Sunday morning—catching Rohan utterly off guard—to participate in Rohan's first meeting with the matchmaker. Most were family or close friends. Obviously, Anju Auntie and Asha were notably absent, but Shanti had arrived, smirking and claiming she was his legal counsel. Shanti slugged back a mimosa in favor of chai, and she wasn't the only one, although the requests were subtle and directed to Rani, who often played bartender. A pundit from the temple had folded himself in a chair but had so far weighed in on nothing but how delicious the food was.

"Your Mount of Jupiter is quite pronounced," Mrs. Bukar said after careful study of his palm.

A ripple of "ahhhh" circled through the crowd. Rohan doubted more than one or two people knew what that meant—not that it meant anything scientifically—and he wasn't sure if it meant what Mrs. Bukar thought his mount of whatever meant. "You have a lot of confidence and leadership capability," she nodded her head sagely.

No duh. He'd soared through medical school. He'd published as a resident and presented at conferences. She could have learned that from a two-minute chat with his mom or a thirty-second Google search.

"Your Mount of Saturn too shows well. Wisdom and integrity define you."

Not if she could read his mind.

"These are all traits that will attract an equally accomplished bride."

"Of course Rohan's bride must be accomplished. A doctor. Or graduate school in something intellectual." His mom frowned as Rani handed him a glass of water and asked him if he preferred beer. He didn't. Then she scooted closer to him.

"Good family. Punjabi. Cosmopolitan. Ambitious, but eager for a family," his mom ticked off the qualities. "Confident, but not stubborn or arrogant. Rohan needs…"

"Yes, yes," his father waved his hand, interrupting his

mother's list. "But he must like the girl. There must be a connection, understanding."

"That comes with time." His mom said, shrugging. "You and I only had a chance to meet twice with our families. Then your father demanded a yes or no from my father," his mom sounded so casual about marrying a stranger. "Rohan is decisive. Clever. And very fastidious. You saw his closet. The bride must be organized. Know how to run a household. And be from the right kind of family so that she will fit seamlessly into Rohan's life and career and social demands."

Not subtle code for rich.

"Ah yes," Mrs. Bukar seized back the reins of the conversation. "Look here, the Mount of Mercury. You are social. Thrive at parties and work events. You will want a social bride to be your equal. Not too quiet of a girl. A girl who can organize your home, but also who can entertain and shine." Mrs. Bukar smiled and leaned back a little. The crowd erupted with comments about parties. How Rohan loved to dance. His stint DJing at parties—the sanctioned ones. Only his cousins knew about the raves and house parties he'd snuck out to DJ in high school and his first couple years of college.

"She must be confident. Hold her own. But reflect well on Rohan," his mother stated. "There will be many parties and much social networking where Rohan's wife must be an asset."

No pressure on the poor mythical bride.

"It sounds sexist," Rohan objected. What exactly was he bringing to the union? Why did the woman have to carry the burden of the house and lifestyle? Was some poor woman having her palm read to find her the perfect mate? What traits was that "suitable boy" supposed to offer up?

Well, he had a date, so it was not going to be him. Not today. Not anytime soon.

"No, no, beta. We are just being practical. You don't know. You will see. Mrs. Bukar and I will find you a woman who will complement you and help you achieve all that you want to accomplish."

Surely his career goals were on him. And he wanted time to make other, less work-oriented goals for himself, not meld his yet unknown dreams to someone he barely knew.

The only thing he wanted to accomplish now was to get out of the house. Breathe. And lose himself in Solei's green eyes and smile. He wondered what she would make of the palm reading game. Was it any less weird than Rani's spirit animals and greatest fear, embarrassment, and achievement questions last night? And what had been up with the L-word play? Why L?

Rani's words from earlier echoed—that he wasn't being fair because his parents were set on arranging a marriage for him, and he and Solei hadn't even had a true date.

But he'd have the ultimate say—yes or no—to some shadow women Mrs. Bukar did or didn't have lined up waiting to meet him.

"Oh," the long pause from Mrs. Bukar caught everyone's attention. Rohan winced as the visual of her and his mom walking into his room when he'd been but half-dressed flit across his retina.

"Your Mount of Luna. That illuminates the darkness," she said gravely, and Rohan barely managed to not squirm away from her scrutiny. Shanti was on her second mimosa or was it her third? As his unasked for but designated legal counsel, she sucked. Mrs. Bukar had both his hands palm up, and she bent over them like she was reading an ancient scroll, weighing his character right now against his potential.

"You have not exercised your imagination much," she said sternly.

"Who needs that?" His father wandered closer, immediately cluing in Mrs. Bukar and everyone else as to why Rohan's imagination, intuition and psychic powers were flaccid.

"But this does not have to be your future," she intoned. His father snorted like a racehorse and mumbled about mumbo jumbo. He took his opinion and headed for the whiskey likely to spike the lattes Rani had made her father and uncles. "All this talk," his father called out, and his mother barely hid her grimace. "Rohan just needs a good girl from a good family. Well educated. Ready to be a good partner. A good mother. What else is there?"

His eyes met Rani's. She was nearly bouncing in her seat.

"Tantric, up all night sex against the wall," Shanti, a

fresh mimosa in her hand murmured sweetly.

Rohan choked in shock. Mrs. Bukar frowned.

"Excuse me, Auntie," Shanti said politely to Mrs. Bukar. "Rohan is parched."

Shanti tipped the mimosa into his mouth and just kept pouring so that he had to gulp.

"Are you trying to waterboard me?"

"My bad," Shanti stood up. "I thought that might be a preferable form of torture but by all means continue your way. Thank you, Auntie. Can I get you anything?"

"More chai, please."

"Certainly," Shanti said, all sweetness and light, but she nudged Rani up and out of her ringside seat to go get the chai for Mrs. Bukar. Shanti took Rani's place, feigning interest. "I hope Mrs. Bukar uses a different set of tools from the last matchmaker," Shanti of course greeted the elephant in the room. "I'd hate for us to be zero for two." She smiled brightly with just enough bite.

"I have an impeccable record." Mrs. Bukar sat up straighter and eyeballed Shanti sternly. "Mistakes do occasionally occur. All of us are human," she said with great dignity.

"Here you are, Mrs. Bukar," Rani returned. "I too am interested in the psychology of love and of creating the perfect match," Rani said. "I am writing my doctoral dissertation on…" She paused.

"Of course, betee," his mom said dismissively. "But we

are focused on Rohan today, and Mrs. Bukar's time is short. We have sent you his numerology chart. And astrology."

Rohan nearly jumped out of his chair. When had that happened? Why had he not been consulted? But Mrs. Bukar held firm to his hands. Her gaze was intense and steady but not unkind.

"By exercising your compassion and empathy, you can strengthen your Mount of Luna, encourage new insights," Mrs. Bukar told him.

"Of course. Of course." His mom nodded vigorously as if she were going to design him an educational program to do just that.

"This is all very interesting, Mrs. Bukar," Rohan said, realizing that if anyone were going to save him, it would have to be him. "And I appreciate your insights and time, but I am needed at the hospital this afternoon at Duke Medical Center, and so I must…"

"There is much more to the reading," she said. "Much more, but this makes me want to look at your heart line, Rohan, because that line has marked differences from your left to your right."

"I'm left-handed," he said.

"Oh. Yes. I see. You have the natural tendency to forge deep friendships and commitment, fidelity, a deep bond, but the way you are living your life, actualizing your potential, so to speak, reveals that you are holding back. The heart line starts at your middle finger on your right hand, showing a potential for restlessness," she said so softly that even Rohan had to strain to hear. "You have such a deep, loving heart, Rohan. What is it you are looking for in a partner? What would it take for you to fall in love?"

Her gaze bore into him with the butter-smooth slice of a scalpel. He felt everyone looking at him. Words eluded him, but he could see Solei's vivid green gaze and her smile when they'd been painting together. She'd been playful, fascinating and encouraging.

"I..." His mouth was too dry to speak, and he wished he'd not cut off Shanti's mimosa torture.

"He's had no time for love," his mom objected. "Love will come. We need to find him a suitable match.

"Do you want to love?"

"Yes."

He heard a feminine chorus of oohs, ahhs and "so sweet."

"The Mount of Venus," Mrs. Bukar boomed. The room quieted. Rani leaned forward, sloshing chai on the table that she wiped off with the sleeve of her brightly patterned blouse.

"What about the Mount of Venus?" Rani demanded.

By the rapt attention, this area of his palm located at the base of this thumb that he'd never once in his life thought about, was the superstar of the reading. He felt a frisson of worry. It didn't really mean anything, right? Mrs. Bukar wouldn't be able to tell that he'd lost his virginity in the pool house changing room on a Monday afternoon during his senior year of high school while his mom and dad had been at work and Shanti and Rani had been at their various afterschool activities. "Very pronounced. You will have a strong interpersonal connection with your bride. Strong emotional connections and sexual attraction are most critical for you. You are very sexually driven, but also a man whose heart must be heard."

Mrs. Bukar's intense gaze bore through him and Rohan felt slut shamed. Shanti toasted him and tossed back the rest of her mimosa.

"Lead with that."

"SO," TULA SAID Sunday morning as she and Solei carefully loaded the now dry street art and poetry drenched drywall sections into Rand's truck. "Any juicy stories from the hottie yesterday or don't you kiss and tell?"

"We didn't get a chance to kiss so there is nothing to tell," Solei said, wishing she weren't thinking about Rohan quite so much. She'd felt certain the night would have ended with him driving her home and at least kissing her good night, but instead of Rani leaving last night like Solei had thought, she'd stayed at the bar discussing cocktail recipes and patrons. Rani had driven Solei home and then Rohan. It was laughable, like Rani had been guarding his virtue.

But her test questions for her potential doctoral dissertation had been unusual, sparking interesting conversations. She wondered if Rani was going to make a dating app or something. Solei had never tried online dating. She was too instinctual—not that her instincts had led her to love Nirvana. But she went by the vibe. And Rohan had definitely vibed every cell into overdrive.

"You going to see him again?"

"I hope so," she said. "I'd like to. He grew up in Charlotte but works in Durham so it would be sort of a long-distance thing, but," she shrugged feeling embarrassed, "I'm getting way ahead of myself. We exchanged numbers. He said he'd try to swing by the park to see me before he headed home."

"You liked him?"

Solei nodded. "A little too much," she admitted. "Being with him felt natural, like we were longtime friends but with wowza chemistry."

"I could tell," Tula laughed. "It was good to see you with someone. I feel like it would be lonely traveling alone from city to city or state to state to complete a commission."

"It's an adventure," Solei gave her stock answer. And she did enjoy it, but just as she'd craved a home base when she'd been a teenager even though she'd loved her parents and was grateful for all that she had seen and experienced, Solei had the same urge now—to stay, to create a home, build friendships.

Charlotte could work. She liked the city. It wasn't impossibly far to the beach. It wasn't particularly artistic, but there was a youthful vibe. Her income would take a big hit as she'd have to decline more commissions. Other artists would fill the void. She might be seen as losing her edge.

But she might develop a different edge or style if she had more time to reflect. Stand in one place and breathe.

"Are you still thinking that you might stay in Charlotte even if your contract for next year isn't approved?" Tula asked curiously with a note of hope as she slammed shut the gate of the truck.

"Yeah," Solei said thoughtfully. "I am considering it, but I am hoping to get the teaching job. Part time is great for doing art and volunteering, but if I teach art full time, I'd qualify for benefits and retirement." Solei laughed. "I sound fifty, not thirty. My parents would think I was speaking an alien language. They are both such free spirits. Even when I was little, I was the practical one."

They returned to the booth that was, for the most part, deconstructed due to the help of a large group of volunteers. The Urban Youth Artist Center had a basement so all of the materials could be stored for the next arts festival or demonstration.

"You want to come to the house for an early dinner?" Tula asked.

"Thank you," Solei said, scanning the now busy park as the art festival entered the second day. "But I'm still hoping

Rohan will have some time."

She should probably go to Tula's for dinner. She wanted to build friendships, and Rohan was not a sure thing. After Zach left and she'd had a heart-to-heart with herself, she'd promised herself that she wouldn't always change her plans for a man or defer to his schedule and his wants.

"Durham's not far," Tula said as if reading her doubts. "Couple of hours without traffic on I85."

"There's always traffic," Solei retorted.

"Not lying," Tula laughed. "But the path to true love always involves a few bumper-to-bumper hours when you really gotta pee."

Solei laughed.

"I have chicken tortilla soup in the Crock-Pot if you change your mind, girl. Homemade salsa too."

"Thank you," Solei said, picking up a stack of art supplies that were in labeled bins, even as she glanced around looking for anything that had been missed.

"Never mind," Tula said softly. "Looks like you have a better offer."

"Huh?" Solei looked up and had to shade her eyes from the bright sun. A shadow moved toward her growing taller, clearer in detail. Rohan. The way her heart flipped was as clear a sign as she could have. Her head might urge caution, but her heart wanted to play this game out—battle as old as time.

"I'll get those and the rest." Tula swept the stack of bins

from her hands and nudged her toward Rohan. "Don't behave," she teased. "See you Monday."

"Oh, ummm." She could barely tear her gaze away from Rohan's advance. He radiated a barely leashed energy that was visceral. He seemed to spark gold and red, and his heated gaze didn't deviate from hers a millimeter.

"Girl, you have it bad, and I don't blame you, but he might just have it worse," Tula teased and them propelled Solei forward.

"Hey," Solei said. "I wasn't sure I'd see you." She tried to keep her voice level when she really wanted to jump into his arms and show him how very happy she was to see him.

"I was beginning to think I wouldn't be able to escape."

She thought he was joking so she laughed, only Rohan wasn't smiling. He looked tense, and before she could react, he closed the distance between them with a thrilling look of intent stamped on his aristocratically beautiful features and then his arms were tight around her and his face pressed into her neck.

"I almost didn't come," his voice was a harsh whisper. "I almost kept driving. I just needed to escape so badly."

"From what?" she asked, confused and concerned. Her instinct was to comfort, soothe. But hadn't she done that for Zach and Miles and Sean? Put them first, taken care of their needs and received nothing in return?

"It doesn't matter now," he said. "I almost made an epic mistake, but I stopped. Took a risk that you'd still be here."

His dark eyes seared her. "I'm happy I did."

"Me too," she whispered. He was alone this time. Maybe they had five minutes or five hours. Who knew? Solei didn't care. She wanted to savor the time together.

She had no idea what was bothering him, but he had come to her. She cupped his jaw and felt him trembling. This stunning man who'd cometed into her world yesterday in a fascinating blaze of color, laughter, contradictions and novelty had come back to her. No one else.

Solei looped her arms around him and pulled him close. She had never felt so strong or necessary.

She inhaled his delicious citrus and sandalwood scent. "I've got you."

Chapter Nine

"TOUGH CASE." DR. Jason Steel elbow bumped him in the locker room Monday night. "The hardest part of medicine is learning how to let go. I'm glad we didn't have to tonight."

"It was a team effort," Rohan said, standing back up even though he had just sat down a moment ago, letting the exhaustion from the emergency case wash through him before he finally left for home after a fifteen-hour day.

It felt good to be back at Duke Medical Center. Back at work and with his colleagues. He belonged here. He knew who he was. He understood his purpose. The clarity after such an emotionally fraught weekend was a relief.

"You have the calm and doggedness of a gifted cardio-thoracic surgeon, Rohan. You do the work and are a natural leader in the OR; even in your green days as a first-and-second year resident you backed up your confidence with skill and preparation."

"Thank you." Rohan often conferred with Jason about his cases, coming to him with questions and ideas. He respected the hell out of him, but they'd never even come close to the line of friendship. They'd attended a few medical conferences together with other attending surgeons and residents on the Duke Medical School cardio division. They'd chatted over beer and ridden in more than one golf cart on an Arizona or Hawaii beautiful award-winning golf course. But he'd been a resident. Not a friend or full colleague.

Rohan enjoyed golf, and it had given him an edge in his career. His father thought golf was a huge time suck. Rohan found it meditative. He'd talked his mom into a package of eight lessons at age twelve, and then he'd ride his bike to the public course and buy a couple of buckets of balls and just hit and hit, finding a groove. His own yoga.

"Heard your article about ventilator splitting is getting published in a few European medical journals as well." Jason peeled out of his scrubs and tossed them in the laundry.

Rohan still stood rigidly at attention, despite the pull of exhaustion, and now that the surgery was over, and his workday complete, the twin, but polar opposite problems of Mrs. Bukar and Solei wrestled for his attention.

"That was a brilliant hack last year, and I hope to God we never have to be that clever again, and if we do, that you're on the floor." Jason peeled off his booties and trashed them.

"You still set in going into private practice with your dad?"

No.

But he couldn't say that. Could he?

"My dad is set on it." Rohan leaned against the locker bay, the cool metal radiating through his scrubs and the T-shirt he always wore underneath. "I...I...don't know," he admitted, strangely relieved to hear the words coming out of his mouth and seeing Jason's movements still as he listened. "It should be a no-brainer," he said quietly, feeling the same dark, wet and heavy cloud that settled over him when he thought about his future.

He hated this. He'd worked so hard. He should feel on fire. Other residents who had a handful of months were already celebrating and lining up jobs. "I've just been on one track so long that I..." He broke off. Jason didn't need to see him as some lost idiot whining about wanting time off, wanting to travel, especially when he didn't even know where. Next, he'd say something absurd about finding himself. He was here. Right here.

"You don't need me to tell you what to do," Jason said, not facing him as he pulled his athletic bag out of his locker. "You're about to complete one of the top programs in the country. You're published. You've spoken at two medical conferences already. You're so damn shiny brilliant you're blinding. Any program or practice would be damn high-five lucky to lure you to sign with them."

Rohan huffed out a shocked laugh. Jason had shucked off his T-shirt that he'd worn under his scrubs and kicked off his scrub pants. Naked, he slid his feet into his shower slides and then paused, toiletry bag in one hand.

"Thank you," Rohan said, not sure where to look. Jason didn't often openly praise. He was his favorite surgeon he'd trained with. They'd all been skilled and generous with their time, but Jason was top dog—the driver in the Duke golf bag, if Rohan were prone to use metaphors, which he wasn't.

"Any practice would be lucky to have you," Jason repeated and paused, clearly feeling his words. "But I'll be honest, Rohan. You have gifts beyond surgery. You're a natural leader. Insightful. Team oriented. You see the big picture, not just the patient but also the team and the group and the program. You have that hunger to gain and share knowledge. You'd be an asset to any medical school or residency program. And you thrive as a public speaker. You engage on all cylinders."

Rohan stared at his palms, hearing Mrs. Bukar's assessment of him and his mount of whatever, as Jason's words hit him hard as if he'd been jolted with a defibrillator.

"You have so many skills beyond the actual surgery. You excel in OR, but you are also a gifted teacher. You communicate and inspire. I know the money's not the same," Jason said. "But you'd be a tremendous gift to incoming students and residents for generations. I've wanted to invite you to at least think about joining the Duke team as a faculty member for a few years now."

"I will, sir," Rohan said startled to his soul. Academia. He hadn't even thought about it as an option. But why not?

His stomach soured. He could just imagine his father's expression, his disappointment. And what everyone else in Charlotte would say at the parties, year after year. What had gone wrong for him to not be hired at a top practice? Why wasn't he making top dollar? Had he washed out? Fallen out with his father? Whispered gossip about how he had potentially failed? He'd had such potential, what had gone wrong?

He could probably earn double in his father's practice. No one would understand him not seizing top dollar and bragging about it.

His father would be crushed. His mom angry. Humiliated. His father and family would become a source of gossip and pity.

"It goes without saying, Rohan, that I am not speaking only for myself. You have many admirers in the department as well as the entire medical school. Every year has one or two residents who rise up and shine, but you are a once in a generation, and you're just starting. For you to have more time and funding to do research... Who knows what innovations you will create?"

As an offer it was a breathtaking acknowledgement of his hard work and acquired skills and knowledge. Duke was one of the top medical schools. And he'd all but gotten a job offer in the locker room by one of the top surgeons in the southeast—who'd been naked.

Jason clapped him on his shoulder. "Think about it," he said. "Let me know if I should talk to anyone, get an offer together."

"Thank you," Rohan said to Jason's back as he strode toward the showers, trim and fit in his late forties. "Thank you. You've given me so much to think about, sir."

"Glad to hear it." Jason didn't turn around. "Sir, my ass," Rohan thought Jason muttered.

Amusement broke through his exhaustion.

ROHAN FINALLY TOOK a shower, visited his last patient— sitting bedside for a few minutes, watching vitals— something the nurses were trained to do, but he didn't want the patient to be alone. That didn't make sense. The patient was alone. And would be alone. No family. No kids. No wife, not anymore. He leaned forward, arms resting on his knees, stretching his neck and spine.

His phone buzzed with a text.

Could be anyone. Work. His mom. Rani. The match-maker. He was too tired to check and was regretting that he didn't drive to work today. He almost always walked, relying on the fifteen-minute walk to settle his head for the day or to clear it at night. But he'd need to walk to Miami to sort this tangle—pressure from his dad about the job. His mom about marriage. And then Solei, a shining beacon flaming between them, tempting him off the path that had been established so long ago.

The path that you said you wanted to step off of, even if only for a few months.

This was dumb, sitting here like he was defeated when instead he'd just been offered the job opportunity of a lifetime—that would devastate and humiliate his family if he took it.

It's my life.

Words he'd actually spoken as he'd rushed to his car yesterday to escape.

"Act like it," Shanti had taunted.

So he had enjoyed a gloriously free afternoon with Solei, holding hands and strolling through a museum of modern art listening to her enthusiastically explaining some of the work, while she took a few notes for a future field trip she was planning for her students. Then they'd walked to an under-construction brewery in Uptown. She'd been commissioned to create their logo—something with a goat—the three former college roommates and fraternity brothers hadn't settled on a name, but they wanted a mural from a "famous street artist" while she was in town before their summer opening.

"Goats are cool," one of the men had said while the other two laughed.

"G.O.A.T, get it," another one had nudged his friend, and they laughed.

Had he been that much of an idiot right out of college? He hadn't had the opportunity, but Solei had listened patiently, then she'd walked around the space and gone outside and stared up at the cement wall of the two-story brewery that had six stories of condos above it for fifteen minutes, not moving, not speaking—likely envisioning possibilities. And as he'd watched her, he'd realized with a jolt, that he did the same thing. He envisioned each surgery—his process, the potential problems, the fixes, each step before he ever made a cut.

Only he would sit or stand meditatively with his eyes closed, whereas Solei stood on the balls of her feet, her body angled toward the blank wall almost like a tuning fork, eyes wide open, absorbing everything visually.

Him eyes shut. Her eyes open.

Wasn't that some sort of cosmic metaphor that should clue him in that he was in way over his head?

His phone buzzed again. He ignored it, needing a few more moments of silence—well as silent as an ICU bed could be with a very sick forty-seven-year-old man alone in the world, coming off of a six-hour emergency surgery.

Forty-seven. Jason's age. Fifteen years older than he was.

Alone. No kids.

Only his upper-level management bank job.

He knew he didn't want that life. Alone. Only his work.

Was a few years to be independent, answering only to himself once he was finally finished with his training, too much to want? Was it, as his mom claimed, selfish?

Tired of staving off the inevitable and his own tired, self-defeating thoughts that looped through his head, he took his phone out of his pocket and stared at the screen, almost uncomprehending.

No text. Just a stylized picture of a goat, glowing white, horns jutting out of the top of its head looking almost like boomerangs. The goat was in a thicket of blackberries chewing, the juice staining its mouth and long silky beard a black purple. It was beautiful, weird and a little threatening at the same time. And the picture filled him with a sense of wonder and longing.

"You like art?" Rohan asked the patient softly, indulging himself in looking at the picture, trying to see all the details so he would have something interesting to say to Solei—so that she would know that he was paying attention, thinking the entire time.

He remembered what she'd told him about praise and teaching—that she would have students articulate what they thought about their work, divine what it meant to them, not seek her opinion or someone else's for validation. And he'd seen her do that in action.

He knew there was probably a lesson in there somewhere for himself.

He couldn't help smiling even though it was probably inappropriate to do so over a man whose chest he'd split open earlier today.

He started to type but stopped. He wanted to be clever. Funny. But he'd never flirted by text. Well, he supposed he had on Tinder, but Solei...he didn't want to get it wrong. And he didn't want to even remotely compare her to any of the women he'd met that way.

Is this my spirit animal?

Is it? Solei replied.

I do prefer blackberries over raspberries. More juice, texture and sweetness, especially in ice cream or smoothies.

Anywhere else?

He read her reply and surged to his feet, taking a moment to look back at his patient, who, due to the ventilator, was still heavily sedated.

"I'll come see you tomorrow morning early rounds." Rohan lightly touched the man's shoulder. Life was an unpredictable bitch. His patient had been a marathoner up until last year when he'd gotten sick. His wife had left him five years ago. The running had cleared his head but had been no match for the massive strep infection that had led to the rare complication of rheumatic fever also untreated. He'd worked through it—even trying to run—popping too much ibuprofen for the pain from his inflammation. He'd damaged his liver and suffered a massive heart attack.

He looked at his watch. It was late.

Can I call?

Please say yes. Please say yes. The fervency of his...what was this...a prayer—practically sacrilegious although he'd prayed for far more ridiculous things when he'd been a boy in the small pantry off the kitchen that his mother used for their pooja.

His feeling of fatalism, exhaustion and sense of not being able to do enough dissipated like mist as he held the lifeline to Solei.

That depends.

On?

Can you?

He laughed.

His phone, on silent, lit up with a picture of Solei outside in the park, shaking a can of fuchsia spray paint looking at him before she'd started on her neon rose.

"Hey," he whispered, leaving the patient's room. "Give me a sec."

"Want me to call back?"

"No." It would be smarter. But no.

"No, now is good. I just want to get out of the hospital. If I lose you, I'll call back."

He waved to the night nurses. Ran down four flights of stairs rather than taking the elevator because he hated being boxed in, and stairs were always the healthier choice.

"Are you running?"

He was. He probably sounded like a stampeding buffalo as the acoustics in the stairwell were loud and echoey. He exited a side door and breathed in the night.

"Sort of. Yes." Why lie? He'd already proved how massively uncool he was Sunday in the park when he'd all but clung to her like he'd been kicked out of a storm.

"How was your day?" they asked at the same time.

"You first," he invited.

"It was rewarding. The kids who'd shown their artwork got feedback from the jury, which we discussed constructively. All of my students who attended the art festival made a few quick sketches of artwork they liked and interviewed at least one artist. They took the assignments seriously. No one dialed it in, so we had active discussions and came up with the next art assignment. The kids are taking more ownership of their artistic journey and we still have two months of school so today really felt like a win."

Her enthusiasm was contagious. He walked toward his apartment, his stress from the weekend—first Asha's suffering and then his mother's desperate brainstorm to quell negative gossip and marry him off—faded.

"How about you?"

"I had an emergency case toward the end of the day. Critically ill patient who was transferred from Charlotte. Everything went as well as it could."

"That's a victory," she said. "What are the top three things you love about your job or is that too limiting?"

He huffed out a breath and picked up his pace. "Has Rani been brain picking again, or are you creating your own meet-cute survey?"

Solei laughed. "I would not have pegged you as knowing that term, Rohan."

"I mostly have female cousins. Desperately outnumbered."

"I've never thought about potential dating applicants filling out a survey," Solei said. "If I do go that route, three things they like about their job will be number five."

"Why the fifth? Oh. Right. So they wouldn't incriminate themselves."

"I wasn't thinking constitutionally," Solei said. "And I think reveal works better than incriminate when discussing a job, at least I would hope so. If you don't enjoy it, find something else. But maybe I should move it lower on my potential list. Seventh or eighth."

"You don't think a person's job tells you a lot about them?"

"Not necessarily what I would want to know," she said softly. "What I would think most important." He could feel his heart flutter.

"Let her go," he could practically hear Rani entreat.

Hard no.

The force of his reaction brought him to a halt on the middle of the sidewalk on the heavily treelined thoroughfare of Duke's campus that he preferred to cut through. "What do you want to know?" he asked curiously.

All his life, his future career had been his main selling point.

"Is this theoretical or about you?"

Her voice was velvet stroking his skin.

Me.

"We can start with theoretical," he said cautiously and held his breath.

The pause had his heart slam. He stood in the middle of Duke's campus. This late at night the Gothic beauty of the stone spires and the juxtaposition of the cultivated gardens enveloped him with a quiet peace on the outside while inside his emotions and thoughts were in turmoil.

"I don't think the two are necessarily separated," she said after a significant pause. "I would want to know the person's thoughts and hopes and goals. How they navigate the world and how they want to grow and change and what they want from being with me."

"I want to see you again," he spoke without thinking— from the heart—something he'd maybe done a handful of times.

"I want to see you too," she answered immediately. No hesitation, and everything in him settled. He began to walk again, this time feeling the night air, the hint of warmth in the cool, and the fragrance of the flowers.

"Tell me about the goat," he invited.

She laughed. "How much time do you have?"

"I'm walking home," he said. "That takes fifteen minutes if I hustle, but you can have as long as you want." He could talk to her all night. He'd gone without sleep before but never for such a sweet and sexy reason.

"Did the goat look hungry?"

"He was chowing down and looked smug as hell."

"It's for that new brewery that's opening in the South End where we stopped before going to Hawkers, which is my new fav restaurant in Charlotte now, thank you."

"Mine too," he said softly, remembering sitting on the patio with her and talking until the restaurant closed. He'd driven home in the dark, hours after he'd intended. "And the goat?"

He looked at the picture as she spoke, wanting to understand her through her art.

"I sent them a sample and now they've settled on Hungry Goat Brewing. I'm drawing some different mock-ups for their logo and also the mural to look at next week. They are three frat bros who've done pretty well for themselves in investment banking so they're thinking they're all that and want creative ways to part with their money. I'm happy to help."

"How'd they find you?" he asked curiously. He'd avoided googling her, wanting to unwrap her layers by himself, not through social media.

"They want something unexpected, a little edgy. They saw my Queen Presiding mural and…"

"Wait, that was you?" he demanded. It was the mural outside one of Charlotte's most iconic buildings and home of the jazz club. God, he pressed his hand against his forehead. She must think he was dumb, dumb, dumb.

"Yes. It's what brought me to Charlotte, and then I wanted to stay for a while."

"Thank Krishna and the whole crew for that," he murmured just to hear her laugh.

"I've been researching goats—so evocative and historical and contradictory in folklore. I haven't settled on what the goat should be eating. It should be symbolic, and yet I was inspired by your jacket last night to go purple. They want neon too as they saw my first mural where I employed that technique in Chicago."

Rohan felt a bout of unaccustomed nerves. She really was successful. Talented. Sought after. And he had to up-the-fuck his game.

"Jacket," he mused, lowering his voice to far away thunder. "Would this be the jacket you stole from me after so nicely returning the pink one the day we first met?"

"Borrowed," she whispered. "You were again chivalrous as we walked last night. I'm wearing it now. It still smells like you," she whispered.

"Will you send me a picture of you wearing my jacket?"

He heard the floop sound. She wore his jacket and jeans and from what he could tell no shirt.

"You are killing me."

"Figuratively, I hope."

"Total cardiac arrest—not good branding for a cardio-thoracic surgeon."

"So we shouldn't FaceTime."

"We should definitely FaceTime."

"When you get home," she said the flirt leaving her voice. "I don't want you distracted when crossing the street."

"Been doing this walk for six years, distract away."

"I love the ombre of this jacket. Your friend's sister is a skilled designer."

"Since you like my coats so much, I'll hit her up for another. It looks better on you than it does on me," he admitted.

"I'm giving it back," she said. "I accidently on purpose kept it so that I would have an excuse to see you again because no one lets a jacket this fine go."

"You don't need an excuse, Solei." He FaceTimed her, only two blocks now from his apartment.

They were quiet for a moment, just looking at each other.

"Sure you'll be safe?" she asked.

"I always pay attention," he assured her, touched by her consideration. Every family member would have kept yammering at him, not thinking about if it was a good time for him to talk. "Besides I'm almost home. Hey, you'll like this part. It's one of the reasons I decided to rent here and haven't left even though I could have found a much bigger apartment. Check this out."

He flipped the screen to show her the sprawling, lime-washed brick building and then lowered the view to the fountain out front. He loved the splash of water. It was a rusted-looking welded cube that had water cascading out of the slits in the sides of the cube but at night there was a flame on top.

"Two elements," Solei said softly. "I would just want to

sit there and think or maybe sketch every day."

They could sit there together when she visited—if she visited, and he definitely wanted her to. She could sit and sketch, and he could pretend to read so he wouldn't look too creepily obsessed.

Rohan dropped down on the wide but low wall that surrounded the water feature. "This is where I like to sit after a long shift before I head up to my apartment. After the walk, the water helps me decompress. I love this building. It's a refurbished textile mill so the ceilings are tall and it gets a lot of light—not that I'm home much during the day."

His apartment was spare. Functional. Clean. He'd splurged on a king bed for the one bedroom and for two low Scandinavian designed couches that both became queen beds in case any of his family came to visit. Only Rani had come and spent the night, which had been his unacknowledged intention. His parents didn't do less than five stars. He had two upholstered stools for the butcher block island and an empty small loft above the great room that was unused because he didn't need an office, and he had no indoor hobbies—not even gaming.

Solei would fill it up with her art supplies.

He nearly bit his tongue as if afraid he'd say that out loud. What was wrong with him? His mom had hired someone to match him in marriage to a stranger on the day he'd met the woman of his dreams. He couldn't play this game. He sucked at deception. He didn't want to hurt Solei, but he also had no intention of meeting up with a procession of approved women either.

Was it cheating?

Why had he met Solei now? Why not last year or two years ago when they could have had some time together? The bitch slap of fate stung.

"I've heard hours for residents are crazy long," Solei said, centering him again. "What do you do on your days off?"

He was going to sound so boring.

"I...ahh." He stretched his legs out and laid back so that he could see the sky. The flame and golden lights around the fountain blocked out many of the stars, but he could still see a faint twinkle that had always reassured him. He was not that important. The stars had seen so many men like him come and go, and they would remain long after he was dust.

"I'm still working on developing hobbies, or I will in a couple of months. I like to work out and run, especially on the trails outside of Durham and Chapel Hill. Did Rani send you her questions about elements?" He'd ignored his.

"Yes," she said. "Her questions seem so random. Is there a method to her madness?"

"Not sure. Story of Rani, unfortunately," he said. "I think her wild mind is her charm, her superpower so to speak, but I'm definitely the outlier of the family on that one."

"Some of her questions were definitely out there, but they made me think. They were fun to discuss with Tula, a teacher at the school. Rani should consider turning her questions into a game. It would be fun to play with friends or potential love…dating interests," she corrected. "Did you answer the element questions?"

Damn. She was not going to let that go. He angled his head back to look at the fountain—the cement wall cool on his back. "Now that I'm here, the fountain has four elements. Water. Fire. Air. And earth. There are polished stones that hold the base of the sculpture. Rocks count for earth, don't you think?"

"Does Rani wanting to practice her questions bother you? There was tension between you."

She nailed that perception.

He was about to say no. Laugh it off. But he didn't. Instead he tucked one hand behind his head and stared up at the sky. His ever-present backpack rested on the ground.

"Yes," he said. "It's probably stupid. I don't do a lot of self-reflecting, and now I'm realizing I'm woefully unprepared for it when I need it the most. I feel so black and white like there should be a definitive answer for the types of questions she asks, but I often come up blank, and yet Rani and my family have no trouble answering questions for me," he said in a spurt of bitterness, remembering how he barely got a word out during Mrs. Bukar's visit and what he had said had been ignored or mis-explained by his mother or someone else.

"But that doesn't mean their takes on you are right, Rohan."

Her softly spoken words soothed. He picked up his backpack and propped it on his stomach and legs so that he could rest his phone on it and still see her.

"I've always aced tests. Always. But I totally stumbled at the first question. Others are even worse. 'Are you at peace with yourself?' What does that even mean? If I'm at peace, would that mean I'd just sit around on my couch feeling peaceful so that I accomplish nothing? I've got a fire inside me that I don't want to bank." Even he could hear the frustration in his voice, and he ran a hand through his hair trying to shut down his agitation. "I'm at the beginning. I shouldn't, should I?"

"I don't think the questions were meant to be so literal." Solei tilted her head, her honey hair falling over her shoulder, and the jacket parted in a way that was uber sexy but seemed utterly unselfconscious. "Or so permanent. You might feel at peace with who you are and what you've done now, yet still have goals. Then at another time in your life, you may find yourself restless so that your peace eludes you again."

He nodded, liking her explanation. It didn't seem so black and white or right and wrong.

"Are you restless, Solei?"

"I was, but not now. I feel calm, but I still have goals for my life, for my art."

"What goals?"

"I'd like to settle in a place at least for a while, build a life, see how that changes my art. Your turn."

He wanted to tell her everything but had no idea how to start. He wanted to travel, but where? He wanted to get a job that challenged him and that he enjoyed but didn't want to work with his father. He loved his family and didn't want to be far from them, but he didn't want to live and work with them. He wanted a woman he adored and who adored him, and he was scared that she didn't exist.

"I disagree with Rani's diagnosis that my spirit animal is a butterfly," he avoided what was really bothering him and went with what had been irritating him since Rani's prognosis of his spirit animal Saturday night.

"Your answers lead to butterfly, Rohan."

"What about me screams butterfly?"

"You enjoy vibrant colors. You wear them. You observe your environment but also move around in your space. You're rarely still."

Damn. She had him there.

"I didn't buy those blazers," he defended. "My college roommate's sister Clarissa designs them."

"She's very talented, Rohan, but you are the one who still wears the jackets even after she has the pictures for her website or you walk her show."

Damn. She was smart. "Nailed it."

Solei laughed. "I wasn't trying to nail you although I will confess that your friend's sister beat me in that I have been thinking nonstop about how I would like to sketch you."

He sat up intrigued. "You want to sketch me?"

"So much."

Where to go with that? Naked came to mind. He was a guy. But he wasn't a jerk. At least he hoped not. And he didn't want Solei to think he was some kind of a player. He hadn't even browsed Tinder in months.

But he was unofficially officially on the Indian marriage market. He had to get his mom to slow her roll, which would be like trying to stop an avalanche by standing in front of it waving one of those airplane orange wand thingies and saying please stop.

"I want to see you again," he said. "Next week is Holi. It's an…"

"Indian festival to welcome spring."

"Yes." He said pleased although he didn't know why because he hadn't gone in years, and he was working next weekend. He was going to have to promise someone something big to have them switch weekend call shifts.

"Would you like to go with me?"

"I'd love it. Here or in Durham?"

"I'll come to you," he said. Maybe he could catch his mom alone and convince her to hold off for…for what? Six months? Would that be sufficient time to kill this magic that was brewing between him and Solei? Would he no longer feel trapped?

"It's late," she said.

"I know. And I have surgery at seven, but there's so much I want to ask you. So much I want to know about you and your art. I want to watch your work again."

"How about we play a modified Rani game and ask each other three questions on the nights we talk? Maybe Rani can use some of them for her dissertation."

"That's a lot of nights you'll be talking to me."

"Poor Solei, late night chats with a butterfly." Solei laughed.

"Agree to disagree on that one. Ladies first."

"Why did you pick cardiothoracic surgery?"

"It picked me," he said sarcastically, and then he stopped. "Well, my dad is a cardiologist, and so it seemed like a good fit, but…I…it's one of the hardest residencies to get. And I got into one of the top programs; so I think it was a bit of a flex on my dad who always pushed so hard," he said slowly. "I think I'm just realizing this now," he paused, letting the knowledge wash over him. "Luckily I loved the challenge and how the body all works in concert. It's very delicate and technical."

"And you said you weren't good at self-reflection. Your turn."

"No, you can keep going." Before he lost his nerve.

"So polite. What is the top thing you'd like to explore once your residency is completed?"

You.

True, but not subtle.

"I'd like to travel," he said. "The plan was to take four or six months and travel before accepting a job offer. My father is planning for me to join his practice as soon as I finish up at Duke."

"Now I have a dilemma. Two juicy follow-ups, but I can ask only one."

"You can save the other for tomorrow."

"Where would you like to travel—what is first on your list is what I meant to ask."

"I don't know." He ran his hand through his hair. It was always flatter after a day of wearing surgical caps.

"You don't have a plan?" Her astonishment did not shine him in a positive light.

Being enigmatic, which he'd been accused of more than a few times had its benefits, but he wanted to know so much about Solei, and even though it was uncomfortable, he wanted her to know him—the real him. Not the him he showed most of the world.

"Out of questions," he said lightly. "You travel a lot for your art. Where is your favorite place where you painted a mural?"

"An art school in Paris."

"Oh. Damn. So much more I want to know. Put a pin in it. Did you always want to be an artist?"

"I don't think I thought of it as a career. I just always drew what I saw or what I felt. I grew up on different yachts. My dad was a captain for wealthy clients when they sailed, and my mom was their private chef so there wasn't a lot of space for toys. I had a duffel bag of clothes and a backpack for my homeschool and art supplies. Art seemed to find me, but I received an MFA in studio arts at UCLA and also got my teaching certificate.

Wow! He was blown away by that outlay of information. Her life was so utterly different and far more fascinating than his. "That's wild! Has that made you thrifty with space?"

It was a ridiculous question. He cringed, but Solei laughed.

"That sounds like a good relationship question for Rani's list," she teased. "For someone who wants a woman or a man whose life will fit into a duffel bag under the bed when they visit."

"I hadn't thought about that, but that could be a dealbreaker," he played along.

"I do live light, considering," she said. "It's a habit, and I think a bit of a curse."

"Why a curse?" He leaned closer to the screen.

"You had your three questions," she said quietly.

Somehow the mood had changed, and he didn't know why.

"Thanks for calling," he said. "You made my day."

"You too. And Rohan," her voice oozed over him like honey, and he found he was holding his breath waiting for her next words like they were lottery numbers. "The butterfly is not a literal butterfly but more a representation of your ideal self. A way in which it could benefit you to change. A metamorphosis of sorts. A possibility if you want to seize it. Good night. Talk tomorrow."

She disconnected and he stared at the black screen for another five minutes while her words rolled around in his brain, and just an inkling of what she'd said, and what Mrs. Bukar had said that had upset him so began to make sense.

A glimmer.

And that was so much better than the darkness.

Chapter Ten

ROHAN HAD BEEN able to swap his Sunday shift with another sixth-year resident for a Saturday twenty-four hour on shift. He'd done his final rounding early, taken a shower and changed and then had driven south to Charlotte. There'd been no traffic that early on a Sunday. He'd be lying if he said he didn't feel nerves feathering in his stomach all the way to low in his throat and anticipation kicked his heart rate up from his usual low sixties to high eighties.

He clutched the bag of pastries and another of fresh berries tightly in one hand when he knocked on the saffron-colored door of the address Solei had texted.

Play it cool. Relax.

When was the last time he'd been nervous about a date? He couldn't remember. He'd always enjoyed dating—the conversation, flirting, doing something non work-related, which happened far more rarely than he'd care to admit.

But he hadn't felt like anything was at stake. No spark, no foul.

He hadn't even felt this nervous walking into his MCATs.

"Hey." Solei opened the door, honey-blond hair loose

and tumbling over her shoulders and covering to just below her small, pert breasts. Gulping in a breath he jerked his gaze north to her vivid green eyes. They looked like two precious gems on a mountaintop, glittering in the warm early spring sunshine.

Damn this woman had him thinking in poetry.

She looked lit from within. "It's good to see you, Rohan." No criticism for him being late.

Solei wore a thin white fitted T and white denim shorts that were cuffed high on her thighs, which he was trying to ignore. He'd been smoother in high school.

"Fantastic to see you too." Massive understatement. He stepped up on the final brick step so that he was even with the door. Uncharacteristically he hesitated, not sure if he should give in to impulse. Not liking this tentative new self, he mentally "ah fucked it," and leaned forward and lightly kissed her cheek.

"Sorry I'm late," he said. "Indian time."

"What's Indian time?" she asked as she stepped back inside her small bungalow-style house.

"Indians are notoriously late. We joke about it. Or maybe it's just my family," he laughed. "In my family we call it Anju time because my aunt is always an hour behind on her best day. So, if we really need her to be somewhere, we tell her an hour ahead. This is cute," he looked around the generously sized open concept-style room. It was eclectically furnished with things that seemed to come from various

172

Asian countries. There was a small backyard with an overgrown collection of flowering shrubs and trees. Beyond the fence, he could see the start of Charlotte's downtown. "What an amazing location. I grew up in Charlotte and didn't know this neighborhood was here. I would have thought a developer would have swooped in and knocked everything down to build high-rise condos."

"I'm sure they've tried," Solei said, taking his hand and leading him farther into the room. "I rented it for a year from a professor on sabbatical. Not much in here is mine except the fold-up drafting table and the blanket that a friend hand loomed from her alpaca herd," Solei pointed to a colorful stripped blanket draped in a hanging rattan chair shaped like a giant egg. "The homes on this street and the next one over are mostly owned by professors. You can't beat the location. This has been one of my favorite places to live. The yard gets a lot of sun but there is shade and a water feature and an outdoor shower and..." She opened the door so they could walk out on the small patio with slightly uneven and mismatched pavers. "There's an outdoor grill and fireplace and best of all a salt water hot tub."

The idea of an outdoor shower and a hot tub was giving him all sorts of ideas he shouldn't be having since he'd driven up to participate in a Holi ceremony. Not that Hinduism was sexually prudish—duh the Kama Sutra—but in his family, he'd been on his own to figure out his body and sexuality. When he'd been fourteen, his mother had propelled his father into his room for the talk. His dad had wandered around his room, touching his things like he'd never seen them before while repeatedly clearing his throat. Then he'd looked him in the eye, said he was a smart boy, and he'd figure it out and had fled. His hovering mom had asked if Rohan had any questions, but he'd waved her off, promising that his papa had been very explicit.

"That will be convenient when we come back and need to wash off." He felt aroused picturing them—multi-colored and wet rinsing off under warm water in the sun, Solei's white T-shirt clinging to her small curves.

"I already have the towels and body wash ready," Solei said. "And in case we're feeling creative and have color left over, I strung an unstretched canvas between two small magnolia trees so that we can throw some of the bags of color on it and see what we create together."

"I should have suspected you'd turn this into an art project—always a teacher."

"I've only technically been a teacher this year," Solei told him. "I've taught guest workshops at colleges and museums for a few years as my reputation started to grow, but I've wanted to work for a while now with younger artists and artists who might come from less advantaged backgrounds whose families might not be able to afford art supplies or classes. Arts are always the first things cut in public schools, and kids need to have safe and healthy outlets to express themselves, so I went back to school last year to get a teaching certificate so that I could teach in public schools."

He listened, feeling guilty. He'd mentored new residents, and while he'd been at Davidson, he'd worked at the tutoring center helping in the math and sciences, but he hadn't done any community outreach.

You could.

The thought was like an arrow lodged in his skull. He could do a lot of things. Soon. His career would always require long hours, but he would have more freedom to make different choices—not only work.

"What are you thinking?" Her fingers brushed his and she took a step closer.

"That I'm glad to be here," he answered honestly. "That I feel lucky I met you and that..." He paused, not sure how to express what he was thinking or feeling. "I am just realizing that I'm coming to what I guess would be called a fork in the road because in two months, I'm finished with my training. I will have to study for my boards, but I'll be done and will have so many choices ahead."

Solei listened with her whole body. She always waited, not jumping in with her opinion or answer. It was a relief, but also a little unnerving because he could hear himself think. He was accustomed to being interrupted—by his grandparents, his father, his mother, his cousins—all telling him the path he should take or how he should feel. Solei just waited as if expecting him to come up with his own conclusions. He'd craved autonomy and space for years—trying to drown out the din of his over-involved family with distance and dodging phone calls and texts, while not cutting himself off completely—but now he was disconcerted by Solei's steady, interested regard.

"I'm not really." He ran his hand through his hair. "I've haven't had a lot of…" This was embarrassing to admit to a beautiful, brilliant and talented woman who embodied making her own choices. "My family has a lot of opinions they've had no problem sharing over the years, so I haven't been free to choose…" He was sounding lamer. He wanted to tell her about his new job opportunity—how it was the one he was by far the most excited about, but that felt traitorous. He hadn't shared the information yet, not even with Rani and likely never would with his parents.

"Let's just say not being in school or training and making some long-term career and life choices on my own will take some getting used to."

"Choice can be overwhelming." She paused. "When I have trouble deciding what to do or how to approach a problem, I go for a run or a long walk and listen to music. Or because I always need a plan, I'll give myself permission to not think about it and draw and let my subconscious process and burble something out. Usually the answer will feel right, but it won't necessarily be the easiest choice."

"I run," he seized on that. That might be something they could do together. She looked very fit. "But I don't have a lot of hobbies. I do love to swim." He loved everything about the water.

"Me too. Hobbies and interests evolve. You'll see things or hear about something, try it, give it a chance and see if you like it."

"Yeah." He wasn't sure.

She laughed. "That is not the face of a man agreeing with me," she teased. "Like birds," Solei pointed to a stone birdbath set in a tangle of flowers he had no idea the names of. A hummingbird feeder hung off a branch above it. "I used to love looking out for birds when I was little, and we were sailing because it meant we were closer to land and might be pulling into a port. Now that I live on land, I always like to put food and water and plants out to attract birds to see what's native to whatever area I am in. I like to watch them interact and go about their day, and maybe someday I'll actually take hikes specific to birding and have binoculars and guides and whatever or travel to places to see specific types of birds, but right now, just seeing them in their natural habitats is a bit of…maybe not a hobby but definitely something I enjoy. Who knows? Maybe I'll illustrate a bird book someday."

He nodded, understanding dawning.

"I like golf," he admitted after absorbing the impact of her words. "It was the first activity I pursued that wasn't pushed by my parents. I don't have much time to golf. Sometimes I head to the driving range if I don't work too late, but I can see how I might play more once I'm in…" He broke off. He'd been about to say "private practice," but Jason's offer kept whispering for attention—tempting him. Taking on big cases with Duke's resources, being able to research. Working with residents and sometimes teaching sounded pretty perfect. And Durham was close, but not too close. "Once I'm working," he amended.

He needed to make a decision. Sooner rather than later. His father had his contract ready to sign. He had more offers to interview in several major cities. And Jason had said the interview would just be a formality.

Pressure built in his chest.

"Today is supposed to be fun." Solei's hand lightly stroked his chest as if she sensed his turmoil. "Heralding spring's arrival. No major decisions required except, are you going to share any of that?" Solei looked at the two white bags he still clutched. "I made coffee as you said you might be operating on no sleep."

"I did get some sleep," Rohan said, "Sometimes I don't so I hope the other res I switched with doesn't get beaten up today, or she'll be out for my head."

Solei crossed both fingers. "Wishing the good karma of not too many surgical demands today holds. Let's eat and then make our Holi battle plan."

"THIS IS PRETTY epic," Solei said as they walked toward the

university's downtown campus. "I've never played paintball or laser tag, but I feel like we're gearing up for a battle."

"I always feel like I'm heading into an audition for Mr. Clean," Rohan said. He also wore white shorts and a white T-shirt.

"Do you do this every year?"

"I haven't in a while," he admitted. "This is the first time I've tried to get Holi off in years. Holi is aligned with the Hindu lunar calendar. It's later this year. Next year the full moon is much earlier in March." He looked at her, and she wondered if they'd be attending Holi together next year. They were so new, and she kept telling herself to stay in the moment—especially as their lives were in such flux.

Enjoy what you have now.

But his inky liquid eyes had her heart fluttering like a high school freshman discovering boys.

She wouldn't have thought it possible, but Rohan looked even handsomer in his highly stylized black-framed glasses. He'd looked a little embarrassed when she'd commented on them, which seemed sweet. He was so handsome and confident that she imagined he could barely walk down a street without women trying to hit on him. He'd admitted he had to wear contacts like it was some kind of flaw, but with bags of color being flung about along with blasters of colored water, he didn't want to risk it.

"I'm surprised you haven't experienced Holi before."

"I've seen the after-effects when I was at UCLA. The Indian Student Club always sponsored Holi—there was music and dancing and delicious food. It looked like fantastic fun, and as I grew up with no religion, I'm always drawn to spiritual things, but I felt like I didn't belong."

He shot her a look, and Solei felt exposed. Her and her need to connect. Did she sound pathetic? "Plus, I was always working," she tagged on.

"I can relate to that." His expression turned wry.

"Does your family attend a temple? It seems like a ceremony like this would be celebrated at the local temple."

"I'm not sure if anyone is going this year," he said vaguely. "You can hear the music already," Rohan said his steps quicker, and even holding a massive blaster filled with colored water in, he lifted his up arms and danced along to the beat for a few steps.

Solei was stuck on his answer about his family. Rani had made it sound like they were all really close. Why wouldn't he know how they were celebrating today or want to celebrate a religiously significant day with his family in their place of worship? But the beat of the music and joy in Rohan's face pushed her worry aside. She was seeing problems where she shouldn't. She and Rohan were just getting to know each other. During one of their many late-night phone calls this week, they'd agreed to enjoy what they could of spring together. Easier said than done. Solei liked having a plan. She needed to feel safe and have an escape route if necessary. But this year had been about staying in one place, making connections and trying to enjoy the moment.

My plan is to not have a plan until June.

The festival officially started at noon, and the color play started at one, but it was just past eleven and the campus quad was already jamming. There were several Indian food trucks, a DJ, a few henna artists doing mehndi tattoos, and tables full of baggies of dried paint for sale. Solei had already packaged up pigments for them—red, blue, yellow and green, but she could see baggies full of orange, pink and purple.

"Not traditional, but just as fun," Rohan said looking at the bounty. "I'm sure Krishna won't mind."

They waded deeper into the crowds. She tried not to read too much into it when Rohan held her hand. But she loved the feel of his palm against hers, his fingers intertwined with hers.

"Is your family very religious?"

"Not really. My grandparents immigrated so that my dad and uncle could attend high school in America. My mom came for medical school so they are very Americanized." His face closed off for a moment as if thinking of something unpleasant. "But both of my grandparents are founding members of the Charlotte temple. My mummyji often leads the prayer chants along with some of her friends, but I think attending temple is, for many people, a time to catch up and share a meal. Indians are very social."

Even though they'd eaten some fruit earlier and split a

twice-baked almond croissant that had been one of the most delicious things Solei had ever eaten, they lined up for some saag and channa to share.

They sat on a wall, shared the food and watched as more people poured in. The music was so addicting that Solei pulled him closer to the DJ to dance.

He held her hand up. "Think about screwing in a light-bulb with your right hand up and unscrewing a lightbulb with your left hand at your hip. And the beat. That's all you need to know."

Solei laughed. "There's a lot more going on in the dance than that," she objected. "I googled Bhangra and also classical dancing and how the hand movements and facial expressions tell stories."

"The only story we need to worry about is the one where we have a good time."

They danced song after song, moving closer and touching each other more—hands brushing and bodies brushing until Rohan reeled her in, hands anchoring on her hips. She could feel his arousal. It sent a shaft of heat through her. Solei had always been physical with a strong sex drive, but for the past few years, she'd felt too burned to try again—it hadn't been worth it. Meeting Rohan had tossed her caution out the window. Logically she knew this might be oh-so-fleeting, but it didn't feel like it would. It was hard to explain, but something deep inside of her responded to him—like he was a key to open some secret, dormant part of her.

Had there been a question covering anything like that on Rani's survey questions she was creating and sending out? In the words of Rohan Kapoor, "hard no."

"Thank you for coming with me today," he said.

She could feel his heat through the thin cotton of his white T-shirt and the warm, hardness of his quads though his pale denim jeans. His taut stomach aligned with hers. They were both slightly sweaty, and Solei had never felt sexier.

"I'm having a blast. You're so much more than fun."

He looked like he was going to say something else, but then his gaze slid to her lips, and Solei felt like the temperature notched up higher between them and around them making it harder to draw in a full breath. Her lips parted.

Yes. Definitely yes.

Tension snarled through her as his onyx eyes questioned.

"If you don't kiss me, I'll burst," she warned.

She loved the way his eyes lit up when he was amused. She wanted to make him laugh just to watch the way the sun rose in his eyes.

"Can't have that. The mess doesn't start for another ten minutes at lea..."

Solei kissed him, blocking the last syllable in his mouth.

He whispered her name against her lips and Solei gently took off his glasses and tucked them on the front of her shirt so that nothing got in her way. She'd wanted to touch his face since they'd first met. She hadn't expected their first kiss to be so shockingly intimate. She'd hoped for a few fireworks. Instead it was like diving off a cliff into warm, embracing water that caressed her entire body and made it tingle.

His lips were firm, magic and assertive enough for Solei to lose herself. His tongue dipped along the corners of her mouth, and she lightly licked along his upper lip. The groan and tightening of his arms around her shot an excited heat that curled her toes.

They both dropped their blaster squirt guns filled with colored water, and her small backpack filled with pastry bags of dried paint fell at her feet as her fingers finally took the opportunity to spear through his shiny, thick blue-black hair that sprang back from his square forehead like a work of art. His hands were in her hair and Solei pressed herself closer against him and deepened the kiss.

The music swirled around them, the beat pulsing in her core. They were jostled by other dancers or people moving to the large grassy area in preparation to throw their colors but none of it mattered. Solei had never lost herself so completely in a kiss or in a man before.

Finally, they broke apart a few inches, both breathing hard, Solei feeling dazzled and dazed.

"Explosive," Rohan murmured, running one thumb over her bottom lip. A countdown started as if in agreement—she and Rohan created a bomb together.

"Massive understatement," she said, licking along his square, jutting jaw and nibbling with her teeth. "I want to experience Holi," she admitted. "But I also want to drag you back to my place."

She wasn't usually so forward, but it was challenging to keep her thoughts and actions anywhere near PG. Rohan had her not only breaking her rules about PDA, but not even remembering that she'd ever had any.

He kissed her again, keeping it lighter this time, his hands on her shoulders, his thumbs tracing her collarbones, and who knew that was an erogenous zone for her?

"You can have both," he said. "We have all day."

"A day is not enough for what I want to do."

The way his eyes widened and breath caught was thrilling.

"Solei," his voice ached, "don't tell me that. Trying to behave."

"Eight, seven…" the crowd chanted.

"Oh. It's going to start," Rohan seemed to snap back to reality more easily than she did, which was not particularly flattering. "Let's go."

Go? Where? Solei was still trying to stick her landing back on Earth. Rohan swooped up both of the blasters, and her backpack and retrieved his glasses from her front, his fingers lingering along the deep V or her T-shirt. Seizing her hand, he pulled her into the crowd and up the stairs to the upper level of the quad where there was a large grassy area with people lined up several deep on all four sides.

"Here." He handed her a red pastry bag. "Wow. That's kinda cool." He gave it an experimental squeeze and as the crowd shouted out one, a puff of red exploded out dousing her chest. "Genius hack," he commented. "You okay?" He had to shout over the noise of the cheering.

"Isn't becoming Technicolor the point?"

"One of many. Let's stay together," he pulled her into the center of the quad.

Staying together wasn't as easy as it sounded. It was all-out color bomb war. And it was the most beautiful, vibrant experience in Solei's life. She held a saffron-yellow pastry bag over her head and squeezed it up in the air just to watch the blast of color contrast with all that Carolina blue like a firework that drifted down over everyone in their immediate vicinity.

Rohan seemed more intent on targeting people squeezing as they ran by like it was some sort of a pigment gauntlet to run. The predominant color seemed to be crimson red and Solei held out her arms as a puff of red she'd shot above her head drifted down over her.

"Ready to gear up?" Rohan pulled her closer to him as the crowd swelled. Solei blinked at him—he was covered in blue and red and yellow. Not so much green. She could fix that.

"What do you have in mind?" She dug a forest-green bag of pigment out of her dwindling supplies in her backpack.

Wow. She'd thought she'd packaged so much that they'd be handing it out to people, but she and Rohan had overly indulged on their exploration of the colors of the rainbow, although Rohan had told her not to pack purple—one of her favorite colors—because it wasn't traditional.

Not everyone was so old school since she saw a lot of purple splattering people. She wondered what other traditions were adopted and adapted as more and more people immigrated from India over the past five-plus decades.

"Trust me," he called out, and swung her onto his back.

Trust me. Two simple words that had always been a warning flag to Solei. Trust was earned over time and actions. She never took trust lightly as it had been broken so often.

But with Rohan's call echoing in her ears, and her front pressed against his back while his arms looped over her legs to hold her in place, 'trust me,' didn't sound any alarm bells.

Like he was in an action movie, Rohan used the blaster full of thick, dark blue water to soak people as he ran the length of the quad. People shrieked, laughed and called for more. Other people had brought squirt guns and blasters and started pulling them out. Getting into the spirit, Solei hunched over Rohan to make it easier to run and she started aiming at people instead of the sky.

Rohan had made three passes along the quad until they were laughing too hard to stand. He staggered over to the side and went knees down in the grass, rolling the two empty blasters away from him.

"Best day ever," Solei sprawled half on top of him and looked down into his multi-hued face. "Absolutely the best day."

"And it's not even two in the afternoon," Rohan said softly.

"I have one bag left," Solei said.

"What color?" He eased a clump of hair that stuck to her cheek, gently out of her face. He curled a lock around his finger and pressed it to his lips.

He was so tender. She'd never had tender. Not really. And she felt another barrier around her heart wobble.

"Green," she said, trying to keep her voice matter-of-fact.

"Perfect," he said, closing his eyes. "Bathe us in it. Green means new beginnings."

Her heart lurched alarmingly. Life had become too perfect. The serendipitous meeting last weekend—encouraging him to venture out of his shell artistically. The fascinating conversation. The fun. The chemistry. The nightly phone calls that unspooled over hours.

Don't forget the living in different cities and no contract yet for next year.

Shut up. They had the spring. She wasn't that young girl who ached for a home and had walked on eggshells around her grandparents afraid they'd change their minds and send her back. She wasn't the college student barely making ends meet and always, always worried about making rent. She'd built a reputation. She had money in the bank and an inbox full of requests. She could relax a little. Not need a plan A and a plan B so that she could sleep at night.

Solei rolled to her side, and then sat up and straddled him.

"To new beginnings," she sang out and aimed the last green-filled pastry bag up at the sky and squeezed as hard as she could.

HAND IN HAND, they walked along the edge of the quad. People were still throwing colors and dancing. Solei took some video and pictures, amazed at how beautiful and surreal it looked.

"It looks like an alien landscape," she mused aloud, just staring at all the colors everywhere and the people walking around like they were covered in some sort of outer space moon or planet dust. "This is what I imagine life on Mars would look like."

He liked the way she thought and how she was so observant. She helped him to see the world through a slightly different lens.

He heard someone call his name. Dammit. He let go of her hand. He figured everyone he knew would head to the temple to celebrate Holi. He didn't want to be part of community gossip or Solei to be subject to intense, critical scrutiny.

"Be right back," he said casually and jogged over to Mr. Pawan, a long-time friend of his family. "Uncleji," he put his hands together. "Good to see you."

He turned his back on Solei, wanting to kick himself as he did so.

"I had an unexpected afternoon off and thought I might just catch Holi." Obviously he had. He was blindingly Technicolor and quite wet with colors running off him. He stayed clear of Mr. Pawan, as he had clearly been more of an observer and just had a bit of red and yellow dusting.

"Of course." Mr. Pawan was cordial as always. "Your cousins always come to this celebration. It is bigger than the one at the temple. Can you believe it?"

Double shit. Rohan glanced around warily almost expecting Rani to pop out from behind a bush. He and Solei had to get out of here.

"The young people prefer it. The music. All of the food trucks. Indian culture's gone mainstream. Can you believe it?"

That was one of Mr. Pawan's catch phrases. Unfortunately, it now put him on edge, which sucked because Mr. Pawan was a wonderful man. He also had two very marriage eligible daughters, and Rohan had been dodging questions about finding a nice girl to settle down with from Mr. Pawan and over a dozen of his cronies for years. And news of his mom hiring a matchmaker would be chum in the water.

Damn. He shouldn't have come. Or he should have ignored Holi. He should have had Solei come to Durham. And he definitely shouldn't leave her standing by herself. Four or five more shoulda coulda wouldas galloped through his head.

Politeness dictated that he ask about Mr. Pawan's health as well as about his family. He did, nearly dancing with impatience. He heard the commiserations about Asha's wedding and congratulations about nearly finishing his residency.

"Your mom and Asha are planning a party to celebrate your accomplishments. We have been hearing of it for months. She even sent out save the date cards as if we could forget, can you believe it?"

Rohan stared at Mr. Pawan, probably looking comically stupid. He'd forgotten about the party—celebrating him finishing residency and joining his father's cardiac group, and now, no doubt his mom was planning to announce his engagement to some yet unmet accomplished Indian woman from a "good family." He didn't want the party. His chest compressed against his spine. He didn't want any of it. He wished he could rewind time to five minutes ago when he'd been happy and totally in the moment, enjoying a beautiful day with Solei. No other expectations shoved down his throat.

"Uncle, it's so good to see you. We will catch up soon," Rohan said, cutting the conversation painfully short. "I am so sorry. I need to go," he kept the rush vague and mysterious. At least with all of the colors, he wouldn't be able to tell anyone anything about Solei except she was female. She didn't even look white.

Holi. The great racial equalizer.

"Sorry about that. One of my family's friends," he said easily returning to Solei, careful not to stand too close or touch her even though he desperately wanted to. To reassure her or him? Their kiss earlier had blown his mind and most of his control wide open. He'd never made out with a woman in a public place before. Never. Ever.

"You called him uncle."

"Oh, everyone who is older and a family friend is an uncle or an auntie, even the real uncle and aunties. It's surprisingly easy although I'm sure it sounds weird and confusing. But at a party that is absurdly huge, it's a lifesaver. If you've forgotten someone's name, just toss out an uncle or auntie. Works like a charm."

Solei laughed. She slid her hand into his. "Hey isn't that Rani?"

He barely bit back the curse.

"She said she had other plans," he said, unintentionally kicking up the pace.

"It is," Solei said. "She's waving."

Rohan swallowed his sigh. "Can't seem to get you on my own," he said as a form of apology for acting like a selfish idiot.

Her smile was beautiful and hilarious because she had Krishna blue on her teeth. He could just imagine how Technicolored he looked.

"Ro, Ro, Ro," Rani chanted. She was drenched in color and sucking down a smoothie. Too late he saw her friends' smoothie truck. Worse, Shanti was with her, flicking her stick-straight hair over her shoulders and pointedly looking at Solei. "Why didn't you tell me...oh..." Rani broke off comically, her eyes so wide they looked like they'd pop out of her head if she got jostled. "Hi, Solei."

The dagger look she shot him hurt.

"You said you had to work," she accused.

"I was able to make a last-minute schedule switch," he said, narrowing his eyes in warning. Rani was his cousin. His younger cousin. Not his mom. Not his keeper. Not his judge, jury or executioner.

"I'm Shanti," Shanti said. "Rohan's less nosy and less interfering cousin," Shanti said, looking more amused by his predicament than irritated. "I tried to get Asha to come with me to get her out of the house but only runt joined me."

"I'm not even that much shorter than you... Well, at least when you're not wearing heels, which is hardly ever."

"Solei," Solei said her gaze not sure where to settle: him, Rani or Shanti. He didn't blame her. He was feeling edgy himself. Charlotte was a city with nearly nine hundred thousand people in it, and he ran in to family and friends within a few minutes.

"My stilettos serve as one weapon in my arsenal," Shanti said. "When I'm deposing potential witnesses, men crumble under the dueling pressure of sexual fantasy and fear. Four-inch heels throws them off their game every time." She looked at Solei's formerly white canvas tennis shoes. "You should try it."

Then she leveled the death stare look she'd perfected when she'd hit her teens on him. Rohan had never personally experienced it before. Rakesh was probably sterile by now he'd been subject to hundreds of Shanti's radioactive glares, not that Rakesh had been fazed, but Rohan had reached his limits of his family's "do it my way." Two more bossy Kapoors was two too many.

"Aaaaand, we're done," Rohan announced. "Catch you all later."

"Not likely," Shanti drawled. "Since we caught you first."

It took him halfway back to Solei's house to get his heart rate back under control and snap a leash on his temper. He only had himself to blame. He'd been stupid to bring Solei to Holi in his hometown. But why the hell couldn't he make friends with anyone he wanted? Why should he feel guilty? It wasn't like he was consorting with drug dealers. But he felt dirty. He'd disrespected Mr. Pawan. He'd lied to his cousins. He hadn't told his parents he was coming up. And worse, he'd treated Solei like she was a secret he'd stashed under his bed.

Damn. Damn. Dammit. He wanted to howl at the full moon that would rise tonight and somehow bust out of himself and his life. Scream at the unfair sky. He'd done everything he was supposed to. No trouble ever. Top of everything—the goddamn golden one. And yet he couldn't catch a breath without someone pointing a finger and telling him hard no to this and hard no to that.

His internal rant circled round and round, and it took him until they turned on Solei's street to realize that she hadn't spoken once since they'd left the park. Dammit. Rani's unexpected appearance—always in the wrong place and the wrong time, and Shanti's cutting snark had ruined a beautiful afternoon.

No. Your reaction ruined it.

The accusation hit hard. Each word a hammer to his head. His heart.

"I'll show you the shower," Solei said.

Her voice sounded final.

"I'm sorry. I'm sorry." He faced her in front of the iron gate that led to her backyard. "I can explain. I hope. Maybe I can't. Solei," he gulped in a breath. "I'm sorry." When did he become so socially clumsy and inarticulate? "I just wanted you to myself today. Longer actually," he laughed ruefully. He took her cold hands in his. "My parents are great. They've been endlessly supportive of me, but they have high expectations. Make a lot of demands. It's a lot of pressure, and I just wanted to have time to get to know you before my large, opinionated extended family becomes omnipresent."

He felt the pressure of the apology and explanation snake through his body chilling him with its poison. For a man who was lauded as being cool under pressure, he was wildly off his game, and as he met her cool, assessing green eyes, he felt he was fighting for his life.

This was a test. One of the most important of his life, and he wasn't going to fuck it up.

"I've been running flat out my whole life." He ran a hand impatiently thorough his hair as if that would pluck out the right words. "And now I'm nearly done with school after fourteen years of higher education, and I wanted time to just be. To think. To travel. To do something for myself before jumping into my career, but my family is already trying to play that out too—join my father's cardiac practice. They even built a whole second house underneath theirs. Fuck. The symbolism of that!"

She stepped into him, her arms looping around his neck like she'd done a few times before. She didn't say anything. She just held him. Her body was warm. Her closeness and touch steadied him, and his heart rate that had been slamming uncomfortably, began to settle. He caught a breath, held it, released and then another.

"It feels so selfish, but I just want time to be with you. To learn who you are and what you like. I want to know what makes you laugh and what inspires you and yes, what you fear. You never seem to judge me, and you have no idea…none," his voice cracked. Holy shit. He felt like he was going to cry. He sucked in a deep breath and pinched his nose. "No idea how much I need that right now.

"You know how you told me that you like to play with your mural concepts before you let any other voices weigh in? I've never had that space. Never. I'm finishing up residency and my family expects me to jump into the job they created and live in the house they built and never once, not once did they ask me what I want," he said bitterly while Solei nuzzled his hair. "Hell, my mom's already hired…" He pulled back from the brink just before disaster.

He couldn't tell her that.

She'd think he was a douche.

A cheater.

Am I?

No. They hadn't declared themselves to be exclusive. But he felt exclusive. The thought of touching another woman, even sitting with another woman over coffee or dinner just felt wrong to his very core. He'd already deleted his two dating apps. No more swiping right for him. And as long as he didn't meet any of the women Mrs. Bukar found, that wouldn't be cheating. Cheating was with intention. Desire. He'd rather slam his balls in a drawer.

He'd have to tell his mom no.

Not that she'd accept that. His burst of determination soured.

But he could and would call Mrs. Bukar. Tell her he was

not ready to look now.

Feeling more settled, he let his hands slide down her arms. He was so far gone on Solei he didn't even mind that they still stood on the sidewalk outside her house.

"My dad is a twin. I grew up with three of my cousins—Asha, Shanti and Rani either in the same house or next door to each other. They are more like my sisters. There was a lot of family pressure on all of us. And sibling rivalry. It nearly broke Rani because she's always been a free spirit, different, and differences are not easily tolerated at least in my family, but I hear the same thing from friends. I also have other cousins. My mom has two sisters and a brother. Rani's mom has two sisters with kids in Charlotte and Atlanta. Then there's the whole Charlotte Indian community."

He huffed out an exasperated breath. "I could go on and on about that. The thing is. They're great. So much social support. And everyone jumps in to help when needed, but it's also cutthroat competitive. Status oriented. Gossip thrives, and I just…" He wondered if he was getting through to her. He was saying this all so badly when it was so important to get it right.

"I don't want to live in a fishbowl," he said. "I don't want everyone to know everything about me. They already think they do, but I've held so many pieces back—like a game of poker. We all do probably." He gently smoothed her hair out of her face as an afternoon breeze swooshed around the corner. "I want you to know me. All of me. I don't want to hold back with you, but I was…I am being selfish, wanting time alone with you."

Her eyes bore into his searching. God, he hoped he was worthy of her time, that she could see into his heart, and his soul, flawed as it was.

"I can understand that," she said, her voice quiet and thoughtful. "My parents are far away. They call me every time they reach a port and have service. And email, but they are not a daily part of my life so I don't have to curate myself or my life for them. They were loving and supportive and let me go live with my grandparents when I was fourteen because I wanted a more permanent home. They left me alone to make my own choice for college and career. My grandparents seemed happy to have me, but they had their own lives and were busy, and I felt like I didn't want to cause worry or trouble. But I never once felt like my life wasn't mine to live."

"I know families can be challenging," Solei said. "My mom ran away from an abusive home when she was sixteen, hopped on a ferry and got a job in a kitchen at a resort in the Charlotte Islands the next day. She earned her GED and learned how to be a chef on the job. My dad grew up on the water in Newport Beach. He went to college, but always sailed and piloted boats and then ferries and yachts. Neither of them had any specific expectations for me to fulfill. Culturally, I can see how your life was so different, your dad being a doctor and you being an only son."

"Both parents are doctors. I was double teamed."

She mussed his hair a little. "And here I thought the whole Indian doctor thing was a stereotype."

"Unfortunately not," he said, relaxing a little, as she wasn't pulling away. Her fingers stroked his neck, and he loved that. "It's getting better somewhat, but not so I or any of my cousins have noticed. Shanti just made partner at a very prestigious international law firm—youngest partner ever, and her mom is still hesitant to talk about what she does."

"That's awful," Solei breathed. "Oh sorry. I shouldn't judge. It's just so different, unexpected from my experience."

"Judge away." He waved his hand, suddenly feeling hot, sticky and itchy now that the storm of emotion had passed. "My mom should have had twelve kids," he said. "Then we would have had a chance to breathe occasionally."

Solei laid her head against his chest.

"I didn't mean to disrespect you. I'm sorry if it felt like that. I just didn't want Mr. Pawan to..." He spread his hands, fingers wide. The damage was likely done at least a little bit. His parents would know he was here. They would know he didn't come to the house.

Shanti would keep her mouth shut. Probably. But she'd probably want a favor. He could deal. Rani was a wild card. But she loved him. She was also unfortunately obsessed with her matchmaker idea.

"Rohan, I won't push you on this, but I think if you

share your feelings with your parents, they will eventually understand. But it's your choice, if and when," she said, her voice grave. "Now, let's wash away and start over." Solei opened her gate and led him up the stairs toward her back garden.

Solei walked to the side of the covered patio, and Rohan followed, not sure what to expect. The shower was open to the elements from the top and one side. The three sides were finished wide teak slats. Solei turned on the water and it came down in a wide spray.

"It takes a minute to heat up. Do you want something to drink? I can still taste the pigment in my mouth. I have bottled water or flavored sparkling."

"Plain water. Thank you." Rohan still wanted to kick himself for acting so awkward at the festival. Solei deserved better. Mr. Pawan deserved better. Rani and Shanti deserved better. Mrs. Bukar and any women she was potentially contacting definitely deserved better.

He closed his eyes and pinched the bridge of his nose hard.

He had to ensure that he never behaved so disrespectfully again.

Man up so to speak—something he'd never thought he'd have to personally counsel himself to do. He always took responsibility for what he needed to do—study, prepare, execute. But he'd never had feelings crowding in, tripping over each other and making him a dysfunctional mess. Why was it so hard to do the right thing?

And why couldn't Solei be the right thing for now?

Seeing a woman shouldn't be a group activity.

She retrieved two bottles of water from an outdoor cooler that looked like an old-fashioned Coke machine and walked back toward him. A shaft of sun caressed her. Her hips swayed enticingly. Her smile lit him up inside, chasing away his angst.

The right thing forever?

It felt so easy with her—if the rest of the world would just shut up for a minute, stay still.

"I can feel you thinking from here." She handed him his water and then twisted the cap off of hers. "Usually, I am the one with the groove." She traced between his eyebrows with her finger. "Thinking the entire time. Making plan A and plan B. You take me out of my head, Rohan."

"You launch me out of mine," he confessed and then twisted off the cap and drank deeply to hide his nervousness at his honesty.

His relationship with his family was complicated. Solei had had freedom to please herself since she was a teen. She had no hope of understanding all the pressures he faced. He didn't even understand it. Rakesh and Shanti had always seemed to roll with it. Or push back. Dhruv had middle-fingered everyone and joined the army. He'd been gone for twelve or more years and was now inexplicably back but making no move to integrate into his family. Rohan hated that his actions had caused Solei to doubt her feelings for him. But his emotions were so fresh, new, outside his experience. And he felt like a giant clock was ticking down.

"You thrill me," he admitted softly. "And terrify me."

"Rohan," she whispered, and never had he loved his name more.

"I feel like I've been shot out of one of those cannons at an old-time circus, and I'm about to splat. I feel like we're running out of time—like I met you too late, but maybe the timing is perfect." He was rambling. He finished the water. He needed to shut up. He was freaking himself out. He could just imagine how she felt listening to his melodramatic lunacy.

He loved the way she looked at him—trying to understand—not telling him how he felt.

"You said you have the spring," she reminded. "We can see where it goes." She bit her lip as if worried she'd said too much.

"The spring," he repeated. He did have two more months at Duke. More if he wanted.

He settled a little.

"I applied to stay on at the school," she admitted against his chest. "I haven't heard back yet, but I have money and choices." She looked at him—a beautiful, rainbow in human form. "There are other high schools. I love teaching, but I can support myself on commissions alone at this point. We could..." She paused, and the light shining in her eyes dimmed a little, and her soft, sweet gaze slid away from his, unsure. "See how it goes."

He didn't like that. It sounded half-assed. Uncommitted.

And he'd never been uncommitted about anything in his life.

Except for his parents' plans for him once he finished his training.

"Yeah, the spring. Then we can see where we are, reevaluate," he said. It sounded mature. Practical.

But felt stupid.

The way he felt when he was with Solei—happy, full of promise, full of life—didn't seem like something that would run its course like a flashflood.

He needed to talk to his parents. Tell them he wanted time. He didn't want to interview a parade of women for the position of his wife. He wanted to explore other career options.

His stomach cramped. He'd never once disappointed them or gone against what they'd wanted. The thought of losing his mother and father's esteem was unthinkable. He just couldn't go there. He couldn't cope with seeing the disappointment in their expressions, the fraught quiet when his name came up, the shame they'd feel at parties that he hadn't reached his full potential.

He knew falling out of favor would suck because he'd seen it happen to other kids he'd gone to school with— Dhruv, who'd known he'd never measure up by middle school and so had made every effort to show that he didn't care. He'd seen the same look on his aunt's and uncle's face with every Rani error, and now Asha would be an object of pity and gossip and disappointment through no fault of her own.

He was in uncharted territory with Solei, and about to be caught up in a tempest when he spoke to his parents.

"The spring," he repeated. "My favorite season in Charlotte."

"We'll make the most of it," she promised sunnily and stepped away. Immediately his arms felt empty. He had it bad for her, and he found he didn't care.

He closed his eyes and fully clothed stepped under the water.

And then Solei was there. Next to him, her head tilted back to get the spray. She lifted up her arms as if in supplication to the water, and even with her eyes closed, her expression read pure pleasure. He'd never showered outside, and even fully clothed. It felt decadent. Solei's thin T-shirt clung to her body, outlining her perfect palmful breasts. His palms nearly buzzed with the urge to caress her small curves.

"Still multi-colored?" Her lips curved in a smile even as her eyes remained closed.

"Let me check," he murmured and then wrapped his

arms around her and kissed her again, and everything flowed down the drain—the anxiety, guilt, regret, irritation—washing him clean.

SOLEI LOVED HOLDING Rohan close, but it never felt close enough. She always wanted more. She wanted to be skin to skin. Feeling daring, she slid her palms under his T-shirt. He ducked so she could pull it off.

"Wow," she breathed out reverently as her hands explored his torso. "I've been jonesing to sketch your face, but now you've given me a whole new fantasy to draw obsessively."

"All yours." He held out his arms. "Anytime. Anywhere."

Solei hesitated, remembering the way Rohan had hunched into himself, looked back furtively when he'd spoken to the man as they were leaving the festival. But Rohan's gaze smoldered now, and his hands anchored at her hips, aligning their bodies so that she could feel the length of his desire scattered her worries. He looked at her like she'd hung the sun, and she'd never had that before. Rohan was fun, and he wasn't making any promises. She needed to embrace what she had now. She missed being touched and the pleasant buzz of sex; except with Rohan desire felt more like a burn.

She jumped into the fire, kissing his sharp jawline that

was still smooth from his shave. She nibbled down his neck and then tongued one of his nipples and then the other. He had no chest hair—from nature or preference, and all that hard-plank smoothness and definition was a visual and sensual feast. His erection jumped against her body, heating her more. She then licked a path down his ribs. Rohan hissed in a breath and groaned her name.

Her fingers played with the button on his shorts and dipped down along his waistband. She looked up at him, questioning. Rohan hissed out a breath, giving her full access.

"You going to let me return the favor?" his voice raw, his breathing ragged. The warm water rained down on them, and Rohan leaned back against the shower wall.

Solei hummed a little as she unbuttoned his shorts, slow-ly sliding down the zipper. Her heart hammered in time with the water hitting her, drowning out the sounds of the city, of the birds that often flitted through the backyard because of the birdbaths she'd added and the several feeding stations.

Boxer-briefs.

Her mouth dried.

"If this were a game of strip poker," he watched each move she made with an intensity that made her feel sexy, bold and adventurous, not vanilla as Zach had complained, trying always to push her beyond her comfort zone, "I would definitely be the loser, and yet I feel like I'm winning."

She eased his shorts and underwear from his narrow hips,

and down his strong thighs. God, the muscle definition—he'd said he liked to run. And then his shorts were at his ankles. He kicked them away, and she gently palmed him, rubbing her thumb gently over his velvety tip.

"Wow," she breathed reverently once again, completely captivated by his masculine beauty, and then she looked up at him, aroused, watching her with the intensity of a predator, water raining down on the beautiful, brown planes of his chest. He looked like a god.

"I've sketched a lot of naked men," she confessed. "You are by far the most beautiful. Your friend's sister may be a talented designer but covering you up would not be my first choice."

He laughed, breaking what was fast becoming a thrall.

"Seriously, Rohan, you have beautiful bones." She kissed the tip of his erection, tonguing a circle before standing up.

"You like my bones, my boner, what about the rest of me?"

It would have been easy to laugh. He probably meant her to, but she'd heard a note in his voice, something, that caused her heart to pinch in sympathy.

"The rest of you," she kissed his forehead, then the tip of his nose before licking along the seam of his lips, "is the best part," she assured him.

He jumped into the kiss—hungry, demanding, and Solei let him take over, reveling in his passion and the no longer repressed intensity that so often hovered around him like an aura. She'd wanted to know what Rohan would be like if he lost control. Now he felt unleashed.

She could still taste him on her tongue—salty, hint of spice, and hard heat, and she wondered if he could too, but the desire for more—more heat, more sensation, all of him seated deep within her, powerfully thrusting drowned out her ability to think.

"Do you want to take this off?" he paused long enough to ask her, as his hand dipped under her shirt, palm hot against her tummy.

"Yes, everything," she told him, looking deep into his eyes. She always felt like she was looking into a star-spangled night sky with Rohan. He had so much life inside of him. So much light.

He hesitated, as if to speak, but Solei didn't want to play it safe. She didn't want to wait. She pulled off her shirt and flung it far across the yard.

Yes, please.

Rohan looked a little startled. She would have imagined that he was so hot that he had women regularly wanting to get naked, sweaty and horizontal with him, although they were currently vertical. And outside.

Vanilla no more. She felt safe with Rohan, like she could be her true self, not needing to censor her thoughts, her spirit, her talent.

"Before we go any further, and I really, really want to," he leaned down so that their foreheads touched. It felt so reverent. Solei closed her eyes, letting her arms wrap around him, holding her to him, instead of exploring him sexually. "I didn't bring any condoms," he said. "I didn't want to assume or push it or…"

She kissed him, interrupting the flow of words. "That's okay. I have a package of five in my pocket." She told him, feeling heroically adventurous and singing one of Billie Eilish's early hits "Bad Guy," against his mouth. He reached into her pocket, palmed her ass, and then her shorts and panties hit the floor.

They crashed together, mouths exploring, hands pleasuring, steam rising, and the sun slanting down across their bodies creating light and shadow and more pleasure and intimacy than Solei had imagined existed.

HOURS LATER THAT felt like days, they laid curled up together on a lounger on Solei's patio. Rohan felt like he was still trying to fully back into his body. The day, and the early evening still had a dreamlike feel. Usually after sex he felt physically relaxed, but mentally invigorated—ready to get home and prepare for his day. But Rohan wanted to stay with Solei. He wanted to eat with her. Fall asleep with her. Wake up wrapped around her body.

Shouldn't that raise some sort of alarm?

He and Solei had talked about spending spring together—at least April and May in his mind—as much as their busy schedules would allow. Solei's work schedule had been a revelation to him. With her teaching, volunteering at the youth urban arts center, and commission work, she was as busy as he was. Usually women he met had been hookups or their schedules were so out of sync—him often working sixty to eight hour weeks—that it hadn't been worth it to try.

But with Solei, he wanted more than just to try. He wanted…he wanted…his mind stuttered to a halt as if afraid to express how intense his longings were. They shouldn't make sense, and they didn't intellectually, and yet for the first time in his life, his head was not leading.

They'd made love in the outdoor shower, her bed and again in the kitchen as they'd prepared dinner together. Rohan should have been on the road an hour ago. Or more. But instead, they'd watched the sun set over the city over a dinner they'd prepared from an online recipe after shopping for the ingredients at a small locally sourced grocery store a few blocks from the house Solei rented. Solei had even lit candles.

"How is your goat coming along?" he asked, running his hand lazily under the strap of her tank top. Her skin gleamed enticingly in the glow of the candles that still flickered on the picnic table.

"The logo design is approved—no blackberries—just hops and barley and a few thistles," she said. "I'm still working on the mural design. That's all mine. I talk to clients and essentially interview them to get a feel for who they are and what they want or what the history is of the building or city or company, but with a commission, generally the idea for the artwork is all mine. I might add in something specific like a pet or something with symbolic meaning for them, but I have a lot of artistic license. I still do a few company logos or music label artwork for fun if I like the project and have the time."

"So different from my career," he mused. "Mine is far more prescripted and bound by rules, tradition, research, biology, technology."

She kissed his jaw. She did that a lot. He had no idea that was an erogenous zone for him. His body stirred to life, and he didn't try to hide it. Solei didn't seem to mind that she was turning him into a sex addict—well more like a Solei addict. And again, as a man who prided himself on his self-control and discipline and meticulous planning, all sorts of alarms should be sounding.

"Not really." Her fingers played with the buttons on his shirt. "Ostensibly our jobs are totally different, and yet you have developed your knowledge through study. I too studied different artists and techniques. You developed your surgical skills through hours and hours of practice as did I. I bet you've come up with some innovations or some flair that mark your surgical technique as unique. I've developed my own techniques as an artist. You are always pushing to improve and innovate to improve outcomes for your patients. Me too. You will probably attend educational seminars or present at some medical conferences as your career progresses to keep current and to improve. I too need to always be learning."

Now it was his turn to whisper a "wow" against her bare skin.

"You must think me an arrogant ass," he said. "I never thought about art like that, but what you say makes sense. There is a tremendous amount of skill you bring to your career, and you have the same sense of pride and determination that I have. I like that," he said slowly.

He liked that she was ambitious for herself and her career. She wouldn't sit around bored and frustrated waiting for him to come home so that they could do something... Come home? He was really jumping out in front of the car.

But instead of getting fidgety and wanting to escape, he savored holding her. Relaxing, something he rarely did. Well, one part of him wasn't exactly relaxed. Solei noticed.

"I like that you have so much energy," she said, playfully rolling so that she was partially on top of him. "You're tastier than gourmet handcrafted chocolate."

"I'll add that on my CV when I'm applying for jobs." He played with her hair that was sexily mussed. "That will make me stand out from the pack."

She smiled, and then rested her chin on her balled-up fist. "You will always stand out, Rohan," she said softly.

His heart actually felt gooey, which would make Rani

laugh, but he didn't care.

"I'm finished with my residency the first week in June." He voiced the thought he'd been trying to ignore since they'd started texting and talking for hours every night over the past week. It should feel insane. He'd only known her a week. But it felt like she'd always been there with him, always been a part of him that he had just needed to discover and release. "When does your school let out?"

"The same week," she eyed him curiously.

"What will you do if the school doesn't rehire you, will you stay in Charlotte and look for another teaching job or will you return to LA?" He forced himself to say the two letters.

She paused. He held his breath. "No," she said decisively. "I don't want to go back to LA. At least not now."

He felt like fist bumping the sky.

"I've been a part of the LA art scene since college. I've done a lot of work there and taught a lot of workshops and guest artist stints in and around the city. I want something different, but I want roots. I like Charlotte, but I can't stay here." She looked around the backyard, her eyes sparkling in the candlelight. "The professor's returning in August. It's weird," she said. "I'm usually such a planner. I'm booked out for commissions months in advance. I'm so organized, but this year, I just wanted to flow a little. Not make a plan. I haven't even started looking for another teaching position. I've loved teaching at the high school, but I can definitely comfortably support myself with commissions."

"That means a lot of travel," he said.

She nodded, her eyes searching his, likely wondering where he was going with this. Hell, he should be wondering where he was going with this. He hadn't intended on going anywhere. Only this afternoon they'd reiterated the spring fling idea, although fling didn't come within shouting distance of what this felt like. Usually when women started talking about seeing him again, he was quick to politely shut it down. Now he was the one trying to figure out how to ask what he wanted to ask.

And what he really wanted to ask.

"I've been thinking about traveling for a few months before I sign a contract," he said.

"You mentioned that. Where are you thinking of going?" she asked curiously.

"I'm not really sure. I've traveled with my family growing up—we always did a big two or three-week summer trip and then a Christmas holiday skiing trip. And in school I've gone on weekends with friends or to weddings, but I've never had time to just visit a place that I wanted with no agenda other than enjoying myself."

"Where would you like to go if you could go anywhere?"

"I don't know. I haven't even clearly thought about it...yet," he tagged on so he didn't sound so lame.

"Maybe you don't really want to travel anywhere."

"Now you sound like Rani."

"She would couch it much more creatively."

"That's true," he said ruefully, wanting to get off the topic of his cousin.

"Where are you looking for jobs?"

"My dad's expecting me to join his practice in Charlotte."

"Where do you want to live and start a practice?"

She made it sound so simple.

"It should be," Solei said.

"Didn't realize I said that out loud." He sighed. "I love my family. I'm close to them. I want to remain close to them—all of them. My parents, grandparents, cousins, friends I grew up with. I don't want to miss most of the family gatherings so I'm looking someplace close-ish. I've interviewed in Austin. Atlanta. Miami. Charlotte," he made a face. "The chief of the group at Duke has offered me a place on faculty. I'd be able to continue my research and surgeries, and I'd be working with the residents. I could even teach a class at the medical school on occasion."

Even he could hear the enthusiasm in his voice.

"I think you know what job you want to take," Solei said after a pregnant pause. She began to unbutton his shirt with her teeth. She kissed his sternum. "Listen to your heart."

Chapter Eleven

ROHAN HEADED BACK to Durham around eleven. Stupid when he had to be at work at six in the morning, but for once in his life he didn't care.

He could still feel Solei's arms around him, still taste her in his mouth. Smell her. Solei was imprinted on his skin and bones. His body felt alive in a way it never had, still attuned and vibrating with the pleasure of the sensation of sharing her body and hearing her gasps of pleasure.

Best day of his life. Absolutely best. By miles.

Best… His phone rang. He scowled seeing Rani's name on his car's screen. But he knew she wouldn't let up.

But damn. He wished his buzz could have lasted until he got on the freeway.

"Yeah," he answered.

"Why are you still driving?"

"Why are you calling?"

"Rohan," Rani's voice was nearly a whisper, and he had to close his sunroof so the night air didn't tear away her voice. "I'm worried."

"Why?" he straightened. "What's wrong? What's happened?" He could turn around. He could…

"I'm worried about you and Solei. You didn't see yourself with her."

He shook his head at Rani's logic. Or lack of it. "I was with her," he said, striving for patience. He might not be a man particularly in touch with his feelings according to Mrs. Bukar. But he wasn't totally divorced from his reality.

"Rohan, she's really into you," Rani said slowly as if he'd suddenly lost fifty IQ points.

"What woman wouldn't be?" he teased, wanting to deflect Rani. He had, after all, been accused of being the golden boy and the golden son of Charlotte by more than his immediate family.

"And you're really into her," Rani said. "This is going to be a disaster for you both," Rani was still loud whispering, which over his speakers sounded melodramatic, like the middle school emo band that Rani had formed for a hot minute.

"Rani, I am not some clueless high school kid at a dance crushing on the popular girl. We just spent a couple of days together."

Everything inside of him rejected that characterization.

"Rohan, she's an artist. She's spontaneous. She's free-thinking and casual. Everything you're not."

"And you know this how?"

And why am I engaging?

"I emailed her my first survey, the one about love languages and hers is totally different from yours."

"You didn't email me the survey."

"I don't have to, Rohan. I know you. And you wouldn't have taken it. You know you wouldn't have."

"Pretty busy finishing up my residency."

And the fact that Rani felt like she could take his survey didn't sit well at all.

"You use work as a shield. And Solei's love language is spending time together. Opposites may attract but they don't last."

"Reminding you that I met her last Saturday." He merged onto the highway home.

And spent most of today with her, making love for hours.

But it hadn't been all sex. They'd walked to a grocery store, Solei googling recipes. Then they'd cooked together. He'd never spent such a relaxed, enjoyable afternoon and evening with a woman. They'd watched the sunset on her covered back patio and then made up a few more pastry bags of the powered paint, added a little water and then had had a free-for-all squirting a large canvas that she'd had. It had been fun squirting paint and pretending to find shapes in the paint and trying to outdo each other with trying to link the shapes to tell a story.

It seemed like a game kids would have played at a summer camp. Something he'd never done.

"Rohan, you're not even listing to me, or taking me seriously," Rani complained.

That stung. Rani was often dismissed. Still if he wanted to claim his life, he had to draw his line in the sand. "You wanted to play matchmaker, right?"

"Yes," Rani snapped. "Which is why you need to cut things off with Solei. She's absolutely beautiful and creative. She makes me wish I were gay. But she's totally wrong for you."

"You brought me to the art fair. I met Solei because of you. You made the match."

"That was not my intention," Rani gasped. "Solei wasn't who I had in mind. Meeting her was a mistake. You wandered off."

"Too late, matchmaker."

"Rohan stop goofing. I'm warning you…"

"Consider me warned," he said, firmly. "Talk later."

He disconnected.

A COUPLE OF weeks later Solei watched the last of her students at the youth center reluctantly walk out of the studio. They were heading to the common area to do homework or another studio to work with one of the other volunteers. She was leaving early today so that she could make it to Durham when there was still some light. Rohan wanted to take her to a nature park so that they could have a short hike and work up an appetite.

For what? The obvious answer was dinner, but when So-lei thought about Rohan, her first thought had nothing to do with food. It might technically be only a few weeks that she'd known him. A blink. A whirlwind. Everything was still so shiny and fresh, and yet in some ways it seemed as if he'd always been with her.

They'd often text during the day. She loved to send him pictures of things she saw or was working on. At night they'd often talk for hours. Last Thursday, he'd been post call and had driven up to meet her after her morning classes had finished. They'd visited the art museum because she was taking her students there later in the month and wanted to do what Rohan had humorously called a reconnaissance mission as they hit different sections of the museum to create a scavenger hunt and assignment sheet.

Rohan had walked the galleries with her, looking at the artwork, asking for her thoughts and coming up with creative questions to ask the kids. He even thought of an activity that she'd been too engrossed in the exhibits to think about—have them do a quick five-minute sketch of a kid they either didn't know or had hardly ever spoken to. She'd been touched by his thoughtfulness, and his companionship had made the two-hour chore fun.

Then he'd looked regretful because he had to go—he needed to touch base with someone and see his family. That's when he'd asked her if she'd consider coming to Durham the following weekend. And now it was happening.

"Oh good, I caught you." Tula poked her head around the door just as Solei packed up her backpack. "Did you hear about next year yet?" Her face was alight with hope.

"No." Solei had to fight the urge to slump. "The board of advisors for the school and administration hasn't set the arts curriculum budget for next year so no idea what the arts program will have and if they want to offer street art," she made the air quotes, "and mural painting as if that's all I've been teaching this year."

She sighed. She sounded bitter. She never wanted to be bitter. Win some lose some, her father had always said philosophically, but he was such a warm, confident, athletic and socially engaging person that he usually won at everything. He definitely lived life on his owns terms as did her mother—something she too had always strived to do.

"I know I'm only a first-year teacher, but I feel that I have made a real contribution to the program."

"Are you kidding? You've collaborated with the teachers in the music, humanities and science programs this year. Total interdisciplinary projects. You've made the studio art program come alive."

"Exaggerate much?" Tula's quick defense cheered her. "I guess I was too arrogant. I loved teaching and the school so much I thought they'd be eager to keep me on at least part-time. I actually told them I'd love to teach full-time. Maybe they aren't as into me," she admitted the possible truth. "And they don't want to tell me until closer to the end of the year."

"Please," Tula scoffed and fully entered the room and gave Solei a quick, hard hug. "They'd be stupid to let you go. Everyone on staff, the kids, the parents, we all want you to stay. Even though we're a private school, budgets are always tight because payroll is the biggest expense. You helped me and Marisa write two grants that came through. You are a famous street artist. And a team player and active in the arts community in Charlotte. Of course they want you."

But they hadn't said so. And she was really starting to worry.

"Famous is over the top," Solei said. She was renown, and she was building her reputation. "But I'd really like to stay on as well." Solei looked around the studio that had been her teaching home since late August. "I love feeling like I have a home in Charlotte. I love the school and kids and staff. The program. I've especially loved collaborating with y'all here."

"Y'all," Tula laughed. "Now you've got to stay. I've made a Southern girl out of you."

"I will if I can," Solei said. "I've liked having a home to come to each night—not so often in hotel rooms or studios or my van when I'm working on a commission. It's been really lovely to just have time to enjoy the city, make friends and know I don't have three commissions in three different cities over the next seven or eight weeks."

"I thought being a working artist was so glam, but you

make it sound like a chore," Tula said. "I'm not that into traveling, and I wouldn't want to leave my husband that much." Her expression turned sly. "Maybe a certain hot Indian doctor is your reason for wanting to stay," she teased.

"I'd applied to stay on before I met Rohan," Solei blushed.

"Busted," Tula laughed. "Have fun with him this weekend. And try not to worry about the contract."

"Oh, next week I'm starting on the mural for the Hungry Goat Brewery. I ended up sending several renderings, and they loved the purple goat chewing blackberries—not for their official logo, but the blackberries did inspire them to start a cider line and have some beer with a touch of fruit 'for the ladies,'" she did finger quotes. "They want a portrait of the blackberry goat, but with more 'beer greenery,'" again she made air quotes, "for the logo, and then the mural can be anything as long as the goat's in it. They started to draw ideas on cocktail napkins, but I had to hard no that."

Hard no. Yikes, she was even starting to talk like Rohan.

"Frat boys and their trust funds and investment banker jobs," Tula laughed.

"Their money works just as well as everyone else's. Plus, they're building their space sustainably and paying to off-set their carbon footprint."

"Did they pay you for the renderings?" Tula asked curiously. She was a poet and didn't consider herself a working artist; Solei had been trying to slowly chip away at Tula's misperception about herself.

"Yes, 25 percent down, and a mixed case of beer. I'm bringing the case to Rohan today."

"You better get going," Tula said. "Drive safe and text me when you get there. Are you driving your hippie mobile?"

"I would make a lousy hippie," Solei said. "My vibe is all wrong, but I love Frida, my classic VW camper bus," Solei said fondly.

"You're going to freak him out. Make him think you're a turtle, who's going to live in his driveway."

Or his parents' driveway. Rohan had let slip a few times how much pressure his parents put on him still, even though he was an adult. That seemed so foreign to her. From a young age, her parents had let her "pilot her own craft."

She wasn't sure which side of the road Rohan would come down on. She had to keep reminding herself not to have her own expectations or push what she wanted onto him.

She was supposed to be trying to enjoy the now.

"His driveway is safe."

"You stay safe, Solei," Tula's voice softened. "You don't know this guy all that well yet."

"I feel like I do." Solei slid her backpack on her shoulders and grabbed her thermos that she'd already filled with coffee for the road trip. "He's so lovely, Tula. Warm. Kind. Besides, I've met his cousin, and she texts me as much as he does. She's a whole different fruit from that family tree. She's working on her dissertation in psych. She sends me the most unexpected, thought-provoking or kooky questions to answer and then discuss. She's thinking about either creating a dating app or a relationship game or something along those lines for her thesis. She's trying to get to the truth of a person—discover their true heart and then help them find their perfect match once they understand themselves. She's also delving into love-at-first-sight, or she may have moved on. She's always in flux."

"Sounds crazy nosy to me."

Solei laughed. "That too. Rani's already had three of her research ideas rejected by her committee. This might be strike four so I want to help her. She's really funny and sweet and vulnerable. She seems so deeply loyal, and I admire that."

"Give me an example of one of her questions," Tula asked curiously.

"Here's today's question. It just arrived so I can mull as I drive. They sort of build off of each other, but the gist is… Do I think my preferences in a mate are based on my own insecurities?"

Tula just stared.

"I know, right? I feel like I need to take a philosophy or psych class just to keep up. And then she wants me to choose one of my insecurities and create a plan to tackle it so that it impacts my life less."

"Head shrinker." Tula rolled her eyes. "That's a fun drive topic. Not. I suggest putting on Taylor Swift and singing with the windows down."

"More my jam than dwelling on my insecurities or secret longings," Solei said. She wondered if Rani had given Rohan a question of the day.

"Text me when you get there." Tula insisted.

"Yes, Mom," Solei laughed. "Even my own mom wouldn't have asked that. See you on Monday."

"THIS IS NICE." Solei leaned back on a flat rock along the Pea Creek Trail. She'd kicked off her hiking boots and her slender pale feet lightly kicked in the water. She wore lightweight, stretchy, olive-colored athletic pants with lots of pockets, a deep pink tank and an olive zip hoody that was tied around her waist. Rohan could not keep his eyes off her. She was a magic, exotic creature, who fascinated him. He craved her company. Her touch. And the time apart had proved what a liar he was. There was nothing casual or short-term about Solei.

He was in deep.

All the "we just met" and "we're just having fun," he'd been telling himself and Rani to try to appease her wasn't cutting it with him anymore.

He'd tried to call Mrs. Bukar to cancel her search, but

she refused to discuss anything on the phone—she wouldn't even take his call. Instead, he'd been foisted off on an efficient, rather judgey sounding assistant. Mrs. Bukar would only meet with him in person. For the past two weeks, she'd been in Jacksonville with a client and then Boston, and when she returned to Charlotte, Rohan's schedule hadn't allowed a trip home except one Thursday afternoon, where he and Solei had kayaked at the US National Whitewater Center and then spent the later afternoon wandering through several art galleries. Seeing art and the world through her eyes had won hands down over trying to wrestle an appointment with Mrs. Bukar, who'd been busy and had coolly informed him that many would-be brides and grooms got cold feet. It was "expected" and only his mother could cancel the contract.

The talk with his mother loomed large and ominous.

God, he was acting like an anxious teen, something he'd never been—nervous of disappointing both his mom and dad when he was a grown-ass—as Shanti would say—man in charge of his own destiny. Theoretically.

"Do you come out here often?" She leaned back, her face catching the last rays of the setting sun that made her look like she was spun from gold.

"Not as much as I'd like."

"What do you mean?" Solei asked in that curious tone she had that always seemed to act like a key to all the thoughts tangled in his brain.

"What do you mean?" he repeated, feeling defensive. She

knew the hours he kept.

Solei had been arched back, face catching the last rays of the sun, her eyes closed like a temple offering. Now she looked at him, and he felt exposed. Fraudulent.

"Do you want to hike in the woods more, or do you think that you should want to hike in the woods more?"

"That sounds like something Rani would have on her survey," he deflected nervously.

"Is she finally including you?" Solei faced the river again. "I had an interesting question to mull on my drive down."

"You don't need to help her with her crazy survey." Rohan kicked into protective mode that in recent years had been mostly employed in diffusing criticism aimed at Rani about everything—the college she chose, her major, switching her major, university transfers, working at a coffee shop and then a bar. Rani never seemed to please anyone. Even Rani felt like she was flailing—"wrong dance, wrong music, wrong party."

But now he would be dissected under the white-hot spotlight if he didn't take the "right" job and marry the "right" bride. And Solei... She would be seen as some...some...he didn't even know what, luring him away from the light.

"I want to help Rani out. And the questions are thought-provoking and entertaining," Solei said. "And also humbling."

"What do you have to be humble about?"

"Someone has stars in their eyes." Solei pulled her feet

out of the creek and shook them off. The water droplets danced in the sunlight, contrasting with the shadows from the trees overhanging the creek. She walked toward him, beautiful, fluid. "There are always areas for growth. I feel like I am on the cusp of a change within my art," she said softly.

"Like what?" He wanted to see her paint again live. He'd looked at some TikToks she'd posted as well as her BSolei artist Instagram, and some YouTube videos. She was starting on a goat mural in the next couple of weeks. He was trying to rearrange his schedule so that he could watch her while still keeping their relationship private. Solei didn't need to deal with his mom and family now. And he didn't want to either.

Solei reached out her hand, and his worries floated away on the breeze. He engulfed her hand in his, marveling at their contrasts. He turned her palm over and looked at it. Did it really tell her story? What was innate and what was possible? What would Mrs. Bukar think about Solei and what her palms said or didn't say?

Rohan raised her hand to his lips and kissed her, his gaze holding hers that was such a vivid green in the sunny forest. His skin had a deeper tone. Solei's was a lighter gold like toast.

"You look like a forest nymph. Do you feel drawn to nature? An earth element?" He laughed. "Forget I asked that. Too much Rani influence."

Solei was too smart. She was going to figure out something was up with the Rani inquisition beyond a doctoral dissertation.

"I love walking and running in nature. Bird-watching. But I've always been drawn to water—maybe too many years on the ocean mermaided me. I never thought I could leave the West Coast or the beach."

"How about lakes?" Rohan asked without thinking and then wanted to kick himself.

He wasn't thinking about moving into his parents' house. He hadn't decided to take the partnership with his father. He clung to the idea that he had time to think about what he wanted.

"Lakes are like nature's bathtubs. I love to swim or paddleboard in them, but rivers appeal because the water's always moving. It feels more connected to the water cycle and the cycle of life, ebbing and flowing and there's the mystery or what will flow by and the adventure ahead."

It was the perfect answer.

Rani didn't know what the hell she was talking about.

"How did Rani want you to grow?" he asked curiously. He had only heard of Rani's quirky questions that were supposedly thought-provoking because Solei would share them when they'd talk at night often starting during his walks home. Or she'd do a quick illustration of the question or the answer like a one panel comic. Sometimes she'd send those to Rani who would then call him wanting to dissect the image.

"I don't think it was her wanting me to grow in a specific way," Solei said, sounding a little somber. "It was more like a nudge for me to do some mental and emotional house cleaning."

Rohan laughed bitterly. "She should start with herself."

"Are you not getting along at the moment?"

"No." He immediately felt guilty. "I love Rani. She's got such a pure heart and soul. She just wants so much to be loved and included. You remind me of her a little, only you have more confidence and direction. Rani's always been a free spirit, I think, impulsive, in the moment, and her parents…and mine…have always wanted to tether her. They want her to take the flight path they think is best."

"Just Rani?"

"Ouch," he said.

Solei pulled him to standing. He kept hold of her hand. Her remark had hit home. Lodged deep. Which mount on his palm covered intuition—the one he lacked?

"Do you believe in magic?" he asked.

"If magic is used as a blanket word for a force that we can't necessarily explain, then yes," Solei said. "I think science is powerful to divine many things that were once mysteries, but I think that we as humans definitely have our limits on understanding, and that there is something much bigger than us."

He liked that explanation.

"I would have thought as an artist, you wouldn't adhere

to scientific principles as much."

"Why? Art requires so much science and math—chemistry, physics, proportion."

Rohan listened, more amazed by Solei than before, and feeling his lack of creative and art knowledge deeply. He was much respected at Duke and he'd been an excellent student, but his knowledge base, his world experience was limited and specialized. He'd never cared before. Or questioned it, but between being with Solei and having Rani yammering about Solei's responses and running potential questions by him—she was thinking about a board game now—he was feeling for the first time in his life, out of his depth.

"From the outside I am considered to be so smart and accomplished," he said slowly. "And yet I am realizing that my life is too narrow. There's so much I don't know," he said. "I lack creativity."

"I don't think you lack it," Solei objected. "You haven't perhaps exercised your creativity as much as I have. It is a muscle, a voice inside you that you can listen to or ignore. But you are a spectacular dancer. Your body really moves with the beat and music. And you said you used to DJ at parties in high school—that's creative. Blending the songs together, the playlist. The build the flow, that's creating."

He'd never thought about it like that. "Really?" He felt a spark of something. What was it, hope? Hope that he wasn't hopeless and utterly out of his league with Solei. Too boring? His family had always made him feel—ridiculously he could admit to himself—like a prince. With Solei he wondered if what he brought to the party, so to speak, was enough.

She leaned into him and kissed his jawline, letting her teeth nip a little. "There's no rule as to what is creative. People can be creative with cooking, gardening, home design, teaching, computer programs and fashion." She soothed the nip with her tongue and a kiss, that should not have jacked him up to the point that he was totally hard. "Mister Pink and Ombre Jacket Man."

"Guilty of a bit of fashion flash," he admitted. "But I don't create them. I just wear some of Clarissa's designs. I don't create or consult about them."

"You make a choice what you put on your body." Her hand stroked down his chest, and her gaze heated and slipped lower. "And what to take off," she teased, brushing her fingers against him.

"We're just going to ignore that part of my anatomy for the moment and keep walking," he said. He didn't want her to think that sex was the only thing he was interested in.

Usually it was. But with Solei, she made him see different possibilities. "I wanted to show you the best viewpoint. I always thought of creativity as this ephemeral thing hovering in the air like a hummingbird…or a butterfly, landing on some with a gift and avoiding others."

"A muse. It comes to grace you and you listen or it flies away. Some people are blessed and others aren't." Solei made a face. "That's just artists trying to build themselves up, make themselves appear better than others, special, blessed. It's like that Calvinist precept that rich people are rich because they are closer to God, more deserving."

"You've really given it some thought," Rohan mused, wondering at her tone.

"I don't like people to put others down to make themselves feel better. Art and creativity reside in everyone. They just need a chance—and time to listen to their voice and give themselves permission to play and to fail and to try again. Being creative should have personal meaning—no one else should weigh in."

God, she was so sweet. And a little naive. Artists might be able to do that, but surgeons couldn't go into their profession thinking about playing and failing. Going in for the win was the only attitude a surgeon could have when they split open a sternum.

But many of the Duke surgeons he worked with had hobbies. Sports. Music. Time to do something more than work.

"If we keep going up, this trail meets up with the loop that will take us back to the parking lot." Because he didn't want to kiss her in public even though they hadn't seen anyone for a couple of miles. He was not an exhibitionist, but with Solei, he didn't trust his self-control. She lit him on fire and made him forget where he was.

"This trail, the one you didn't want to take?" she teased as she put her socks and boots back on.

"It's closed," he said. "Due to erosion. Not a rulebreaker." He kissed her palm before finally releasing her.

The closed sign hadn't detoured Solei. She hadn't even paused, whereas his heart had thundered with apprehension. The loop trail was closed for a reason. What if a ranger caught them? What if the trail just abruptly ended? Fell into nothingness? But Solei had charged up it.

Watching her he'd felt a frisson of something unrecognizable that had skittered through his blood, almost like champagne. And then she'd turned around and grinned, and the tentative protest about the closed trail sign died in his mouth.

They continued to walk the trail then wandered along the creek sometimes side by side, sometimes him behind. He loved to watch her. She seemed part of the wooded landscape. Natural. Beautiful.

"You never told me what insecurity Rani wanted you to contemplate."

"I haven't decided."

"There can't be that many," he objected.

"We all have them," Solei said thoughtfully. She stopped walking and laid her palm over her chest. "All of us. Even you."

"But I don't want to discuss that with Rani."

"Or me?" Her gaze searched his, serious, but warm.

"I...maybe," he admitted reluctantly. "But I think it's myself I'm hiding from."

He hated that he was shutting her down. He expected her to be disappointed. Maybe walk off in a pissy mood. Rani would have. Or maybe she'd make light of it like it didn't matter when it did. But not communicating wasn't fair when he wanted to know everything about her.

"Or maybe from others who are close to you." Solei leaned into him and then stood on her tiptoes. She sweetly kissed him, shocking him with her tenderness. "Maybe later we can both play doctor—I'll show you mine if you show me yours."

It took him a moment. "You're on, Beals," he laughed. "But not today. Today let me pretend to be Superman to impress you."

"You don't need to impress me, Rohan. Just be you."

Thankfully she turned around and walked up the steep incline toward Buckquarter Creek Trail and the falls because he wasn't quite sure what do with her comment—how to arrange his expression or process all the feelings battering around his head and his chest.

Superman, my ass.

He was fooling no one.

He stopped walking. He wasn't. Certainly not himself anymore. And not Solei. But did he need to? Was he, for the first time, really enough?

Chapter Twelve

THE TRAIL KEPT climbing, and it felt good to exert herself. Solei loved the sound of the water as it rushed over the flat rocks in the creek, and the last of her week's worries fell away.

"Do you mind if I take pictures?" She looked at him over her shoulder. Yup, he'd been looking at her butt and flushed at getting caught. It was endearing in a way it wouldn't have been with another man. Rohan was so polite and controlled that getting caught doing something so like a guy was sweet and funny.

"Eyes up, Doctor."

"Sorry, not sorry?"

She stopped so that his next step brought her flush with his chest. "Good answer." He'd taken off his long sleeve wicking athletic shirt and tied it around his waist so that his arms were bare. She loved the way he looked—always fashionably dressed and well-groomed. He was very fit and took care of himself, which made her feel safe, like he wouldn't indulge in anything self-destructive.

"I missed seeing you this week," she admitted.

"The distance sucks," he said. "But in a way, it's made us really have to put time aside to be together and make an effort. I never bothered to do that before."

"Really?" She'd imagined Rohan had had his pick of so many women. "What's different? Why me?" she asked curiously. Might as well jump off the cliff early as a form of self-protection.

"You. You're different," Rohan said and caught her hand and looked at her palm. "I told myself I had to be focused solely on academics and building up my resume during high school to get into college and then did the same thing in undergrad for med school and then academics and seeking out research opportunities in med school so that I could get a top residency position. I didn't ever try for a relationship. I couldn't afford the distraction. It had been drilled in me growing up, and then as I got older it was my own voice exhorting me to work smarter and longer than anyone else.

"But really, that was an excuse. I never met anyone like you," his voice resonated with sincerity. "If I had met you in college or when I was in med school, I don't think anything could have stopped me from trying to get your attention."

Solei's heart soared, but she tried to tamp it down. Rohan made her feel so special. He was busy with so many demands on him, plus he had a large, close-knit family, and yet he was dedicating so much time getting to know her. "You got it," she whispered.

She didn't know who initiated the kiss, but they both fell

into it, but instead of it heating up like their first kiss in the shower when they'd been so desperate for each other that Solei had felt feral and out of control for the first time in her life, this kiss felt sacred. Their eyes were open. Their breath mingled, and she felt that as she breathed him in, he became a part of her and she of him.

They slowly broke apart. He smiled, and it lit his face. She loved the light creases that radiated down his cheeks when he smiled like this. She traced them lightly with her fingers, closing her eyes so that she could really focus on how his face felt, remember his skin, his bones, his smile.

"I want to remember you and this moment," she whispered reverently.

"Why do you need to remember?" he asked. "I'm right here," he whispered. "Right here, Solei."

It sounded like a vow.

Determination and steel edged his expression. "I'm so lucky I met you," Rohan spoke in a rush. "You are magic. I was lost but had no idea. I wandered off and turned a corner and looked up and there you were—a living flame. A miracle that plucked me out of my life and plunked me down in a different universe, ostensibly the same but different. I felt as if the world tilted on its axis, but then you were there, holding me up, and I want to hold you up too when you need it."

She couldn't breathe or swallow. No one had ever said anything so wonderful to her. Never. Ever.

"I feel the same," she whispered, feeling warmth and happiness and belonging bubble through her as if she'd just downed an icy bottle of Topo Chico. "Never say you're not a poet, Rohan. Never say you aren't creative," She pulled him to her tightly and held on.

"I'm not," he said, his lips against her hair. "But when I'm with you, I feel like I could be anything."

"Rohan," she caught his hand and held it to her cheek, "I feel like I'm falling in love with you." There. She'd said it. Probably a dozen weeks too early. But why hide? She was tired of hiding, playing it safe. It was better to know where she stood. Where he stood. And full disclosure, she wasn't falling anywhere. She'd stuck that landing somewhere on that campus field when she'd clung to his back like a monkey, and he'd run through a barrage of shooting colors, and she'd felt him laughing as her chest pressed against his muscled back.

She could easily see her feelings deepening over time. "But I'm in love with who you are, not some version I think you should be. I. Love. You. Rohan Kapoor." She pressed his palm against her chest.

"What...what made you say it like that?" he whispered, his black gaze drenched with silvery stars and full of questions as if he were struggling to believe.

"Something Rani asked me—texted me last night. She asked what was one thing I would change about you, and I said nothing. She pushed. Said there must be something. But no. Nothing, Rohan."

He held himself so still, his hands on her shoulders, his gaze intently drilling into hers. She held herself stone steady wanting him to believe, to know he could trust her to be careful of his precious heart just as he took so much care with the hearts of his patients. His expression slowly morphed from confusion to disbelief and then to hope. Solei's heart thudded with the gravity of the moment. His eyes filled with tears, and he blinked them away.

"No one has said that to me before," he whispered. "Not ever."

She brought his hand to her lips and kissed the pad of each of his finger as she uttered each short sentence.

"I said it. I feel it. I mean it. You can trust me to always be honest about my feelings," she finished, placing a kiss on the knuckle of his thumb.

SOLEI SMILED AS Rohan explored her light blue VW Vanagon. He couldn't seem to get over the conversion to make it a traveling home. He'd popped up the roof several times, and opened and closed drawers, marveling at how everything fit together, the functioning sink, the composting toilet, the small shower, the two-burner cooktop and the fridge.

"It's like a Swiss Army Knife," Rohan said. "Ingenious, useful and attractive. I always wanted one, but my parents wouldn't get me one when I was a kid. I can stand up in here." He rose up and down on his tiptoes.

Solei had to hold back a laugh. He was enthusiastic like a kid would be. "A Swiss Army Knife or a camper van?"

"Swiss Army Knife," he grinned. "My parents wouldn't have camped ever. My mother's idea of roughing it is room service that closes at midnight. But this...what do you call it...a camper van? A Vanagon? This has me jonesing on a whole new level." He jumped out and walked around Frida.

Solei remained where she was—sprawled on one of her two camp chairs in the parking area of the park, letting him have his fun. He climbed back in and unfolded the bed and put it back up again and then down. He looked at her, and she could practically feel him estimating if they would fit. She blushed.

"Why didn't they want you to have a knife?" she asked to distract herself from his jumpability factor.

Judging by Rohan's clothes, car and demeanor, he seemed pretty steeped in money. She'd never wanted for the necessities growing up but had worked in coffee shops since she was a teen and had worked full time at Starbucks for several years out of college while she built her artist resume in Southern California.

"My mom was convinced I'd injure myself—hurt my hands. My dad too. He thought the knife would be a waste of my time and my brain," Rohan said while he examined the way the drawers opened and how they were organized.

She loved her van. She had the money to upgrade to a newer, slicker and more spacious model if she wanted, but she'd bought the van in college and had fixed it up over time, learning how to do things from mechanics and contractors and the internet and sometimes trading art for different projects. She'd escaped more than a couple of dodgy living situations and had lived in her converted van for a few weeks or a couple of months more than a few times until she found a safer or more affordable living situation. She'd learned how to do her own engine maintenance and some basic repairs so that she only had to rely on herself. Plus, with Frida's short wheelbase, she was easy to drive in cities, which was where most of her commissions were.

"A Swiss Army Knife is a tool. And useful."

He'd jumped back inside the van. "I know. Sleek, stylish and nearly infinitely useful. This is amazing." He lowered the top and then raised it again, looking up. "It's tight, but yet so functional, and with the top popped," he looked up, "it doesn't feel as claustrophobic as I would have imagined. You even have a skylight in the roof," he was awed, "for more light. Do you paint in here?"

"Usually outside. I have a fold-up drafting table. Did you ever buy yourself the knife?" she asked, curious about Rohan's family dynamic. Her parents had indulged her childhood requests for art supplies, encouraging her to try different mediums, and when they were in harbor, they'd taken her to galleries and museums. Because space was always tight in their crew quarters, she'd had to be judicious when buying something new, but her choices had been hers, not her parents'. She was beginning to wonder how many choices Rohan had had. Had he always wanted to be a heart surgeon—is that what had driven him so fiercely?

He paused whatever he was doing in the van. The space between her question and his answer was awkwardly long.

"I haven't thought about wanting a Swiss Army Knife in a long time," he finally said, his voice sounding flat and diminished.

A variety of potential comebacks rolled around in Solei's head, but she kept silent. Clearly Rohan could buy most anything he wanted, especially when he finished his training and took a job. With a jolt, she realized he could take a job almost anywhere.

So can you.

Logic dictated that it was too soon for her to factor Rohan into her future plans. They had talked about spending the spring getting to know each other—that was part of the reason she'd come down for the weekend. Rohan didn't have a lot of weekends off, and the two-hour drive did complicate seeing each other regularly. So logically she should just enjoy the moment, not worry about the future.

But Solei's heart wasn't guided by logic.

"You would have bought the knife," Rohan said, sitting down next to her and handing her a bottle of sparkling water after twisting off the cap. He had a bottle of still water.

She would have, but she could tell it bothered him that he hadn't. She didn't like seeing his earlier enthusiasm doused.

"Cool fridge," he deadpanned.

"I have solar panels on the roof so I can operate on solar power—not as long in the Pacific Northwest I found out last year when I was there for a couple of weeks on a job."

She took a deep drink of her water, savoring the effervescence of the bubbles. She tilted her face back to catch the last rays of the sun before they slipped behind the tree line. "I'm not sure I would have bought the knife."

"You would have," Rohan sounded certain. "You exude confidence and independence."

"You do as well."

"With work. With academics. With my family and social expectations, I'm more…not sure what words work here." He shot her an uncomfortable look. "I'm more…squirrely… They… I love my family. But the weight of what they want and the constant pushing feels…crushing. Sometimes I want to…escape."

What was he trying to tell her?

He leaned forward, elbows on his knees, water bottle dangling from his fingers.

"You would have bought the knife. You wouldn't have cared what your parents thought."

"Not in that instance maybe," she began, feeling like she too should tell him more about the weight of her history. "I still think about each purchase. I still live light. I grew up with my father piloting clients' yachts, and my mom was their private chef. I had one duffel bag for clothes and a backpack for school and art supplies. If I got something new, something had to go until I moved in with my grandparents for high school. But still I lived light because I was worried if I made a mess or was an inconvenience for them, they'd send me back."

She sipped her water. "And I'd have had no place to go. I've never met my mom's family, so I tried to stay small and quiet, tucked in my room, but I also got a job and saved all my money and bought a used truck with a shell first so I'd always have a place to sleep, and then in college I bought Frida from an art professor, who converted vans on the side, and she was his first."

Rohan listened with his whole body, and Solei couldn't remember any of the men she'd dated ever doing that. Usually it had been about them, and why had she allowed that?

"I have a lot of money in the bank. And a condo in LA. I could afford a bigger, newer, more tricked-out van, but still I get…anxious making bigger purchases, something I can't carry in Frida. All of my clothes still fit in the same duffel bag I bought in college."

She hadn't meant to say that. She'd never told anyone that ever. She didn't want Rohan to think she was strange. She wanted him to admire her—realize that she was just as strong and accomplished in her world as he was in his—that they were equals.

Rohan set the bottle down and reached for her hands. He gently pulled her up and on to his lap. For a moment, she stiffened. She hadn't meant to be that vulnerable. She always tried to be strong, standing on her own, never needing support. But it felt so good to be held. She'd had boyfriends. She'd always enjoyed sex, but she hadn't had this before—this tenderness and warmth that had nothing to do with foreplay.

It was like he understood her on a level she barely understood herself.

Rohan's hand was soothingly stroking down her back as he held her close to his body. His chin rested on her head. "Frida," he said softly. "Frida Kahlo. Of course you named your van."

She relaxed against the steady thud of his heart, feeling safe and cared for, something she hadn't even known she'd wanted.

"You've had to be so much more self-sufficient than I've had to be."

"Since I was five or six and have memories, I knew I couldn't get in their way, and had to take care of myself. My mom and dad were working. I had to stay out of the way and entertain and teach myself. When I was old enough, I helped my mom in the kitchen and helped with serving and washing the dishes. It was a fun but unconventional life, but I was happy to get off the boat. I wanted to put roots down and have space, and yet I still haven't managed to make a home," she whispered. "This is the first year I haven't traveled a lot, staying in Frida or a hotel room or guest room of a client, but I still can't put down roots because I don't know if I have a job, and I feel like the energy in LA is too frenetic right now. I feel played out there. I rented my condo to an arts college for visiting professors, which covers my mortgage so again I'm just looking down a long, lonely road."

She swallowed hard, shocked she'd confessed all that. She'd never told Zach anything about her childhood, and he'd never asked.

"But you're not alone now, Solei," he whispered.

And she so desperately wanted to believe that, but she couldn't quite trust. They were new. He was clearly wrestling with something. Both their lives were in flux.

"I grew up so differently," Rohan said. "You had so much freedom, and I had very little along with clear, explicit expectations that were also my expectations," Rohan mused. "It's not like I didn't have the drive to excel. I did. I'm ambitious. Competitive. But there was never time or encouragement to explore other things. Everything I did as a kid was to get into the right high school. And from there, college. And from there, med school. And from there residency and from there I wanted to shine and publish so I got top offers for jobs even though the assumption was that I would join my dad's partnership and earn top dollar."

He picked up his water from the folding camp table, unscrewed the cap and took a deep draw, before screwing the cap back on. For a long moment, they didn't say anything, the silence warm and comfortable, but Solei's mind started to race, thinking back over his words and tone and John's warning she'd shrugged off the night she'd first met Rohan because it had been absurd at the time. Rohan was so different from other men she'd known, but she couldn't shake the fear in one essential way he was the same. He'd leave.

"So you've really slept in Frida?" he broke the silence.

She loved the way his voice sounded in the dark, the way it rumbled up from his chest and tickled her cheek. He would be a popular late-night DJ.

She nodded. She still hadn't decided how the night would go. Would Rohan want to camp out in her van, or would they go back to his apartment? Or would she stay in Frida alone? She felt a little raw. "I love to road trip in her." Solei went for honesty. "She's small enough to handle like a car in towns and cities, but because of all the modifications for camping over the years, she can really go off the grid and get into nature. She's sturdy and reliable."

"You've never lived in her, have you?"

"Not as a permanent home." She tried to push away a few memories, but they elbowed forward. "But the van offered an...escape hatch more than a few times early on."

"Solei," he breathed, once again pulling her closer and

nuzzling her hair. He started kissing her softly almost as if she had a hurt he was trying to kiss better. "Did that happen…often?" He seemed barely able to ask the questions, and he held his breath, and she found herself relaxing. Her instincts weren't wrong. He did have a protective nature.

"A few." She didn't want to talk about it. She was in a good place now. "But not for a long time. I've worked hard to get where I am, and I invest and save most of my earnings."

"I have a feeling you are whitewashing it."

"It's in the past," Solei said. "I've worked hard to build my reputation. I receive plenty of commissions for my street art-style murals now. I have money saved. The van is more a…" She paused not sure how to describe it. She usually laughed off questions about Frida. People had thought it weird that she still kept it, and that she continued to improve on it and keep it in such excellent mechanical and physical shape. It was always fully stocked, ready to get back on the road at any time. "I guess she's my security blanket," she admitted nervously.

She winced. She worked so hard to be strong and independent. She could take care of herself and plot her own future. "But I do love to camp and Frida is a great camper." She forced cheer into her voice, feeling like they'd delved too deeply tonight although she craved that with him. But she'd opened herself up so much and felt the need to scramble back on higher ground. She was also afraid about what he'd say about camping. He'd grown up privileged, traveling to five-star resorts. She could do that now if she wanted. And she might. But she'd always crave the quiet of nature.

I'm tired of always being alone.

That realization hit hard.

He leaned away from her, his gaze clearly searching hers. His lips tilted up in a sad smile. "I hope you never need to use your van as an escape hatch again," he said. "Only as a means to find new adventures," he said seriously. "And I hope that we can share some of those."

It was hardly a commitment.

But it wasn't a dismissal.

"I like the sound of that." Solei clinked her water bottle to his. "To future adventures." Solei would be lying if she didn't imagine Rohan by her side.

Chapter Thirteen

THE TIRE INDICATOR light flashed on his Audi's computer screen. Rohan swore softly and pulled off the road onto a gravel shoulder. Fields spread out all around them. At least he had cell service.

"Sorry," he apologized to Solei. "Something's wrong with the tire. Figures it would be when I choose a farm to table restaurant out in the middle of nowhere. It will take Triple A a while to get here."

He hated to miss the dinner reservation. Laurel Farms was a new restaurant, but it already had people driving from all over North Carolina's Triangle area to sample the unique offerings of two childhood friends who had attended culinary school and then opened their own farm to table restaurant after inheriting one of their grandma's farms.

"We can change it." Solei popped out of the car.

"Wait. What?" Rohan, already scrolling to his Triple A contact followed her. "I've never changed a tire in my life," he confessed. It seemed like it was one of those essential skills that parents taught their children forty to fifty years ago, but with the advent of cell phones…

"Pop the trunk," Solei said.

"But…" He stared at her, feeling a weird mixture of shock, awe and shame. "I can just call Triple A."

"We can do it," Solei said. "Get your owner's manual."

Rohan swallowed and walked back to the driver's seat. The owner's manual. The thing he'd never opened. The car was fairly new. The car told him when it needed servicing. He had an expensive maintenance plan at the dealership.

"But couldn't you be hurt?"

"Not if you know what you're doing." Solei smiled. "I've driven Frida cross country and have changed a lot of tires, oil, spark plugs and more. A tire's no big deal."

While Rohan watched, helpless and fumbling, as he tried to help, Solei changed the tire and sent him a text reminding him to buy a new tire and have all of his tires checked and rotated. She even picked up the dusty tire that was not noticeably flat.

"At least let me do that," Rohan objected. His job might be all cerebral, but he worked out. He wasn't useless.

"No point in both of us getting dirty." She loaded it in the trunk of his car, and then less than fifteen minutes later they were back on the road.

Solei pulled out a small package of wipes from the backpack-style leather purse that she always carried. She wiped off her hands, and then wadded up the wipe and tucked it back in her purse.

"I feel like a useless idiot."

"It's just a skill, Rohan. No one is born knowing how to do that. Most people learn from a parent or friend. My dad was a boat captain. He had a lot of mechanical knowledge and knew how to navigate his way through any equipment breakdown. I learned about sailing, stars and engines from him. My mom was a chef. They passed on their skills, just as your parents passed on theirs."

Had they? His nanima and mummyji had done so much of the cooking, but they hadn't taught him. He'd been shooed out of the kitchen. His grandfather had taught him chess, cribbage and backgammon. He'd had instructors or tutors for most everything else.

"I'm pretty sure I'm the only Kapoor in my family who has even watched a tire get changed," he said. "And that is not a brag."

"That's a start," Solei laughed. "If it bothers you, I can teach you how to change oil, batteries, headlights and wiper blades and messy and mysterious car things and you can teach me how to make chapatis or how to start an IV. Practice makes perfect, right?"

"Okay," he said. "You made your point. If I take any road trips, I will definitely not go out of cell range so I can google my own fixes. And I'll know where my owner's manual is."

"It was right where it was supposed to be, just not out of the factory packaging, but I bet a lot of people never crack the spine of those things."

His father certainly hadn't. He never needed to. He bought the latest models for him and his wife, drove them for two years max and then turned them in for new ones to mitigate the risk of anything going wrong. He thought Solei's Vanagon was older than she was and kept his mouth shut about his family's relationship with vehicles.

"Also, you might consider buying a basic car tool and emergency kit."

"I suppose I should get a tool kit for my apartment as well."

Solei kicked her sandals off and tucked her legs under her. The red and yellow sundress she wore rode up her thighs a little, and the breeze from the open window tugged at her hair that she held back from her face with one hand.

"That's a hard yes, Dr. Kapoor." She grinned.

And his feeling of inadequacy dissipated.

"WOULD YOU RATHER…" Solei paused dramatically, sipping sparkling water as she sat next to Rohan on an Adirondack chair that looked out over Laurel Farms. She'd enjoyed the vegetarian meal, and she and Rohan had opted to have coffee and dessert in a beautiful Tuscan-style courtyard that overlooked the farm's vegetable gardens and orchards. Beyond that, on top of a small rise, sat a large white barn where the goats and sheep were beginning to congregate as evening drew near. Solei wondered if she and Rohan could walk to the barn so that she could take a few pictures of the goats that she'd use for inspiration for her mural. She'd started researching goats as soon as she'd decided to take the commission.

She couldn't remember the last time she'd seen a goat. Maybe in Bluebird Canyon in Laguna Beach a couple of years ago. She had a friend from art school who lived in the canyon and opposite her house was a few hundred acres of dedicated green space. To mitigate fire risk, goats would periodically graze the land. She'd loved walking along the faint animal trails and talking to the goats, who were quite affectionate. Picking ticks off herself after the first hike had been gross and enough to encourage her to bundle up even when it was beautifully sunny and warm.

"Is this a Rani game? I'm not sure if you've yet dissected the insecurity she demanded of you, but I have a new one now." Rohan's head was tilted back to catch the last rays of the sun. His eyes were closed. He really had the most beautiful bone structure. She couldn't believe she hadn't sketched him yet. "Spare tires, emergency kits and tools."

"Your man card is safe," Solei laughed. "And I'm enjoying the randomness of Rani's questions. She's sort of a spaghetti-against-the wall woman. She reminds me of those big puppies like the Bernese mountain dogs that burst into a room full of enthusiasm and affection and just want to be loved on but can't stand still and knock into everything with their wagging tail."

Rohan laughed. "That is a perfect description of Rani."

"I can't tell if she's making progress on her dissertation proposal," she said. "I feel like she might want to create categories for her questions—perhaps she could create a board game or a box of questions—like a party game. She could have theme boxes—for teens, for couples, for friends, even coworkers."

Rohan stared at her.

"What?" she asked, a little unnerved by his intense scrutiny and utter stillness.

"That's brilliant," he breathed.

She blinked. The awe was clear in his voice. Had anyone ever been so impressed with any of the ideas that were always banging around in her head? Never any of her professors. Not Zach. Her parents and grandparents had just always accepted her work or ideas with a happy smile and murmured "well done," or "beautiful."

"I love that idea. She could run with that. You should tell her. Maybe you two could collaborate—questions and artwork, and now I've terrified myself by putting together my two favorite women."

Favorite? The word resonated. She looked at Rohan quickly. It was just a figure of speech, right? But he was looking at her, stars in his eyes.

And then the tiramisu arrived—one slice two forks.

Her phone beeped with a message. Normally on a date

she would have had it tucked away in her purse, but she'd wanted to snap a few pictures of the goats playing— challenging each other on the top of a small shed.

"Speak of the devil, Rani wants to know what about you surprises me."

Rohan picked up a fork. "I'm not sure I'm ready for that. Maybe I should have ordered a port." He speared a bite of the dessert. "My culture and general manliness would dictate I order a top-shelf whiskey, but I just can't get the taste for it. I like wine. Wine—maybe that could become my hobby post student and resident years. Traveling could be involved. Learning. Purpose. Art and chemistry and nature. Thoughts on wine?"

He held out the bite for her.

She stared at the deliciousness. She didn't have a huge sweet tooth, but she always wanted a taste. That was usually enough. Zach had always insisted she order her own dessert. He didn't want to share. That right there should have been a warning sign. Oh. That would be a good category for Rani and a humbling one for herself—warning signs from relationships where the person definitely should have swiped left.

"My thoughts on wine," she mused, lips hovering close to the cake, and she loved how heat flared in his eyes and his attention was on her mouth. She looked up at him, happy he was getting as turned on as she was. "Yes, please."

And then she swallowed the bite of tiramisu.

"Oooof," Rohan hit the dirt on his ass, while a playful kid bleated in his face, nuzzling him for attention. Solei had been playing with the farm's goats and taking a few pictures, and more than once, he'd had to rescue her hair from a goat's mouth.

He laughed and jumped to his feet, picking up the kid with him. "They're playful like dogs," he marveled. "And this is coming from a man who never had a dog growing up."

"I didn't either," Solei said, "for obvious reasons. And I think one of the driving factors for me when I applied to stay on teaching at the high school in Charlotte was that I could put down some roots and finally adopt a dog."

"A dog, huh?" Rohan repeated, more than a little deflated, although he had no right to be. He didn't want to take his father's premium job offer in Charlotte, and he was the one who'd suggested them keeping things casual through the spring.

Shower sex and marathon afternoon and evening sex were not exactly keeping anything casual, and even though he'd reminded himself that they were both consenting, healthy and successful adults blowing off some steam, his advice to himself had fallen flat. Making love with Solei had shattered any pretense that anything with her was casual.

It was so much more.

He, who had felt like jumping in his car and driving west until he ran out of road when his mom had mentioned marriage, commitment, settling down and starting a family, now felt the best part of his day was communication with Solei. He'd looked forward to this weekend more than any birthday.

He, who had avoided committing to a job or a plan of action, and instead had used the waning weeks of his residence as a shield, now wanted to make plans. But before he said anything to Solei—possibly scaring her out of her mind—he needed to talk with his mom about Mrs. Bukar and his father about the partnership.

"What kind of dog?" he asked, trying to ignore the nerves that wrestled in his stomach and clawed at his throat when he thought about confronting his parents. He had no idea how they'd react. None. They'd never been angry with him. He'd never fucked up. He ran his hand through his hair and breathed in deeply. He had to take control of his future. It was his. Not theirs, and now that he'd fallen in love... Love. The word. This was it. He'd seen it before with more than a few of his friends. He'd heard them fumble through an explanation about their feelings, justify actions— dropping out of school, breaking up with a long-time girlfriend after meeting another woman playing Frisbee in a park, getting married after a few months, starting a family during residency—that had seemed mystifying. Stupid.

And now he was contemplating breaking his parents'

hearts. Could he do that?

"I don't know." Solei continued to take a few pictures of the goats, wrestling her dress away from one. "Thank you for the cheese with dinner tonight," she said sweetly to the goat. "But you cannot have a chunk of my dress in return." The goat bleated, looking like it was smiling. "Not walking out of here flashing anyone."

"Wait. What?" Rohan homed in on that. "Are you not…" he dropped his voice low "…wearing panties?"

Solei winked.

"We were talking about dogs. Maintain focus." She laughed at him.

He lit up. His life had always been so serious. His family focused on achievements. He'd always been diligent, head down working. Rani had been the only one who brought joy. "I guess we still are," he deadpanned, earning another Solei smile. "Sorry, not sorry."

"I'm just as bad," she admitted.

"If you won't help me focus on anything other than you, you will have to drive us home because I won't be able to concentrate."

Solei's breathing changed. Pink tinged her cheeks, and he saw her swallow.

"The dog," she whispered. "I don't have a breed in mind. I thought it would just arrive in my life—a twist of fate. I didn't want to push it. I thought we'd find each other."

Like we did.

"Sometimes," he stepped closer, the barn, the diners on the terrace patio, the goats all fading away, his world narrowing to just Solei, "you have to push."

"It's a delicate balance. Knowing when to push or pull or be still."

He wasn't sure if she wrapped her arms around him first or if he did, but she felt fantastic. Warm. Strong. Her natural fragrance making him hungry. He pressed his lips against her hair. He loved the color, the silkiness, the body—it seemed alive as it flowed over her shoulders to her shoulder blades. He had loved the way it had spread out over the cushions of her outdoor couch the first day they'd made love.

But he had to get himself under better control. They had a forty-five-minute drive home.

He rested his forehead against hers. "Tell me more about this dog. Distract me so I can walk out of here and get us home."

"Distract you." Her breath was warm against his lips. She kissed the corner of his mouth. Her tongue traced the seam of his lips. "Like this."

"Yes. But not what I meant."

Her expression was innocent as she pulled away a little.

"Let me try again," she said contritely.

He ran his hand down her back, resting his palm in the curve of her spine, wanting to go lower, see for himself if she were wearing panties or not, but not wanting to be a human male version of a dog.

"I've dreamed about having a quirky dog. A dog that maybe not everyone else would immediately see its charms, but I'd want to have some land first so it can run around and have something to protect, and I'd like to hike with the dog, and camp so not too big."

"Quirky and perfect. A statement dog like your art." He'd googled many of her murals in LA, San Francisco, Portland and Seattle. More were scattered around the country. Her images were a visual feast and often had an element of irony or surprise—forcing the viewer to take a step back and think, keep looking. Her art made a statement.

"Yeah," she said, looking at him a little startled. "I always try to have an unexpected twist in my art, so I guess I would want to have a dog with his or her quirk on, an individual, but loving and loyal."

"I must seem so average and boring to you."

Solei, taking a close-up of the goat he had been holding, dropped her phone and quickly retrieved it wiping it off on her thigh.

"Right because boring and average are adjectives that you've heard applied to yourself so often." She rolled her eyes. "I'm sure you are universally adored and admired. And I have proof," she teased, holding up her phone. There were five texts from Rani.

"I think she fears I am a bad influence leading you astray."

"Or leading me where I want and need to go," he answered.

"She's getting impatient about my reply about what about you surprises me," Solei said.

"Not surprised it's taking so long."

She crossed her eyes. "Right. Wrong. No. Wait. Hard no," she laughed and stuck her tongue out. "I've been trying to think what about you doesn't surprise me," she said shocking him. "So, no harshing my musings. I'm an artist—all about visuals. I'm going to create a picture for Rani detailing the many ways you surprise me."

"How do you paint a surprise? Show me jumping out of a cake?"

"Now there's an idea." Her appraisal was openly sexual, and he got hard all over again. "What flavor would you like it to be?"

"Carrot or coconut, but I prefer pie. Pecan or lemon meringue."

"Pie is a messy, sticky, delicious choice," Solei approved. "I'll need you to model for my own personal sketch class when we get back to your house. Naked, and I call dibs on licking you clean."

SOLEI LOVED DRIVING in the dark. Well, she just loved driving. Letting her thoughts unwind. Listening to music or a podcast or a book. This early morning as she drove back to

Charlotte, she was thinking about Rohan. Rohan and their weekend together. She'd had a magical time. Never before had a relationship felt so easy and natural. She'd loved the hiking. She'd loved shopping for ingredients to make dinner and breakfast.

She could see the sky was graying up off to the east as she drove south on I85. She'd spent the entire weekend with Rohan. Initially the plan had been for her to head home Sunday late afternoon or early evening, but they'd been enjoying themselves too much for her to want to leave. Sunday morning, they'd gone on his favorite trail run and then had headed into Chapel Hill to a bakery. Then in the afternoon he'd taken her to a Top Golf and taught her how to hit, and they'd played a couple of hours, making up games for points. Rohan had a killer swing and was competitive, but so was she, and once she got the hang of what her body needed to do during a swing, she was surprisingly steady and hit straight. Rohan had been elated, asking her several times if she were having fun. She'd loved making contact with the ball, and they'd decided that his next weekend off, they'd play a round at a low-pressure public course.

Solei had googled courses near Charlotte and had signed up for four private lessons, determined to not embarrass herself even though Rohan's lessons came with benefits—his body warm and hard behind hers, his sexy, late-night DJ voice tickling her ear, his lips brushing her cheek.

She huffed out a breath. She could not be getting

aroused while driving, and definitely not before six am.

Had she done the right thing signing up for lessons? Was she becoming a version of what Rohan wanted or a better version of herself? Changing herself for a man?

"Stop overthinking," she commanded. Couples adjusted and adapted to each other. That was part of growing as individuals and as a couple. And she felt like she and Rohan were a couple. But did he?

He was definitely making an effort to see her again. He was on call today and had promised to come up tomorrow afternoon to watch her set up for her mural project for Hungry Goat Brewing. She often had an audience when she painted—it was called street art for a reason. Curious bystanders and fans would show up and watch and document, which was why she didn't often announce projects too far in advance on her social media. But clients often did. Rohan had seen her paint at the art fair, but if he made it up to watch her, it would feel more intimate.

As if in tune, her phone rang. She didn't look at caller ID. Who else would be calling her so early?

"Hey," she breathed, excitement curling low in her tummy. Instead of a week or two without seeing him in person, this time it would be only today. And she had seen him this morning. They'd made love and showered together, and he'd made her a gigantic coffee for the road. "I was just thinking about you. I miss you already and can't wait for Tuesday."

"What's happening Tuesday?"

"Rani?"

"Duh. Caller ID."

"I'm driving."

"To work already? That's motivated. I am lucky if I am not fifteen minutes late everywhere. Maybe that's why no one wants to hire me."

Technically she was driving to work. She'd just left from a different city.

"Why so early?"

"Got a lot to do," Solei said vaguely, taking a sip of the still piping hot coffee. Delicious.

"You didn't answer all my 'would you rather' questions or tell me what about Rohan surprises you."

"I answered a few, Rani," Solei said piously, not wanting to hurt Rani's feelings. "But I've been busy."

"Wait, you weren't with Rohan, were you?"

Busted.

"I've been busy preparing for my painting for the Hungry Goat Brewery," she said, hoping she could throw Rani off the scent. Not that she cared, but Rohan was quite private. He said his family was always up in his business too much and that he wanted some space.

"Proverbial shit will hit the fan soon enough," he'd told her darkly last night when they'd cuddled on his couch while sort of watching a show on Netflix.

She'd objected to the "shit" analogy and had offered alternatives such as roses or dandelions. She'd been playing with the idea of dandelions for her goat art. True beer was all about hops and barley, but the company wanted to launch unique flavors. Goats ate everything and dandelions had always fascinated her visually—trying to capture the fluff and whimsical movements as the seeds drifted on the wind. But maybe this wasn't the right project for that. She often played with concepts or images for a while before finding the perfect project to showcase the idea.

She never seemed to have a flash of brilliant insight some of her peers described. Her art was more perspiration instead of inspiration.

"Maybe my muse stutters," she mused.

"Funny. I'd like to see your muse in action. It's tomorrow, isn't it? I've never watched an artist."

"Of course, but I'll just be getting started. I'm doing some prep work today with scaffolding and marking out the site, but tomorrow won't be some visually spectacular feat, and I work in layers, so I won't finish," Solei warned.

She wondered if Rohan had told Rani that he'd be coming up Tuesday afternoon.

"I still want to check you out," Rani said. "I'll take you to dinner."

How would Rohan feel about that?

"Did you see Rohan this weekend?"

"Not kissing and telling," Solei said primly.

"That's a yes. Is that why you were too busy to play the

lighting round game of 'Would You Rather…'"

"You're having other people take your quizzes aren't you?" Solei asked, suspicious of Rani's perseveration. "A dissertation involves a lot of research, doesn't it?"

"Of course," Rani said. "I started with friends and family but now I'm collecting data from people all over the country. I'm really having a blast organizing everything—it's fascinating and I'm looking at the metrics of dating apps. I've interviewed six matchmakers from different cultures. I think finding the right romantic partners is my jam. Next, world domination."

"I'll pretend that that's not scary."

"With me it would be. Total disaster," Rani said cheerfully. "We'd burn or blow up. You didn't give me the prosthetic limb answer after consulting with Rohan, did you?"

"I still don't know why you don't send these quizzes to him as well. You said you wanted to see if you could match people," Solei stopped mid-thought. Did Rani not want her dating her cousin?

"I've known Rohan my whole life. I know his answers."

"Rani, how can you really know what he thinks if you don't ask?"

"I just do," Rani said quickly, her voice certain.

Solei took another sip of coffee. The horizon was now a gorgeous pink orange, and she pulled her phone out of the holder and keeping her eyes on the road snapped picture after picture as she drove, hoping to capture the color tones.

"Okay, what would Rohan rather lose, an arm or a leg?" she challenged softly. She and Rohan had played Rani's game, timing themselves. She'd thought it would end in laughter or Rohan dismissing the questions. Instead, they had scooted closer and closer, answering instinctively, knees touching, gazes locked.

"Leg," Rani said. "Obviously. He's a surgeon. Hands are imperative. Critical."

Solei felt something in her chest tighten protectively. She would have thought the same thing, and yet Rohan hadn't even pondered his answer. "Rani," she said softly. "Rohan loves to run. He loves to run trails and hike in nature."

"Yeah, but he's a surgeon. And people can get pretty proficient with prosthetics. He'd still be able to walk and run and stuff, but not operate."

Likely true. But the human will was not necessarily bound by rules. It could be enormous. Incalculable. And technology and innovation never stood still.

"You never answered," Rani pushed. "Leg, right. Because you're an artist."

Rani was right but wrong. Her first answer had been leg because she wanted her arms so that she could hold and care for a child, which had shocked her into silence last night, because she had never been one of those women determined to be a mother. And again, women with one arm had loved and raised children. And people painted using their feet, or their mouth.

"Getting close to school, Rani," she said although she wasn't, but she didn't want to reveal anything to Rani before talking to Rohan. "I'll see you tomorrow."

"Wait, don't you think that's a good question?" she demanded. "Should I scratch it?"

"No, it's good, but I think your interpretation lacks a little imagination. You should follow up on your lighting rounds with a why. That way the prospective couple have an activity they can do together, and they can learn something about each other that they might not otherwise learn for a long time. And they might learn something about themselves. I feel like you have an agenda with the way you phrase your questions and construct the activities. Your opinion and agenda will possibly skew your data in a way that will not be conducive to creating something that will promote a strong sense of self and of what one wants in a romantic partner."

Total silence.

Darn. She'd hurt Rani's feelings. That's what happened when she was relaxed, a little bit sleepy and feeling thoughtful and safe driving in the dark like she was in a womb.

"Who's the psych doctoral candidate here?" Rani demanded. "You are brilliant. I would kiss you if I were there."

"I'll take a rain check," Solei laughed, relieved.

"I'll buy you a drink and dinner and name my firstborn after you."

"That's a little excessive," Solei said.

"Pretty sure excessive is my middle name," Rani sang out. "And after I've collected my research and had my dissertation accepted and write my thesis creating a psychologically driven matchmaking something—whatever it turns out to be—I'll find you and me the most fabulous matches. Thanks, Solei."

Rani hung up.

Solei replayed the conversation, trying to figure out what she'd just heard. True Rani's conversations often veered far out of her lane and sometimes over a cliff, but still, why would she act like Solei wanted to be matched with someone else? Maybe she didn't realize how much time she and Rohan had been spending together. Or maybe Rohan had...

"Stop."

She'd just warned Rani about making assumptions. She shouldn't start either.

Chapter Fourteen

"ROHAN." HIS MOTHER walked into her office, her expression mildly alarmed. "What is it? What are you doing here?" She stopped in the doorway.

Instinct rose up hard, fast, to reassure her. It bubbled in his throat. His mouth opened, lips already curving to mutter "I'm sorry." He stomped down the childish impulse.

"I didn't want to do this on the phone."

If anything, his mother looked more alarmed. Her arm, bent at a ninety-degree angle to hold her Birkin bag, went limp. Her bag plopped upright, next to her on the carpeted floor of her office.

"Beta?" she asked.

Despite the cool elegance and sophistication of his mother's dermatology clinic that catered to those with money and desire to enhance their appearance far more than it did now to anyone who had real skin issues like psoriasis, eczema and more, the air felt thick and heavy, and a wave of heat rushed through his body.

"I don't want to get married," he squeezed the words out and shut his eyes like he was eight again and having a panic attack over telling a lie about gaming. The memory of his first panic attack was so vivid, he could hear his mother yelling for his father. His father's fingers digging into him as he checked him for choking. The soft chenille blanket that Nanima wrapped him in while his mother shouted at them all to "slap him out of it." Later, Nanima had made him chapati's and four-year-old Rani had curled up beside him in bed clinging to him like a monkey while his mother had paced in the living room panicked that he was going to be a "head case," like Chirag. He hadn't known what that meant or who Chirag was, but he'd been terrified.

"Oh. My. God." He heard his mother clunk back against her door that snicked shut. "It's true. You're gay."

For a moment he was so lost in the totally forgotten memory he didn't process.

"What?" His eyes opened wide. Stared. His mother looked pale and deflated. He was handling this badly. He always handled his mom badly. She was so beautiful and fragile-looking that he felt he had to walk on eggshells, but no, she was made of steel, and she intimidated him in a way he admitted to no one. "No," his ears caught up to his brain. "Why do you think that?"

"You're not?" She whooshed a breath in relief and touched her chest. Her color returned and her lips curved up in a smile. "Oh." Her perfectly buffed nails, a soft coral blended with her light peach suit, shone as she placed her hand over her heart. "Of course you aren't."

"I'm not. But if I were, it wouldn't be a big deal," he said firmly. Rohan had several fraternity brothers who were gay, one of whom had cried when he'd come out and another whose parents had rejected him for a few years when he'd come out as a sophomore—claiming that he wasn't their son anymore, and the frat had rallied around Cole, taking care of him, helping him to find the means to stay in school and stay in the frat house.

"No, no. Of course not," his mother said briskly, but her smile that didn't reach her eyes said "you'd better not be." If she read his mind about Solei, she wouldn't worry. Well, she would, but it would be about something other than his sexual orientation. "But those flashy jackets you prefer, Rohan. You act like a peacock—strutting. So eye-catching. Maybe that works in Paris or Milan, but once you are practicing with your father, you'll need to tone it down."

He could feel his burst of motivation deflate under her censure.

"You're stylish," he objected getting derailed as usual by her.

"I am a successful doctor. An entrepreneur with a highly lucrative skincare line. On the board of several city organizations. And on the expansion committee of the temple. I need to look the part."

Nailed it.

"Why are you here? Oh. Is today your interview with Papa's group? He didn't tell me." Mystery solved, she smiled, picked up her Birkin bag to put on her desk and walked closer to him. "That is so silly. Papa has planned to hire you since you were born. He's so proud. His group has grown to include so many partners, privileges at three hospitals in Charlotte and several clinics. A couple have hired their offspring. But rules must be obeyed." His mother waved off the concept and she frowned a little—ironic since she laid down so many rules for all of them.

And that quickly, the acid was back burbling in his gut. He hadn't felt the need to pop an antacid the whole weekend with Solei. He stood straighter. He had to take charge. Stop ducking and weaving. His father and joining the partnership was later on his list of problems to solve today.

Tomorrow was his interview for the faculty position at Duke, and even though Jason had practically levitated with joy and had fist bumped and back slapped him at least a dozen times when Rohan had said he was interested in hearing more about the potential job, Rohan wasn't going to count on anything until he'd signed a contract. Tomorrow night the team was taking him and his "significant other," if he wished, to dinner.

He wanted to square things with his mom and his dad before talking to Solei about considering looking for a job in Durham.

He was nervous about that—that he was assuming too much, but he could barely breathe when he thought of disappointing his parents.

"Mom, please. Listen a moment."

"I am busy. I have appointments." His mom's back was to him. "Chai?"

"No, thank you."

His mother had a Keurig in her office. There was an elaborate espresso machine in the lobby for the patients. She began making herself a chai. And…sigh…of course one for him. He couldn't even be trusted to know whether or not he wanted a beverage.

"I want you to cancel Mrs. Bukar, please."

"Why? We are so lucky to get her. She's in high demand. We need the best for you Rohan. This is what we've been working toward."

"Do you hear yourself? We. It's me. My life and I'm not ready for…" he broke off. He'd been about to say marriage, but he wasn't sure that was true anymore. He hadn't been ready for the concept of handing his life over to someone else before he'd fully tasted freedom, but Solei didn't make him feel trapped. She didn't make him feel manipulated. She listened. She shared herself. She was honest with her opinion and compromised. No guilt. No martyr. "I want to have some freedom."

"Don't be so melodramatic." His mother handed him the unasked-for chai latte. "Of course it is time for marriage, Rohan. You've turned thirty-two. Your father and I married after medical school. I was twenty-five. He was twenty-six. You were born two years later. Freedom," she laughed.

"What a thought. What, are you a prisoner?"

"Mom, I just want a few years to…"

"Years! The thought!" His mom's eyes bugged, and her voice sounded like glass being cut. "Years to do what? Debauch yourself? Get off track? No. Not my son. Your father and I did not put in all this effort into raising you to have you stall out. Freedom. A childish concept. You are a man, Rohan. Behave like one. You will marry and start a family. That is how it's done."

"I want a family. I just want to choose…"

"Not this again. Freedom. Choice. Only the Lord Krishna knows what sort of woman you would bring home. Probably some blonde free spirit raised by a single mom who did a semester of community college who would break your heart and take half your money. Do not mistake lust for love," she said.

"Do you trust me so little?" he asked, shaken by the picture she'd drawn—gullible, dumb, impulsive, led by his dick.

"You are book smart, Rohan. But naive about women. You don't know how they are. You can trust me and Mrs. Bukar to find you a suitable girl." She blew on her chai and then sipped it. She smiled. "You have always been a little shy." She touched his cheek. Her hands were cool as if they couldn't absorb the warmth of the drink she'd held. "That gives me an idea. I will have Mrs. Bukar help me invite one or two candidates to the party. You can meet the girls in a less formal setting. Have a choice," she arched a brow, topic closed. "Come for dinner tonight. We can talk about how the 'interview,'" she rolled her eyes and smiled as she did the air quotes, "went. Nanima and Mummyji will be thrilled to see you."

"I have plans," Rohan said darkly.

"Come for dinner." As usual she ignored him. "Rohan, it will all work out. You will see. I will arrange it all. You will marry and live a good and content life together. Excel at your career. Be a man of worth and respect in your community. Raise successful children. What else is there?" she asked.

"I want the chance to find out," he said, and while his mom gaped at him, he took advantage of her shock and left, closing her office door a hundred times more quietly than he wanted.

ROHAN PARALLEL PARKED his Audi and then closed his eyes, pinching the bridge of his nose. He was a coward. He'd gone to have an early lunch with his dad between cases. A thirty-minute lunch in the cafeteria that had been compressed into seventeen minutes and most of that had been a parade of colleagues interrupting to congratulate him on being nearly finished with his cardiothoracic residency. A lot of Duke jokes at his expense as a handful of his father's colleagues were Carolina alums and bled Carolina blue. He took it all in good stride.

He hadn't been able to get in more than a swallow or two of the mutter paneer or vegetable korma, which he hadn't wanted anyway, but his father had extolled the virtues of the Indian food at the hospital—twice a week now—so effusively and the chef had come out to meet him, so Rohan had felt obliged to take a scoop of each. His salad too sat untouched. He'd gulped two glasses of water. His throat was dry, and his stomach still had churned with acid.

His father had commented on his bouncing leg.

"Public jitters will not instill confidence in colleagues or patients and definitely not their families," his father had noted coldly. "From the moment you leave your car and swipe your card to get into the hospital, you are on display. You are a leader. Never forget that."

His father had spoken to him like that when he'd been ten.

"I feel like I'm in a time warp with you," Rohan had said just as another group of surgeons had come up to greet them, and Rohan had had to accept that now would not be the time to tell his father he was considering another job offer.

It felt like a wasted day. He'd failed. He'd even tried again to meet with Mrs. Bukar, but she said she was having chai with several prospective girls for him and another client, and no he couldn't meet the girls yet—like he wanted to. Just thinking about it made him feel dirty, like a cheater.

He was here in Uptown to see Solei start her mural, but the usual sparkling joy that coursed through him when he was about to see her was absent. He felt sick. Numb. Shamed. He climbed out of his car feeling like he was in his eighties, not his early thirties.

He'd wanted to come to Solei today free and clear—no Mrs. Bukar, no looming job he didn't want. But he'd failed. Shanti had been right on the day that they'd moved Asha. He'd let his parents keep their illusions of him from childhood. The dutiful son. The perfect son. He'd only shown them the hollowed-out, sanitized version.

Was the man he'd become, the man he wanted to be, someone they would still respect? Be proud of? Still love?

He didn't know, but if he wanted to be that man, if he wanted to build the life he wanted, he was going to need to cut the cord and find out.

He slid his Robert Marc NYC shades on and locked his car and headed up the block and turned left. The music, a Little Nas X song lifted his spirits. The failure at the hospital and his failure to communicate and fully connect with his mother rolled off his shoulders and splatted on Camden Road, and he found himself grooving to the music. A little of his swagger returned.

"Look who's back," Rani called out, blowing him an exaggerated air kiss. "Charlotte's hottest bachelor."

"Solei didn't tell me you were going to be here." He joined Rani, who stood close to the action.

"Maybe she doesn't tell you everything." Rani lowered her cat-frame sunglasses with rhinestones on the dramatically flaring points and batted her eyelashes at him. "Just like you don't tell her everything."

"Nobody tells someone everything. I want an air of mystery."

"Or secrecy," Rani shot back. She wore vivid red lipstick and a black jumpsuit with blindingly white Adidas. "You're on a collision course, Ro."

"No head shrinking." His eyes were on Solei. She was up on free-standing scaffolding with no safety harness. She wasn't high…yet, but he didn't know how big her mural was going to be. She had the entire brick wall. She'd texted him a few renderings over the past few weeks, and it had been fascinating to watch the goat evolve as she did more research. The owners had given her a tour of their facility, and she'd interviewed them. He hadn't been able to join them, but Rani had. He'd enjoyed the beer samples Solei had brought this past weekend.

About thirty people watched her—some of them teens. Maybe her students? She wore a black racerback tank and black leggings with her usual Docs—these were canary yellow with a face on them with the tongue sticking out. Her tool belt rode low on her hips and held cans of spray paint in the pockets. A woman with long, braided black hair stood on the scaffolding with Solei, and two men stood on either side of the scaffolding, arms crossed, mirrored sunglasses on, facing the crowd. They looked like they should be on the set of an action movie.

Solei looked beautiful and confident as she worked with different tones of green. Her movements were sure and fluid, and he could practically feel himself melt with pride and longing to be up there with her instead of the person assisting her.

It had only been a day and a half since he'd seen her last, but that felt like too long. A two to two-and-a-half hour drive hadn't seemed like a big deal in the beginning because they were both busy, but this past month, the distance had seemed to stretch out, wrap around his ankle and pull him under.

He'd missed her.

"Why do we have to stand so far back?" he asked. Everyone was in a semicircle and a good thirty to forty feet back.

"Security," Rani said. "She has to hire a team when she's working."

More people arrived—some looking determined, like they knew what they were about to see and others drifting up to join the crowd, clearly curious bystanders taking in a novelty. Phones were out.

The fact that she had to hire security was both ominous and reassuring.

Solei conferred with her assistant, and then the scaffolding started to lower. Before it had gone halfway, she hopped over the side, and Rohan, worried, instinctively moved forward. He was immediately blocked by the muscle.

"Oh hey." And then Solei was there, her hand on his

arm. "You made it. How was lunch with your dad? It's okay, Brian, this is my boyfriend."

"Gotcha, sunshine."

"It's good to see you." Her hand slid down his arm, and her fingers tangled with his. She leaned in for a kiss. He loved how she was so affectionate. Her other hand lightly touched his hair, his cheek, knuckles grazing his jaw.

He stared at her, likely looking stupidly dazzled, his mind still hung up on the word boyfriend. Boyfriend. He'd never been a boyfriend, not in the true sense of the word. It said so much, and yet at the same time, not enough. The rush of feelings roaring through him didn't fit anything he'd ever felt as a boy.

"Lunch?" she asked. "Did you get a chance to talk to your dad about considering other job offers?" Her vivid green eyes darkened with concern.

"No." Instinctively he looked around like a bad actor playing a paranoid drug dealer. He hadn't even told Rani he didn't want to work in his father's group. "The hospital was a bad idea of a place to talk."

He was beginning to think he'd need to take his mom up on her offer to have dinner with them instead of spending the time with Solei. Disappointment clenched his stomach.

"I'm sorry," she said, and her warm expression recentered him. "Unusual, as I find most of your ideas to be perfection."

"The idea I'm having now is going to lose you your audience if I drag you out of here caveman style or get us arrested if we stay."

Solei's eyes gleamed with humor and a touch of heat. "Tempting, but I haven't had to dodge cops since I was a young teen, and I'm likely not as fast."

"You didn't?" He was shocked and intrigued.

She winked. "Stick around to learn more."

"I intend to."

"Or do you need to head back home soon?" She nibbled on her lip. "Did you come to see the art or just to say hi? Can you stay for longer?"

"I came to see the artist and the artist doing art." He realized he'd been holding her arms the entire time they'd been talking—clinging to her. So not cool. No one in his family was into PDA. He'd never even seen his dad kiss his mom that he could remember. But he'd also never seen them fight much beyond a minor disagreement or difference of opinion.

He leaned down and lightly kissed her cheek, wanting so much more, but forcing himself to release her and take a step back.

"I'll try to wow you." She also took a step back.

"You don't have to try. You already do," he said playfully, wanting to lighten the moment because he felt too much pressing on his chest and swarming around his head banging to get out.

Solei tilted her head and looked at him thoughtfully. He wondered what she saw. Then she glanced at the crowd, looked back at him, made a heart shape and mimed it exploding.

"What the hell does that mean?" he muttered, watching her walk away.

"It means she's in deep." Rani was by his side, tugging him another few steps back into the crowd. "Deeper than I thought possible."

"Possible?" He looked at his cousin. She looked so dramatic, like she was on a movie set. And maybe in her mind she was. Hell, this whole place looked like a movie set. Heavy equipment, a killer playlist pounding, the beautiful artist star on the scaffolding getting strapped in—thank you, Krishna—like she was going to do a stunt.

"I thought I was your favorite?" he mocked. "You don't think anyone could be crazy about me?"

Rani leaned against him, cocking her head into his arm. "You are infinitely lovable, Rohan. That's the problem."

"Not from where I'm standing." He watched Solei use a lighter green to outline the stems of green she already had radiating out, giving the impression of a thicket. He knew she layered in a lot of different colors in her paintings to give an effect of light and shadow. She worked so quickly that it seemed like magic. He wondered if she were going to go for a neon effect here. So far, the goat—the brewery's namesake—had not made an appearance on the wall.

"I love her, Rani," he confessed the words quietly.

"Ro," Rani's voice was distressed. "I know you think that

all the questions I've been asking are crazy witch mutterings, but..."

"No, I don't," he turned his attention to Rani. "You are smart, observant and insightful, Rani. Solei and I have had some of the most interesting conversations I've had in my life with a woman other than you about our answers to some of your questions. I've learned so much about Solei through the conversations—she has dreams and ambitions that fascinate me, and we have more in common than I would have thought."

"How?" Rani demanded, looking alarmed.

"I feel like a door has finally opened, and I want to walk through it and discover more doors—learn more about Solei and myself."

"Ro," Rani placed her hand on his arm, "it will never work long term. You'll break her heart. You'll have yours broken."

"Good thing I'm about to be a top cardiothoracic surgeon," he mocked and swallowed his hurt and worry that Rani wasn't on board with him and his happiness plan.

"Not funny, Rohan. This is serious."

"I know. It's my life. It's my future. Be happy for me. I love her," he repeated the words firmly, wanting to say them, hear them, share them with Solei and everyone else. "I never would have met her if I hadn't run the errand with you to the art festival. God," he gripped his hair. "What a near miss I had. I never would have met her if I hadn't wandered off searching for the music source, and when I saw her, it was like…I can't even describe it, like the world was shiny gold and different and I finally understood how the universe worked."

"Rohan, you don't even sound like you." Rani's eyes were huge. "This can't be good."

"Why? Why do I have to keep to one path? And it's not even a path I would have necessarily chosen. I'm nearly at the end before I even wondered if I am on the right one. Now I feel like I am at the beginning, like I have choices."

"You are a gifted doctor and surgeon," Rani said on blind faith since she'd never seen him operate. "Solei is an artist. She has no tethers. You've only known her about eight weeks. Have you told Uncle and Auntie?" Rani demanded.

Rohan watched Solei. No. He hadn't. He'd wanted privacy to enjoy the relationship.

"I shared my feelings with you. I thought you'd understand, but you're just like everyone else, shoving me in a direction because you think you know better."

He expected Rani to run off. She didn't jump into conflict the way Shanti did.

Rani blinked back tears but held her ground.

"I just don't want you to get hurt. And I don't want Solei to get hurt."

"That's not how life works," he said. "I'm tired of playing it safe, and I don't think Solei knows how."

They watched the thicket she was painting grow—hops

and barley on the outside but thistles and dandelions shooting through the thicket giving it an almost fantasy look. The painting had texture now, depth, almost like a scene out of a video game.

"If you're really serious about developing some relationship tool, you can't object when a couple finds happiness together. Even if they break your rules or go off-course or it's not the HEA in all those romances you read. You're a scientist. You need objectivity. You can't ignore it if your initial hypothesis isn't playing out."

His words were a lash. He'd probably regret speaking so freely later, but what he said rang true. He didn't want to float through life, but he loved his family. He had to find a way to have both—space to make some choices and his family.

They were both silent for a moment, Rani blinking rapidly.

"Rani," he began after a moment.

"No, you're right. I'm sorry. I have been pushing you. I have made assumptions like a know-it-all. I've never seen you so loose and happy. And I'm happy for you. I am. Happy. Happy, and a little envious, actually, but I'm also scared."

"I am too," he admitted, looking at her. "But I feel alive."

That shut Rani up. He warred with trying to apologize but why? He'd only spoken the truth. His phone buzzed with a text. Jason asking if there was any way they could move up the dinner invitation part of the interview to tonight. Again a "significant other," was invited. Eyes on Solei, he texted back and said he'd ask his girlfriend if she were free. Peace settled into him when he hit send.

Chapter Fifteen

SOLEI PUT THE finishing touches on the goat's eyes—more of a suggestion of silver to add the luminosity she was looking for. A couple of the kids at the arts center had come to take pictures for her from different angles and perspectives and sent them to her phone so she knew how the picture would look as people walked by. A few of the kids and a parent had been enterprising—running to Costco and returning to sell bottles of water and other drinks and some snacks to raise money for the center.

She'd been worried that Rohan would get bored, but he'd watched her intently and had even gone to a bank to get money for change for the kids selling drinks. He'd also bought them some food from Chick-fil-A to "keep the teens' energy up."

He was essentially perfect, which was becoming a problem. She was no longer as eager to keep her position at the school until she knew what Rohan was doing, and that should be a bright red warning flag. She'd allowed herself to base her future plan on what Zachary had wanted. Her passivity still burned, and she'd sworn never again, yet now she found herself waiting—not applying for other jobs—and sifting through potential commissions, basing her interest on geography—how close it was to Durham or Charlotte—instead of what challenged and interested her more.

Not good. She'd promised she'd never again defer her professional aspirations for a man.

"Head in the game, Solei," she muttered as too much silver bled into the goat's dark iris that was black layered with three shades of purple and misted with lavender.

She repaired the work and then sorted the colors back in the stacked carousel that she used on job sites.

Her students whooped below. Solei unstrapped her safety harness and swung down over the railing as Rohan lowered it.

"Trying to cut me out of a job as your assistant?" He greeted her with a sweet kiss. "You jumping over the railing gives me a heart attack, just so you know." He took her hand and pressed it to his chest.

"I don't want to get you paint splattered."

"I like being colorful."

His smile made her heart race.

"I'm almost done," she promised. "I just need to look at the artwork before the scaffolding company takes it away and sign it if it's done."

She felt exhausted and exhilarated like she always did after finishing her work. Sometimes a project took days and months of planning. Sometimes just hours. This had been fairly freestyle and quick. She'd planned out the drawing, but she always left room for a flash of inspiration. Today it had taken the form of a golden glow infusing the top of the painting—a hint of sun and the sunrays shooting through part of the thicket of green lightly kissing the goat. She hadn't planned that at all, but Rohan arriving in a saffron blazer had lit up her imagination.

She didn't think Zachary had ever inspired her artwork. She'd become almost furtive about it. Rohan always seemed so enthusiastic about her art. He watched, jumped in to help and other than fielding a few phone calls and texts and talking to Rani, he'd been so present and complimentary.

"Do you need me to back off for this part?" Rohan asked as she moved around the area, eyeing all the details of her painting that glistened. The goat looked alive, and his eyes seemed to follow the view from all angles.

"No," she answered honestly, wanting to feel him brush against her body, but no way was she going to ruin his beautiful sports jacket. "I don't want you to back off for anything."

He smiled, and Solei felt like everyone else just faded away, except a raspy voice interrupted.

"Solei, I'm Heather Jenkins from Charlotte Art Beat. Wondering if I could get a short audio interview with you for an upcoming segment. The brewery owners said we could go inside."

"Ummmmm…" she broke off. She'd been hoping to

spend some time with Rohan.

"Do it if you want," Rohan said. "It's not a problem. I can wait. Want me to grab you something to eat?"

"No, thanks. I was hoping we could go out or back to my place." She'd grocery shopped, hoping, but she shot a look at Rani. Maybe there was a change in plans. "Unless you need to get back earlier," she qualified since he had fielded a few calls, and he'd said his lunch with his father hadn't been as productive as he'd hoped.

"I actually want to talk to you about that," Rohan said. "After," he nodded at Heather.

Curious, Solei quickly thanked the kids for helping and was thrilled to learn that they'd earned nearly two hundred dollars for art supplies.

Then she thanked the security team and her assistant for today, Leila, who was a local painter finishing up her MFA.

Rohan and Rani followed her into the brewery that was nearly prepared for its soft opening this weekend. They sat at a long bar that looked out over the glassed-in equipment.

Josh, one of the owners, poured several flights of beer for all of them to sample. Solei tried a citrus beer that looked light. It was delicious, but she still didn't think she'd start drinking beer. She'd never really embraced it. Rani seemed to be enjoying the freebie and chatted happily to Josh and his two partners.

"Maybe you can interview the Hungry Goat owners about why they chose a goat as their symbol," Rohan teased

Rani. "In a different part of the brew pub so Solei can do her interview. Ask these men about their thoughts on goats and if they make good spirit animals or guides or whatever else you've been running by Solei the past couple of months."

Rani stuck her tongue out.

"Goats are quite evocative," Solei said. Heather turned on her recorder, and Rani closed her mouth with a snap. Solei kept her voice low and a little mysterious, feeling like she was back volunteering at the local Boys and Girls Club as a teenager reading to kids and doing arts and crafts for service hours.

"Over centuries and throughout cultures, goats have inspired a lot of emotion. Some people think they are weird or spooky—the ancient Greeks sacrificed them along with sheep to read their entrails in myths. They were symbols of virility and fecundity, they have an uncanny ability to yell like a human, their rectangular pupil can freak some people out, but they are also adorable and easily as affectionate as a dog—running to greet you and pushing to get some love."

She definitely had everyone's attention. She had no idea what Heather wanted for her podcast, but she often free associated with words and ideas and images. It was how her brain worked. And she wanted to get out of here. Peel that gorgeous coat off of Rohan. Hopefully Rani would get the hint, but Solei doubted it, so she tried to squelch her libido.

"Goats are quite useful as well. They produce a highly nutritious milk that contains more potassium and iron and vitamin A than cows' milk. And the cheese is tasty as well." She had taken her hair down after painting, but it felt hot and sticky in the brewery as the air-conditioning wasn't on. Instead, the garage-style doors were rolled up, but there was no breeze.

"And then there's the whole historical symbolism that goats evoke. They can represent faith or independence. Dreaming of goats is considered a good omen, signaling a new opportunity and climbing to greater heights. So, they are historically and culturally significant, but also they are cute, funny, friendly, useful to clear out invasive species and to keep fire hazards under better control. Goats can nourish the body and the soul."

Figurative mic drop.

"Rohan," Rani said into the silence. "I totally get it now."

"Damn. We were just playing with goat like G.O.A.T. You know, greatest of all time," Josh said. "She drew that wacky, glowing, mysterious neon looking goat chomping on blackberries as a sample for our brand, and we were just like damn. All in, girl. We're all in."

"Let's roll," Rohan whispered in her ear. "I got a proposition for you."

Solei didn't care what else was happening or what she should or shouldn't do. Business could wait. She followed Rohan outside, before anyone likely realized that they'd left.

"Thank you for coming," she said. He swept her into his

arms and kissed her breathless right in front of the brewery with Rani and the others staring at them.

"How would you like to have dinner with me? A work dinner." His eyes drilled into her, and his breath seemed a little shallow like he was nervous.

"Of course." She'd likely have dinner or almost everything else with Rohan no matter where or when. "A work dinner?"

"I talked to Jason and a few of the other partners and told them I was interested in exploring the surgical faculty position at Duke. I wanted to learn more. I thought you and I could talk about what that means for us tonight, but they have pushed up the timeline to tonight because none of the partners were on call. They pushed back the reservation so that you could join us if you are willing and able."

Solei was still transfixed by the words "what that means for us." An unexpected nervousness sparkled in his inky eyes, and he swallowed hard. "I know it's a weeknight and a lot to ask. I've never…"

She covered his twitching hands. "Yes."

LAST-MINUTE DINNER WITH partners two hours away was easier said than done. As she drove home in desperate need of a shower, Solei cataloged her few sundresses. Rohan had seen two of them, and they seemed suddenly too casual for a job interview dinner at a new restaurant in Durham. She'd googled the restaurant as soon as she jumped in Frida, which was when the nerves started.

Normally Solei wasn't too concerned about her appearance. California was super casual, and as an artist, she had a lot of style leeway, but if there was one thing she'd learned over her year in Charlotte was that going out meant dressing up. The South was more formal. Elegance ruled. Her throat tightened. Rohan had said not to worry. He'd wanted her to follow him home, but she insisted that she'd take a fast shower, change and head out.

Now she felt a little panicked. She knew she was attractive and that Rohan wouldn't put pressure on her to look a certain way, but bringing her would reflect on him.

She hit the number for a higher-end boutique that she'd designed an inside mural for last fall when they'd opened.

"Hey, Stephanie." Relief whooshed through her when she heard the owner's voice. "I have a fashion emergency. My boyfriend is interviewing for a job as a faculty member and attending surgeon at Duke Medical school tonight and we're going to an elegant new Asian fusion restaurant, and I only have a few minutes to find something appropriate."

"How far away are you?"

"Ten minutes tops."

"Park in the loading zone. Shoe size?"

"Eight."

"I'll have three outfits to choose from ready for you."

And she did. Solei pulled up. Stephanie's long curly hair was twisted up away from her face, and she'd propped open the back door and handed Solei a sparkling water with lime. She drank gratefully.

"This Johnny Was Norah short silk kimono just came in. I steamed it. It looks fantastic with this pale lavender bamboo jumpsuit—elegant but a touch of boho and the wedge heels will make you look even more sophisticated and willowy," Stephanie said. "I know you love olive, so I have a jumpsuit in olive that is more revealing and whispers sophisticated and the Kuren cropped kimono will add a pop of color and elegance and the embroidered flower and leaf pattern will tie into the jump suit. The wedge heels will go with both looks."

Solei sipped the water, wishing her heart would slow down. Both outfits were eye-catching. Elegant yet playful. Unexpected. And they looked expensive. For someone who mostly saved, splurging only on art supplies and could fit her wardrobe in one bag, maybe it was time to take a few fashion and life risks.

Always a saleswoman, Stephanie also brought out a long, red-orange sheath dress that buttoned up one side so it could be demure or racy. She'd paired the dress with a wildly patterned silk scarf with fringe, beads and tassels.

"Hard to decide, I know." Stephanie easily read her. "You might need two outfits—one to wow your man's new colleagues and another to impress the parents."

Pretty early for that, although the next time her parents got into a port and called, Solei intended to tell them about Rohan. Today, anything seemed possible.

"I'll take all three," Solei said feeling brave and reckless at the same time. She pulled out her platinum Amex—the one she hardly ever used. "Wish me luck!"

"Unless he's blind or gay, you're not going to need luck. You'll need a broom to sweep up all the broken hearts and paper towels to mop up your man's drool."

"Exaggerate much?" Solei laughed, breaking some of the building tension at purchasing so many clothes all at once. Maybe if she wanted to plant roots, she was going to have to push herself to outgrow Frida a little.

Feeling more settled and confident, she swung by her house to quickly shower and change, even having enough time for light makeup, including a light dusting of powder with a touch of glitter. She chose the lavender jumpsuit with the multi-colored silk cropped kimono, thinking it was stylish but demure. She loved the subtle color. It was so pale it was almost a pinked gray, and as she drove, she wondered what she would mix to create that color and what she would paint.

The drive was two-plus hours. One hundred forty-seven miles. But Solei felt like she was flying into the unknown, and anticipation tingled through every nerve.

"You look beautiful," Rohan said, opening Solei's door ahead of the valet after handing him a tip and telling him he'd help his date.

His date. He still felt like he needed to pinch himself that Solei was his. He held her hand as she slid out of the car. He'd never seen her look so polished. She glowed.

"I feel like I should frame you." He brushed his lips against her temple, not wanting to smudge her makeup.

"Good one," she laughed, slipping her fingers into his as they walked up the stairs and the doorman opened one of the massive, glossy red doors. "Frame the artist. Ha. Ha. You look pretty spectacular yourself. Love the teal suit."

Still holding her hand, he did a four-count dance step, lifting their arms up and turning her toward him.

"Why was I wearing a white shirt when you first arrived?" he smiled. "So boring." He paused at the restaurant's entrance and kissed her knuckles, holding her warm gaze. "Thank you for setting me straight."

"As if you ever need an excuse to glam up. I am not even a tiny bit surprised that you had a lavender shirt," she said.

"You inspired me to match. Thank you for helping me to give the shirt an outing. I bought it last summer and never wore it." He let himself look his fill, still stunned that she was going to dinner with him and his colleagues. "While I love this new polished you, I also love your sweaty paint-splattered look when you are creating."

"You need help," she laughed at him, and then her

looked turned a little shy. "I have a confession," she said softly, a flush staining her cheeks and fascinating him utterly.

"That sounds promising," he said softly, tipping her chin up so he could look directly in her eyes. "Is it the same one you never confessed when I first met you?"

She smiled. "I bought everything I'm wearing in about five minutes at a shop where I painted a mural last September. And I also bought two other outfits. I think just maybe I might be busting out of my one duffel bag a little." She nibbled on her bottom lip that had painted a soft pink and had been tempting him the entire drive over to the restaurant.

"Frida might complain?"

Solei nodded. "She might. You, sir, are looking at a risktaker."

"I like what I see, RT," he said. "Are you going to model anything else for me later?"

"Maybe." Her eyes shone like emeralds.

"Ready to razzle dazzle?"

She nodded and they walked in together and checked in with the hostess.

"Anything I should know?"

She'd asked him this earlier when she'd arrived. He'd been too distracted by Solei's incandescent beauty. Incandescent. He should have led with that.

"We're having dinner at the hottest restaurant in the Triangle area with my colleagues, not walking a pirate plank."

They followed the hostess to the reserved private room, and Rohan walked a little behind her, palm on the small of her back, definitely enjoying the view of her pert ass.

Pull yourself together.

"This is going to be casual," he said, even though the restaurant and private room seemed anything but, and he'd definitely upped his wardrobe game going full suit. He thought he heard Solei huff a laughed "right."

"Hey, you're not nervous, are you?" He slowed and slipped his arm around her waist.

"No." She met his concern with a smile. "I'm looking forward to it. I've never been to a work event with anyone before."

"A first for me too." He savored the moment and her closeness. "Thank you for joining me," he said. "I haven't been out with the partners and their spouses before. Instead of thinking and stressing, I'm looking forward to tonight. That's you," he tapped her chest lightly. "You make everything a little shinier, Solei."

"You too." She looked at him, her cat-eyeliner with a touch of sparkle gave her an exotic and mysterious vibe and the body slimming pantsuit in the subtle color made her skin glow. The color pops of the silky jacket or whatever she wore sliding off her shoulders made her look like she should be strutting down a runway, inaccessible. Instead, she was with him, supporting him. She slipped her arm through his. "Ready?"

"Hard yes."

SOLEI HADN'T KNOWN what to expect exactly. She'd been in her "prepared to go with the flow" mode. Growing up, she'd always been around people with money and power and influence. She'd met celebrities, sometimes played with their children on the different yachts her father captained. She also regularly interacted with clients who had a lot of money and high expectations.

She hadn't expected the dinner to be intimidating, exactly, but she hadn't known she'd have such a good time, especially as she sat across from Rohan and a few seats down, so that she could chat more easily with the wives and husbands while the partners talked to Rohan about the job and his expectations and goals. She settled in, prepared to listen and engage. She had the easy part especially as everyone was so friendly, but when the conversation veered toward her career, she felt a twinge of panic.

Tonight was about Rohan. Not her.

But before she could think of a way to deflect, the chief of the group, Jason Steel googled her and started asking her some questions as he and others started looking at several of her projects online. As she sat there, feeling like a truck was barreling toward her, she became the topic of conversation. She was too nervous to look at Rohan, anticipating that he'd be upset to have lost the limelight.

"You need to see this," Rohan's voice rang out enthusiastically. He pulled out his phone, then he paused. "Is it okay if I show them your rose and mermaid from the art festival and your goat at the brewery?"

The breath she'd been holding and the tension in her shoulders crashed out of her like a wave. "Sure," she smiled at him, and then she looked at Jason. "I got Rohan to paint and write a poem at the Charlotte Arts Festival."

"Really." Jason leaned back in his chair. "I haven't seen the artistic side of Rohan yet, although his surgical skills are often inspired and inspiring. You must have access to some magic pixie dust."

"She is magic," Rohan breathed. "Check this out." He held up his phone with a video of her painting the neon rose the afternoon they'd met. She hadn't even known he'd recorded her. She'd never watched herself create. She often posted on social media, but rarely anything of herself. It was interesting to see her the utter focus on her face and yet her body was fluid and sure.

Rohan played it a couple of times so everyone could see. Everyone seemed dazzled by the rose and how it seemed to "magically appear and glow like a neon light." There were a lot of questions about her career, how she got started, what she was working on next. Solei looked at Rohan. He put his phone away and grinned. Then he fist bumped her across the table and made an exploding motion.

"Told you," he looked around smugly, "magic."

Chapter Sixteen

TWO WEEKS LATER on Friday before lunch, Tula entered Solei's classroom before her last student, Raya, lingering to ask some advice, had even finished packing up a few extra art supplies to finish her final portfolio project.

"I'm going to miss you," Tula said. She opened the small fridge in Solei's classroom and pulled out two cans of sparkling water and popped the tops off.

"Cheers to a great year." Tula clinked both cans and handed one to Solei.

"Bit premature. We still have a week of school, and it's not like I'm never going to see you again. This is just an interview. Not an execution."

"I know." Tula took a deep swallow. "But you're going to get the job. The school would have to be loopy whacked dumb not to hire you."

Solei smiled and shook her head, and then she impulsively pulled Tula in for a hug. "Thanks," she whispered, tears stinging her eyes. "I love how you are always so confident for me," Solei said. "You've been a good friend, and if I get the job and move to Chapel Hill, we'll still be friends. Wednesday is a half day at the school, so I'll still be able to volunteer at the center with you and Rand."

"I know." Tula pulled away and wiped away a few tears. "I have to teach after lunch so don't go ruining my makeup."

"You started it."

"You could have stopped it." Tula hugged her again. "Sorry. It just makes me mad that the school and the parent advisory board are making you wait this long to renew your contract. They really told you to wait until mid-August?"

Solei nodded. She couldn't deny that it stung. The principal had continued to compliment her work, and to reiterate that she was an excellent studio arts teacher and had excellent professional reviews as well as positive reviews from parents and students.

But that hadn't resulted in a contract.

Solei wanted certainty. With Rohan staying in Durham, moving closer to him made sense, and if they didn't work out, she'd still have a tenure job, her art and the friends she intended to make. And if she didn't get this job, she'd look for another one. There were a lot of high schools and community colleges in the Triangle area, and she'd continue to take commissions.

After a lot of soul searching, she'd decided that she'd forever regret it if she didn't give her relationship with Rohan a chance. He seemed to be throwing caution to the wind with her—discussing the future—things they could do and places they could go. She'd met a lot of his work colleagues and their spouses at his job interview dinner a few weeks ago. And she'd met a few of his fellow residents when she spent the next weekend with Rohan and a group of them went to Top Golf and then grilled out at someone's house on a Sunday afternoon.

Rohan had looked around his friend's house as if seeing it for the first time. When they'd driven home, he'd asked her about her condo in LA and the house she'd been renting in Charlotte—what did she like in a home? She'd been shocked, trying to not read too much into his questions. When she landed the interview with a high school in Chapel Hill, she'd worried he'd feel pressured, like she was trying to push into his territory, but he'd been just as excited as she was about her potentially moving closer to the Triangle area.

"Best of luck, although you won't need it," Tula said, walking her out to Frida. "When are you going to upgrade this relic?"

"Frida is a keeper." Solei stroked the door as if Tula's comments could hurt her beloved van. "We've had many adventures together. Rohan thinks her design is clever like a Swiss Army Knife." She smiled, thinking of the gift she had for Rohan—his first Swiss Army Knife, the Victorinox multi-tool plus. That would keep him busy and inspired.

"Tell me you did not force that man to sleep in your van like a hippie."

Solei laughed at the scolding. "Okay. I didn't force him. But he did try it, and yes, it was workable but definitely out of his realm of experience." Solei laughed remembering Rohan's mix of shock and awe and enjoyment versus struggle.

"Ugh," Tula rolled her eyes. "At least upgrade to one of those sleek Mercedes Sprinter vans that somehow magically sleep four. You can do five star now. You have a doctor on a leash."

"He's not on a leash," Solei objected. "And I can do five star on my own if I choose. Rohan is a man, not a paycheck."

"I know," Tula sobered. "Just teasing. Go get that job and your man."

"I intend to." Solei kissed the window of Frida who had traversed many roads—city and back—and miles with her.

She got in the van, turned the key and Frida hummed to life. No matter what, she was heading into another adventure. And this one might prove the most exciting of all.

SOLEI BUSTLED HAPPILY around Rohan's kitchen, making pesto, grilling peppers and thinly slicing pears and Gouda cheese to make some bruschetta for when Rohan texted that he was on his way. She still buzzed with excitement over the interview. After the past couple of months on pins and needles waiting to hear if the Queen City Arts and Sciences would renew her contract and then dismally hearing that she wouldn't know if she had a job until early August, the enthusiasm from the interview team at the Chapel Hill high school had been a confidence boost.

She had been unsettled not knowing her plans for the fall. True she was a working artist who'd made solid bank over the past few years, and she didn't need the teaching job to survive. But she wanted it. She'd loved having colleagues and making a few new friends and volunteering her time and skills at the arts center. The thought of being able to settle into a community, have a purpose beyond herself, collaborate with colleagues, make friends and teach teenagers along with having a job with benefits felt right.

She'd been taking care of herself for a long time, but if she got this new job—which was tenure track—she might finally feel as if she could relax a little. The job sounded ideal. She'd be full time and teaching four studio arts classes. She would have leeway with her curriculum design as long as she met state required standards. Collaboration within the staff was encouraged. The arts department was well funded, and the parents were supportive and involved.

Rohan had driven her through Chapel Hill near the University of North Carolina once, but as she'd driven back to his apartment in nearby Durham, she'd decided to take a more thorough and scenic tour. She'd driven around the cute college town and through a few neighborhoods with more curiosity. She'd felt so positive during the interview although she didn't know how many candidates they were interviewing. She'd shown them a sample of her portfolio as well as a slideshow of the multimedia exhibit she'd co-directed at the Charlotte arts festival. That had clearly blown the interview panel's socks off so to speak—something her father, who rarely wore socks, used to say. The parents on the panel had had so many questions and wondered if she could recreate something similar for the students at the Chapel Hill or Durham art fairs. She'd discussed what had gone well, and what she'd learned honestly. She'd also discussed the hard push for fundraising, which the three parents had looked at each other and laughed and waved that off like it was nothing.

Must be nice.

The positivity and the openness of the interview and the panel and then the tour of the school had her metaphorically crossing all of her fingers.

After driving around for half an hour and enjoying a coffee on Franklin Street and absorbing the energy of the famous street that UNC students frequented, she stopped at a farm stand to gather some ingredients for dinner. She loved cooking. Rohan enjoyed it as well although he rarely did it on his own. She loved looking up recipes online and trying new ones, but it was so much more fun and satisfying to cook and to enjoy food with someone.

With Rohan.

She would find an apartment or small house to rent with a nice kitchen—being a little outside the city would be nice.

Durham was a large, thriving city with over four hundred thousand people. Chapel Hill with sixty thousand people felt more like what she was looking for. LA had been her home base for many years, and it was easy to find opportunities, but she longed for a house with a studio and some acreage.

A knock on the front door surprised her. She looked at her phone. Rohan hadn't texted. He wasn't due home for at least another hour at best. And there was a code to get into the building and elevator so it wasn't a salesperson.

She turned off the heat for the burner where she'd been planning to grill some vegetables and then chill them for a veggie salad. Curious, she opened the door. A woman in a yellow sundress and black, red and yellow blazer stood on the doorstep, a large leather tote casually slung over one shoulder.

"Oh. Hi." She looked at the number on the door and then back at Solei. "I'm looking for Rohan Kapoor."

"He's not home yet," Solei said. "Are you one of his cousins? Asha?"

"No," she looked taken aback. "You know Asha?" The woman's eyes looked her up and down slightly critically. "Are you his roommate or something? I thought he lived alone."

The conversation was starting to feel weird.

"How can I help you?" Solei asked carefully, feeling herself tense.

"I'm Jasmine. I knew Rohan when we were kids, but I

moved away to Boston for college and ended up staying for med school and then Chicago for residency. Our parents are friends."

"Oh. Hi. I'm Solei." She felt suddenly awkward like she was doing something wrong—being in Rohan's apartment, but he'd given her a key and was expecting her for the weekend. He'd said nothing about expecting a family friend. "Do you want to come in? He's still at the hospital but should be home in an hour or so. I was making dinner. There's plenty."

She opened the door wider and stepped back. The woman hesitated, even took a step back herself.

"I don't understand."

"Ummm… What?"

"Are you…do you…work with Rohan or…?" She lost her smile. "I'm home for a couple of weeks for a visit and to interview for a position at the same hospital where Rohan is going to work, only I'm in general surgery. I thought it would be a good time to reconnect before his party next weekend. Sort of get a jump on the competition."

"Competition?"

Rohan hadn't mentioned a party.

The woman was beautiful with soulful dark eyes, and long dark lashes that curled up. Her hair was thick and long and silky midnight black that glinted blue in the light streaming in through the walls of Rohan's apartment. She eyed Solei curiously and then sighed.

"Maybe I should go. I can catch Rohan at the hospital. I have his number. I just thought I'd surprise him. His mom said he wasn't on call this weekend and that he'd love to see me again."

It was hard to breathe, and Solei's chest felt like it filled with ice.

"Your choice," she said sunnily, battling back her reaction. There had to be a reasonable explanation. Rohan would clear it up. "But you're welcome to stay," she said firmly determined to not be rude to Jasmine and to give Rohan a chance to explain. "I could make some chai or a cocktail if you prefer."

"Are you…you're not like a girlfriend or anything like that are you?"

"We've been seeing each other for a few months," Solei said, happy she'd kept the dress she'd worn to the interview on. She'd made an effort with makeup and her hair so that Rohan could have the whole effect. "We met in March through Rani."

Not exactly but if Jasmine were really a family friend, she'd know Rani, and it made her feel more legitimate—not good. Jasmine was making her feel like she was Rohan's secret lover stashed in his apartment.

"Rani?" Jasmine exclaimed. "Why would she… March? That long?" Jasmine demanded. "No one said anything about Rohan dating anyone. Not that a man that fine would be a languishing virgin, but…how did you even get in here?

Did he give you a key to his apartment or are you living here? What the hell is going on?"

Solei was asking herself the same question.

"Why would his mother hire a matchmaker if he's living with you?"

"A matchmaker?" Solei nearly yelped she was so shocked.

"If you're still offering, I think we can both use a cock-tail."

ROHAN PARKED HIS Audi and took the stairs two at a time. Normally he didn't drive to work unless he was on call, but he was excited to get home because Solei was there. He couldn't wait to hear how her interview had gone. He too had news but had deferred the celebratory offers to grab a beer after work because Solei was waiting. He hadn't signed the contract yet, but the job was his if he wanted.

And he wanted.

Now all he had to do was the hard part—sit down with his dad and mom and tell them he was taking Duke's offer. And also that he was seeing Solei and would not be meeting any of the women whose bios Mrs. Bukar had emailed him this week. She planned for him to meet two of the girls next week. That would not be happening, and his mom had invited a family she'd met during residency to attend his party with their daughter, who was a pediatric dentist.

He definitely had to hard no all of that.

He'd put it off for far too long, but a lifetime of keeping his thoughts, feelings and dreams private had died hard. He'd wanted to wait, having his job plan settled, let his relationship with Solei develop—see where it went—before he made waves with his family, but they were as usual shoving him hard to an end goal that they'd established, and he didn't want anyone to get hurt, especially Solei.

He unlocked his apartment, frowning at Solei's packed bag by the doorway. Normally she was so neat and tidy and would already have unpacked her weekender bag in the closet space he'd made for her.

He heard voices. Confused, he walked farther into his apartment out to the small deck on the back that was large enough only for a small grill and table for two.

"Jasmine?" He blinked in surprise, his gaze swinging around to Solei. She looked back at him in a way that unnerved him. No warmth. Lots of questions.

"What are you doing here?" he asked Jasmine and winced because it sounded rude, but he hadn't seen her in years except briefly at a few weddings. "I mean, I wasn't expecting you."

"I flew to Durham for a job interview yesterday and had another in Raleigh today. Monday I'm interviewing at the hospital where you will work, and that's the job I'm really gunning for," Jasmine said, sipping on a cocktail. From her relaxed posture and tousled hair, it wasn't her first—more

317

like her third. And by her smug expression, she was enjoying his discomfort and the coming drama storm. "Your dad and mine have put in a good word on my behalf so it looks like we'll be working together." Her look turned sly. "Your mother thought it would be a nice surprise for me to look you up while I was in town. Your secret girlfriend let me in. Surprise." She toasted him and drained her drink.

Shit.

SOLEI FELT TOTALLY calm—at odds with the hurt and anger that banged around her heart wailing to get out. It was like being in a movie, and yet she didn't have the same script. She'd made a pitcher of cocktails for Jasmine, who'd tossed them back at an alarming rate. Solei had allowed herself only a few sips as she knew she'd be driving tonight.

"Rohan, I'd like to speak with you a moment in private."

"Solei," he looked totally distressed, his hands out, palms up as if seeking forgiveness. Would she forgive him? Was there anything to forgive? She wasn't quite sure what was happening, what he felt about her, but she was not leaving here until she'd said what she wanted to say. She'd been thinking about it the entire time Jasmine had chatted about her family and Rohan's family—their friendship and history, and she'd hinted at an understanding between them, but then after the third cocktail, she'd learned more about the matchmaker who'd been hired *in March* and had been compiling bios of women for Rohan to interview. Like a job. He'd said nothing. The whole time they'd been together—he knew this was happening—Rohan had been sleeping with her while his family had been lining up potential brides for him to choose from like he was some sort of prince.

Jasmine didn't seem to have personal feelings for Rohan as much as she was uber competitive and wanted to beat out the other women—some of whom were invited to his graduation party next weekend—something she pointedly had NOT been invited to.

Solei walked toward the kitchen. She'd fed Jasmine the dinner she'd planned for her and Rohan, hoping it would mitigate the alcohol that Jasmine had tossed back like she was parched.

"Solei, I'm sorry," he said quietly. "I can explain."

She leaned against the butcher-block island. Everything was spotless. Just a plate of food, covered in clear plastic wrap for him. She hadn't been able to eat anything. Part of her had wanted to run away, but no, she'd avoided confrontations in the past. She'd let her own needs be sublimated in relationships to keep the peace. She'd crept around on the yachts owned by others, trying to keep out of the way. She'd tried to be the model granddaughter and not be an inconvenience when she'd lived with her grandparents. She was done with that. She'd tried to be the perfect girlfriend supporting and accommodating her man.

She was done with that too.

Rohan paced, ran his fingers through his hair. He looked gorgeous and miserable, and she didn't understand at all.

"When were you going to tell me?"

"What?"

"That you were a prize being dangled to the single women of good Indian families in the southeast? That you were the golden son."

"Oh. God. Not that. Rani always…"

"Why were you with me, when you were interviewing other women to marry?" she interrupted. She had to know how far he'd gone. That would help her rip off the Band-Aid. Maybe it would hurt less if she knew he too was a cheater. She couldn't believe how gullible she'd been. And how well he'd kept his secret. But why?

"How long were you interviewing perspective wives while you were then making plans with me, spending time with me, making love with me?"

"Never," he said quickly. "I never met with another woman," he swallowed hard. "It's true. My mother hired a matchmaker after my cousin Asha got jilted days before her wedding, but I didn't want her to. I asked her to cancel Mrs. Bukar. I called Mrs. Bukar to tell her I didn't want to be matched," Rohan's voice was low and fast, agitated. "Solei, from the moment I saw you, I…I…couldn't even see another woman, not like that."

"Then why not end the whole thing? Tell your mom

about me."

He recoiled.

An eerie silence descended. He looked more miserable.

"I see."

"No. No, you don't."

"I do. I'm not a secret to keep."

"I know."

"I deserve better."

"I know you do."

This was it. The end. She looked at him one last time. How could she have been so stupid? So blind? But he had seemed as into her as she had been into him—except the day of Holi when he'd met a friend of his parents.

Dumb. His actions that day spoke more clearly than anything else he'd said to her.

She battled back tears and steeled her spine. She'd let herself hurt later—safe in Frida, driving away.

"The thing is, Rohan, so do you."

She picked up her bag and opened the door. He seemed frozen to the spot, not even looking at her, staring mutely at the wall.

He wasn't even going to fight for her. A sob burbled out even as she tried to swallow it back.

Solei took the stairs, needing the speed and the physical action. She pushed open the door to the outside so hard that it hit the wall. She ran to Frida. She opened the door to her van and tossed her overnight bag in along with her backpack and purse. Then Rohan was there, trying to hold her. She slapped him away.

"Solei, wait, wait. Give me a chance to explain."

She held herself rigidly. "I did. You had had more than two months to explain."

"Meeting you was just so unexpected. So amazing. You blew my mind. I've never felt so much for anyone ever," he said.

"So why the secrecy? Why not invite me to the party your family is throwing?"

He looked stricken with guilt, and Solei just couldn't handle any more. The stress of not knowing if she had a job, the thrill with the interview today, the shock of Jasmine showing up and casually discussing Rohan's impending marriage plans, it was just too much. The exhaustion hit her like a wave. And she still had a two-hour drive. Probably more because she'd be hitting the tail end of rush hour.

"Never mind," she said, climbing into her van.

"Solei don't go. We can work this out."

She tugged the door out of his hand and slammed it, but she rolled down the window. "We can't," she turned on her van. "You can. You need to figure out what you want, Rohan. You need to fight for what you want. It's your life. Your future. Your decision. Be the man you want to be." She reached in her purse. God, this evening had gone so differently than what she'd imagined. She handed him the Swiss Army Knife in a cute gift bag that she had created. "I hope you figure out what you want and who you want to be, Rohan."

He stared blankly at the festive gift bag in his palm.

"I hope you do. I want you to be happy."

"I'm happy with you," he said, looking utterly gutted as he gazed up at her. She nearly turned off her van, nearly stayed.

"I was happy too," she admitted. "But I'm not living a lie. I'm not holding back who I am. That's on you."

She reversed Frida and pulled out of the apartment complex parking lot, not daring to look back.

Her phone rang before she even got on the main road. She would not answer. She would not give in. But she glanced at the caller ID.

"Now? Of course," she muttered. Wiping away a stupid stray tear she hit accept.

She got the dream teaching job in Chapel Hill.

But not the dream man.

She nearly said she'd think about it over the weekend. Would she want to live in Chapel Hill, so close to Rohan if he were married to someone else?

That question decided her. She needed to take charge of her own life and happiness.

"Yes," she said to the principal of the school. "I'd love to accept."

Yes to herself. Yes to her future even if Rohan wasn't in it. Hard yes to pursuing the life she wanted even though she was taking the next step alone. Again.

SIX AM ON Saturday morning was probably not the ideal time to drop a bomb when he was hoping for no casualties, but Rohan couldn't wait anymore. He'd wanted to go tearing after Solei, but she was right. She deserved better. She deserved a man who would put her interests and happiness above his own...what...fears, anxiety? It was laughably stupid when he thought about it like that. Afraid of disappointing his parents—at what expense? Solei's happiness. His own. Not acceptable. Not anymore.

He had to come clean.

And then he would go to her. Explain. Grovel if he had to. He'd never done that before. He'd never fucked up to warrant a prostrate mea culpa.

But he'd do it. Again and again if he had to.

So last night he'd returned to his apartment to see Jasmine still out on the deck watching the sun set and finishing the last of the cocktails—clearly in no shape to drive to her hotel much less the two-hour drive home.

"Sorry." She didn't sound it. "I think I fucked up your game."

"I fucked it up." He sank down in a chair. "All on me. And it wasn't a game. I love Solei."

Jasmine had put down her cocktail, looking a little more

sober. "Wow," she'd breathed. "Shit timing."

"No," he said. "The timing was exquisite. I seized the moment and ran with it, but I should have leveled with her about my family and their expectations."

"We all try to dodge them," she said quietly. And then after they sat there silent for so long, she sighed. "What are you going to do?"

"Tell my mom and dad everything. Make sure they listen. And then win back Solei's trust and her heart."

Jasmine had huffed out another breath. "Best of luck. I liked her. She was kind to me when she didn't have to be. She was cool about me showing up and dropping the matchmaker bomb on her. Sorry, Rohan. I always kind of liked you. Well, not always. I thought you were an arrogant prick when we were teens because you could do no wrong and walked on water and were the example that every parent waved in our face like a red flag to a bull. But I always thought you were hot."

"I think I should be held up as the anti-example."

For some reason—probably because she was drunk—Jasmine thought that was funny. She'd laughed and then she'd pretty much passed out, and Rohan had covered her with a blanket, and after opening the exquisite gift bag and seeing the Swiss Army Knife, he examined all the knife's intricacies. He couldn't help but make the analogy that the knife's hidden compartments were more than a little like Solei's mysteries that he'd only begun to discover, and he felt sick and shamed as he'd been forced to wait until Jasmine slept long enough on his couch to clear the alcohol from her body so that he could make her a large coffee, give her a bottle of water and Advil for the road.

And now he was home with a box full of Krispy Kreme donuts. And a stomach full of nerves and acid and an iron will.

He made chai, and after looking at the box of mixed donuts, he made scrambled eggs and cut up fresh berries and melon.

By seven his parents had shambled out to the kitchen, exclaiming at his presence and the earliness of the meal. His nanima, fussing because he'd used "her" kitchen sat beside him, chatting happily about how handsome he looked—except he was too thin, and was he eating, working too hard, and when was he moving home. None of them came out as questions.

"Mom, Dad," he said nervously. "Please sit down. I'd like to talk to you."

"Such drama," his mother said. "We were at a party last night. We've only just been to bed a few hours," she yawned. "I thought you were working this weekend."

"I'm on call Sunday," he said over the sound of his father grinding espresso beans. His father made a latte, steaming nonfat milk both for him and his wife.

"Please," he waved his parents to seats in their own home. "I have something to say. I've had something to say for a long time now."

"Blessed Krishna you are sick," his nanima jumped up and blessed him, waving her hands, touching her forehead and generally fussing.

He tried to smile. "No, I'm fine."

He didn't feel fine. Losing Solei had him feeling like he'd been dragged behind a truck, and he hadn't slept in the past twenty-four hours.

"I'm fine, Nanima." Or he would be after this. "Healthy. Please, relax. I want to talk to all of you. This is important."

His father finished making his coffee and sat on his favorite chair while his mom and Nanima took the couch.

"First, I'm in love."

His mom and Nanima had the same reaction—a quick inhale, and they both touched their hearts, and smiled luminously.

His father took a sip of his latte. "Love," he repeated flatly as if it were an unwanted diagnosis.

"Jasmine," his nanima whispered.

"What? No?" And how had his nanima who barely left the house except to accompany them to the temple or a few select parties at friends' houses heard about Jasmine's scheme?

"Mrs. Bukar came highly recommended," his mother breathed. "She is so good. Anju has yet to get an appointment to work on a match for Shanti," his mother said with satisfaction, and then she frowned. "But really, Rohan, you shouldn't jump ahead like that. You were always the fastest and quickest boy in your class," she recalled fondly. "But we need to meet the family. All of us. All of them. We are going to become a family. I can arrange…"

"Nothing, Mom. You don't need to arrange anything. Her name is Solei. She…"

"Solei. What kind of name is that?" his mom demanded. "It sounds French."

"Pretty?" Nanima breathed. "Do you have a picture on your phone?"

"Who is she? Who is her family?" His mother half stood and then sat down again. "Did you know anything about this?" She looked at her husband.

His father shrugged and drank his latte, not engaging in the relationship talk. His bad news was coming next. Not for the first time did Rohan wish he'd been less evasive and passive. He wanted to kick himself. What was it Shanti always said… "balls to the wall" …but she meant it sarcastically. She always claimed she was tougher than any man, and she was likely right.

His mother stood up and retrieved a file from her desk and began leafing through it. "Which one is she? Mrs. Bukar has sent over twelve candidates, but I see no Solei. Is she someone you work with? A resident?" His mother sounded nervous. "When did you meet her? Just recently?" Definitely hope in her tone.

"Solei is an artist," Rohan said firmly. "And a teacher. I

met her in March with Rani."

"Rani!" His mom would of course seize on that. "Oh, dear God, she could be anyone. So typical of Rani to ruin everything." His mother jumped up, wringing her hands. "How could she? She knew we were planning a match for you, the perfect match. We've been discussing so many options. You had so many, many choices, Rohan. So many. You have no idea how many families have reached out to us. Phone ringing off the hook. Daily emails. You can have the best."

"I've found the best," he said quietly.

"How can you say that?" his mom demanded. "You've known this…this…artist…oh my God, I never thought that word would leave my lips…for a few months. That is nothing."

"Mom, you married Dad after having chai with his family twice and taking a walk in a park with him."

His mom waved her marriage agreement away.

Nanima looked at the open box of donuts—twelve different selections. She reached for a chocolate old-fashioned.

"Rohan, put those on a plate. Have we taught you nothing?" his mom snapped.

Rohan eyed his pacing mom and retrieved a Wedgewood china plate with the "India" pattern and arranged the donuts. He handed Nanima a napkin.

"Do you have a picture of… So…so…how do you say her name?"

"I'll show you in a minute, Nanima."

"Of course Rani would screw up the best match in Charlotte's history." His mom punched in Rani's contact.

This...this drama, this anger, this blame was what he'd wanted to avoid, but of course he'd made it all so much worse.

"No. Mom. Wait." Of course she didn't. "It's not Rani's fault. She was just there. I saw Solei on a stage and..."

"Oh dear God," he'd never heard his mom call out to God so many times. "Is she also an actress? This cannot get any worse."

His heart sank, even as his anger bubbled. His mom wouldn't approve unless Solei was the doctor daughter of a friend of hers. Or a friend of a friend.

Rani must have answered because his mom was rapid firing a complaining combination of Hindi and English and Punjabi at Rani, who likely had only gone to bed a couple of hours ago.

He grimaced. This too was his fault. He'd delayed and delayed and now he dropped the bomb on them at the crack of dawn.

"Mom." He got up and stood in front of her blocking her pacing. "I love her. I love Solei."

His mom stared at him aghast. "You can't." She ignored Rani who sounded like she was confused and probably apologizing reflexively. "It's too soon. We can fix this."

"There's nothing to fix. And love doesn't work on a

timeline. You know that. You and Dad..."

"But that wasn't love. It was practical. We had similar upbringings, culture, family, expectations. Love comes later," his mom said.

Rohan's father continued to sip his latte, looking out toward the lake, not at his family drama.

Rohan knew his parents respected each other. He rarely heard them argue. But he didn't see them love on each other ever. He couldn't remember it as a child. They behaved more like respectful colleagues. Team members.

"I love Solei now."

"That will pass." His mom was sure. "It's an infatuation. Easily forgotten. Oh. God. Is she a blonde? Probably fake like everything else, Rohan. You have no experience. You are so trusting. Your...your..." she waved her hand, her expression of deep distaste. "It will pass."

"I seriously doubt that, Mom." He felt even more certain as his mom rapid-fired her arguments and complaints and blame. "I love her. I want you to meet her."

His mom slowly sunk down on the couch. "Meet her," she whispered, looking at his father for the first time during the entire conversation. "Do you hear him, your son? He wants us to meet this unknown girl. This artist."

"Then let's meet her," his father said philosophically. "Bring her today or next weekend to the party. Whatever. We'll meet her," he stood up. "I'm going to take a shower. Then I will have breakfast."

"Breakfast! How can you talk so calmly of breakfast?" She popped to her feet. "Your son is going to bring some random girl home."

"Could be worse," his father smiled in a rare show of teasing. Or maybe he was being literal. He picked up his copy of the *Wall Street Journal* and the *London Financial Times*.

"An artist," his mom made a face. "A teacher. So…" His mom swallowed, holding her hand to her throat and sat back down slowly as if she were injured. "She went to college?" He heard the note of hope in her voice, and he started to relax just a little.

"MFA UCLA and a teaching certificate."

His mom plucked at the gold fringe of a pale blue velvet pillow. "That could be worse," she whispered after a long while. "I think." Her brow furrowed briefly before she remembered that severe expressions made lines. "Are her parents doctors?" she asked hopefully.

"No. Her mom's a chef on private yachts, and her father is a captain of the private yachts. She grew up sailing around the world, and they are still married and in love."

This threw them. Rohan would have laughed if he'd been watching from a distance.

"Yachts." His father paused his exit. "Like multi-millionaire and billionaire yachts?"

Rohan nodded.

"Like Jeff Bezos? He has a yacht that supports his yacht.

Like that?"

"His client information is privileged. But maybe," Rohan said and pressed his luck because at the moment not only was Solei not speaking to him, the chance of his father getting to walk on a billionaire's yacht docked in a harbor was likely less than zero. "You can ask him when you meet him."

"Oh. My. God," his mom said. "Listen to your son. Love. Billionaire's yachts. A blonde. She sounds blonde. I wish I smoked."

"I have cigars," his father said, leaving the room. "Help yourself. Today's a good day to finally find a vice."

"Papa," Rohan followed. "I have something else to say to you."

His father paused and then turned around.

"Rohan," he said. "All I ever wanted was for you to be the best man you could be," he said.

"I want that too. I wanted to be the best I could be. I wanted to make you proud."

His father nodded. "You need to make yourself proud. All we can do is our best. Your best was better than mine," his father admitted, flooding Rohan with shock. "You were the best of me and your mother. I have always been proud and impressed by your intellect and curiosity and grasp of complicated issues. Your skills as a surgeon are unparalleled. You were published before you nabbed one of the most prestigious residencies in the country. You are a comet that is going to burn brilliantly for decades. Duke would have to be asleep at the wheel to not do everything they could to entice you to stay."

Rohan staggered in relief.

"Papa," he could barely speak. "Are you're okay with that?" He needed him to be okay with that. "I want to continue my research. I want to work with the top teams in the world. I want to train residents."

"Rohan, your mother and I gave you life. It's your life to live."

"It never felt like it was." Bitterness crept in.

"It's our way. We pushed too hard to excel as we were pushed. But you rose to the occasion. You are a gifted cardiothoracic surgeon and will inspire and train residents for decades. Now, I have to go to the bathroom. Enough drama and revelations."

Chapter Seventeen

EARLY SATURDAY MORNING Solei pushed the remote on her garage door and wheeled her stacked, revolving cart containing her medium—spray paint out of her rental house. She was too keyed up to stay inside. She had to create. She had to let all of the hurt and the doubt and the anger and the longing for Rohan out. So, she'd posted an address and a tease—a cinder block wall that had recently been put up as a divider between a new construction building and the Youth Urban Arts Center—on her social media. She'd posted on the center's Instagram and would DM her students, inviting them to show up when she arrived and got organized.

Street art in its pure form. Except she had permission and a permit. She and the students had been discussing painting the wall, but they hadn't set a date.

She hadn't been able to sleep last night, alternating between curling up in the egg-shaped hanging chair and watching the moon or running on the treadmill the professor had in his spare bedroom.

Rohan hadn't texted or called.

She knew because she'd checked obsessively, even as she

vowed that she would not make the first move. That was on him because he had been the one holding back.

His silence was a dagger.

He hadn't been all in like her. He wasn't willing to fight for them. And even as she knew—she absolutely knew—it was better to know where she stood—tossed aside on the road—now rather than later when she was even more invested, Solei ached.

Breaking up with her two college boyfriends had been easy compared to this.

Zachary walking out had been nothing compared to this.

"Head in the game," she murmured, loading up the first cart of paint and returning to the garage to grab three more carts of paint that she used when she worked with the kids at the center.

"Solei. Good morning."

Rani stood near her van, shifting her weight from foot to foot and running a hand nervously through her jagged bob. There was nothing good about it, but there would be once she started painting—she was determined to turn her mood around and move on.

"Are you okay?" Rani asked, taking off the sunglasses she hardly needed yet as the sun was still in the pink fingers across the pale blue eastern sky stage. Rani took a hesitant step toward her.

"You're not my favorite person right now," Solei said. "You should have leveled with me."

Rohan should have leveled with me.

"I know." Rani swallowed convulsively and took another step toward her. "Look, I'm sorry. I kept telling Ro he was going to get burned, but he wouldn't listen. And he is fighting for you in his own way."

"By hiding me in a closet?" She metaphorically sneered at her heart's leap of hope.

Rani looked like she had just woken up—leggings and a college sweatshirt, no makeup and her hair was rumpled. "You didn't come here to apologize for Rohan, did you?" Solei demanded suspiciously.

"No. No. No. He's stuck at home trying to get through to Priddy Auntie," Rani said appeasingly. "I know it sounds strange and weak, but you can't fathom the pressure he's been under his whole life. You've never met his mom."

"That was Rohan's choice."

"I don't think he felt he had one," Rani said. "I know he was avoiding conflict and protecting himself and his family, but he also felt he was protecting you."

Solei stared at Rani uncomprehendingly. She knew Rohan loved his family. He'd said so many times, and he'd admitted that while he'd love to live in Austin or Seattle or LA, he couldn't imagine living so far from all of his family. And she knew there was tension between them, but Rani made Rohan's mom sound like a dragon.

"I love my aunt. I do. And she adores Rohan. He's like her big, blazing ball of light. I think he was just so gobsmacked by his feelings for you that…"

Solei stalked back to the garage to wheel out the second cart. Rani nervously hopped beside her. Solei loaded up the second cart. "Sure Rohan really didn't send you? No more lies."

"No, he'd be pissed at me for interfering. Again." Rani hung her head. "And that right there proves that he loves you because Rohan's never mad at me. Never. He's the only one. He's home exploding his world. And I wanted to make sure you're okay since he can't right now."

"I'm fine." Solei marched back into her garage to grab one of the two new boxes of spray paint that she'd ordered for the center. She might as well bring them in case a large group of kids showed up to paint. She jerked her head for Rani to grab the second box.

"You don't look fine," Rani said earnestly. "You look all puffy like you've been crying."

"What is this, tough love? I am not a therapy client, and if I were, your last comment would not help."

"I get that you're hurt and angry, and I didn't lie."

Solei retrieved the last two carts. She had to get out of here. She couldn't let herself hope.

"You lied or *pretended* to be working on a survey for your dissertation. You had me thinking you were creating a dating app, but I think those questions would be better in categories in a party game."

"A party game," Rani breathed and clapped her hands.

"That's brilliant."

Solei huffed out a breath and rolled out the last two carts. She loaded one in. She would not let Rani distract her from her cleansing rant.

"You encouraged me to help you, and I did in good faith, but all along you were playing some game, just like Rohan was playing with me."

"He wasn't. And I am working on my dissertation." Rani blinked at her, looking so distressed that Solei could feel herself start to soften. "I have a direction now. You did help. I've been working so hard to organize everything and have a meeting with my committee next week to make my proposal, and now with the party game idea…"

"I have to go," Solei said firmly, grabbing up her backpack and closing the garage door.

"Solei, please, Rohan's turning himself inside out for you right now. He's desperate. I want you to give him a chance."

"Rohan has to fight his own battles, Rani."

As if this were a movie, Rohan drove up, his powerful Audi rumbling to a halt on the opposite side of the street. He swung himself lithely out of the car, and her stupid heart vaulted into her throat, racing like it was truly being chased.

He looked absurdly beautiful. Teal blazer, dark washed jeans, peach oxford shirt open at the collar and the sleeves pushed up on both his blazer and shirt. His walk was fluid and sexy as he crossed the street. His hair was perfectly styled and gleaming. How dare he look so fantastic.

"Solei." She felt like he pulled her heart out of her chest and tossed it in the bushes.

"No," she held out her hand. "You have to figure out what you want, what you really want with your life, and that doesn't happen overnight after a visit from an ex determined to get drunk and rekindle the romance."

"What I want is you, Solei. What I've always wanted is you."

"No." She couldn't do this. She'd prepared for it to be over. She felt battered and bruised and while she'd told herself to hold on to the slender thread of hope, she'd truly believed it was over. "You played with me like a toy," she accused.

He stopped walking.

"You pursued me knowing that you were going to marry someone else as soon as you finished your residency. That's why you suggested we see each other this spring. You just wanted one last adventure before you settled down. I was a spring-long bachelor party."

He paled. "Solei, it wasn't like that. Not at all. I..."

"It feels like that." She banged on her sternum. "Here. And now that I've had time to think about how you were sneaking around playing with me while marriage candidates were lined up for your exalted perusal, it was exactly like that. A game to both of you." She pointed at him and then Rani. "You wanted to keep me a secret from your family like I'm not good enough for you. Like you wanted the thrill of slumming."

Rohan looked sick and frozen to the spot. Rani had big fat tears rolling down her pixie face, and Solei hated this—hated how much she hurt, hated the ugly but true words galloping out of her mouth like the horses of the apocalypse. She wanted him to argue. Prove to her that she had it all wrong, but he looked stunned. Probably no one had called him out before.

"Golden one, my ass," she hissed, wanting to hit something. Instead, she all but tossed the last rolling cart into the van. It tipped and several cans rolled away. Screw it. She slammed Frida's door, not even clipping the cart in because if she didn't get out of here, she was going to do something stupid like run to his arms and burst into tears. Or hit his perfect nose.

She was better than that.

She'd made a promise to herself that she would be strong and independent and not pretzel her life and career to fit those of a man. And she wouldn't.

"You had your fun, both of you. Now go run back home to play the role of lying, calculating, but oh-so-dutiful son." She hopped in Frida who was more loyal than any man she'd met, and for the second time in eighteen or so hours, she squealed down the road, not looking back, tears blinding her.

"Arrrrrrrrrgh," Rohan bent over and howled, gripping his hair.

He sucked in breath after breath and spit the extra saliva that accumulated in his mouth. His stomach heaved, and he had to swallow down the bile mixed with chai—all he'd consumed over the past eighteen plus hours.

"Oh, Ro." Rani rubbed his back in circles. "Oh. Ro."

He finally stood up. "I hate that she's right," he whispered.

"What do you mean? You fell for her right from the beginning. I tried to convince you to back away from the car wreck, but it was like trying to separate gravity."

"But I didn't understand what I had with her. I didn't realize what a rare gift I had inadvertently and undeservedly been handed. I didn't think it was real or could be permanent. I did keep her separate from my real," he scowled and made air quotes. "life. I didn't make myself or my feelings clear to my parents. I thought I would just ride it out, have fun while it lasted. But almost from the beginning I was in so deep with Solei. I knew I didn't want to consider being matched. I thought it was about having time and freedom, but it was about Solei. Her. I didn't tell her. I didn't cherish her. And I let her down. She thinks I used her, and I did. I did." He felt gutted and he faced Rani, feeling angry at himself and helpless. "I can't imagine my life without her in it," he told Rani. "I don't want to."

"Tell her," Rani said. "She's hurt. She's scared. She needs

time to process but go lay yourself bare to her. She's so deep in love with you. That doesn't just fall away with one F-up."

"She's not ready to listen. I need to show her. I need to make like a grand gesture."

"No. Don't. Leave the melodrama to me and your mom. Just talk to Solei."

"Dammit. Just dammit." He walked in a circle. "Where the hell did she go?" A sudden horrible thought hit him. He'd seen two boxes in the van. She wasn't leaving was she? He ran to the gate leading to the backyard and opened it. He peered through the windows. But he wasn't sure what was hers or part of the rental. She'd told him she traveled light. What if…he spied her drafting table with papers clipped on it, and one of the rolling carts that she had with her art supplies in it. He pressed his face against the cool glass, and just breathed.

She hadn't left. Yet.

He had to think.

He had to plan.

He walked back slowly to the front of the house. That's when he noticed the three spray cans in the gutter. He didn't really formulate a thought or a plan. He swooped up the cans on instinct. He felt feral.

"Rohan, what are you doing? Are you nuts? Rohan, this is like totally illegal. You're…you're defacing private property."

Rani's voice was far in the background as he pointed the

first spray can that he'd picked up at Solei's garage door. He kept his finger on the trigger and let the colors flow out of him.

"I can't believe this. What is wrong with you? Rohan, you have to stop."

But he was on a roll, and he didn't care.

"I've played by the rules my entire life and look where it got me."

"Risking arrest and losing your entire career that you haven't even officially started," Rani yelped, hopping up and down at his side.

"Alone," he corrected. "I followed other people's plans for my life, never mine."

"So, what, now you're an artist? A criminal? Rohan, you have to stop."

He'd created a giant sun with flames shooting out. He pocketed the yellow. What was next. He aimed the can. He was doing this all wrong, but damn it felt good, right in a way he hadn't felt unless he was with Solei. Pink. He could work with that. He did a rough painting of a working heart. And then began to spray out words that flowed from his heart.

"Rohan, you have to stop. You have to. You're going to get in trouble."

"Bring it on."

"OMG. You're bewitched. You've lost your mind. Rohan." She tugged the can out of his fingers that were now paint-stained. He felt authentic. The painting sucked in skill, but it was the most authentic thing he'd done in his entire life. The most honest moment he'd lived.

"OMG," Rani looked at the garage door, her face comedically horrified. Satisfaction filled him.

Rohan snapped a picture of his work with his phone. Then he sent the picture to Solei.

This is me with you. You make me whole. You make me a better version of me.

"I'm expressing my feelings."

Rani huffed out a breath. "Give me those, you crazy, crazy man in love. Go get your girl." She grabbed the last spray can out of his pocket and tucked it under her arm with the others.

The high from his unexpected crime scene ebbed a little. "I don't know where Solei is," he said sadly. "Her drafting table is still here so she's coming back. I'll just sit here stalker style until she comes home. Keep trying until she believes me. When I want something, I go for it, and Solei is critical to my survival."

Rani sighed in exasperation. "I never pictured you playing drama queen. Not ever."

"Not playing. And all those questions you answered for me, Rani, are you really sure that's who I am?"

"No," she whispered. Then she rallied. "You'll probably be arrested if you stay here. Go home. Give Solei some time to process, and if she doesn't call the police when she gets home, you can talk to her later."

"No, I need her now. I can't live in this limbo without her knowing how much she means to me."

Rani hissed, pulled her phone from her pocket and looked at it.

"Oh. She's here." She held out an Instagram post. "Impromptu mural. She's invited the kids at that arts center where she volunteers—the one that hosted the multimedia..." Rani broke off as Rohan kissed the top of her head and ran to his car.

"You rock," he called out and zoomed away, leaving Rani standing in the road with the spent spray cans tucked close to her body.

SOLEI STARED AT the blank wall. For once no images crowded in her imagination seeking release. She shook the spray paint can, a shocking raspberry pink—a color she would always associate with Rohan—trying to think of something, anything just so she could feel like herself again. This had seemed like such a good idea—escape the house and her thoughts only now she was outside, in public, with the potential of an audience and some of her students showing up to create, and she couldn't be a desert of ideas.

If she were home, she could play around until something happened, but out in public the pressure was intense.

"C'mon, Solei, you're better than this. Breathe out the

doubt, girl."

Her phone buzzed with a message. One of her students? God, she had to pull it together. She pulled her phone out of her back pocket and blinked at the image. A sun. A beating anatomically correct heart and words in the arteries. She read the words over and over again.

Wait. "Is that my garage?" She stared at the picture, willing the weathered gray barn-style double doors with the roses climbing a trellis to morph into something else. But no. It was her garage door. Rohan had painted a mural on her garage door that was only hers for another month. July first she had to find a new place to live.

"Holy cow," she whispered, scrolling closer on different parts of the picture.

Rohan who'd said he knew nothing about art, who couldn't remember doing anything artistic beyond early elementary school, who had gamely tried to loosen up and play word and shape games with her a couple of months ago at the art festival had painted her a picture—her as the sun and him the beating heart with the arteries wrapping around the sun and the words flowing through.

And something inside of her broke.

People were capable of tremendous change.

Rohan may have started out thinking they were only playing, that this was temporary. He'd never made any promises to her beyond spring. But just as her feelings had consumed her quickly, perhaps his too had changed. But she hadn't trusted him.

She'd shut him down because she'd been afraid of how intensely she felt.

So he'd drawn her a picture.

"Solei."

Startled, she looked up. He was there. Still crisply beautiful. His fingers a multicolor of yellow, pink and lavender.

"I'm sorry I hurt you. I'm so, so, so very sorry. I'd rather stab myself than hurt you. I wasn't completely open, or honest with my words. My head was playing games with me, not you, but my heart was and is and always will be yours."

She gave up trying to resist and went where she belonged, into his arms.

He smelled so good. Felt so warm. She blinked back tears.

"The night Asha's engagement fell apart my mother had hired a matchmaker to try to mitigate the scandal—give people something else to talk about. I told her no. I told her I wasn't ready. I wanted freedom. Time alone, but then I met you, and freedom and being alone and traveling were the last things I wanted. I only wanted you. From the first moment I saw you I was changed. Transfixed. All I wanted was you. All I want is you."

She pressed her tear-wet face into his shirt, hoping that her nose wasn't going to get snotty. She'd cried so much last night even as she'd tried to hold back, she should be totally dehydrated now—no tears left, but they flowed—only this time, they were happy tears.

"I did meet with the matchmaker, but again, that was my mother ambushing me. To think is to act with my mother. The day after I met you, I was hoping to see you in the afternoon, and while I was getting dressed, my mother was touring Mrs. Bukar around our house. I was trapped into a palm reading. My family all weighed in on what I wanted in a wife, not letting me get a word in edgewise, and I finally escaped—to you. I've been dodging them since. I could have balled up better in that department, but..." He sighed and kissed her hair. "I've always been a pleaser, not a boat rocker like Rani and in her own assassin way, Shanti. I'm more like Asha—watchful, low key, get shit done right the first time. I had never been in love. I didn't know what had hit me when I met you. I was consumed."

"Me too." She looked up at him. "Only I didn't have to deal with any parental or grandparent expectations. They all believe in living your life the way you want and trying to do some good in the world."

"I'm on board with that, Solei. I'm all in. Please, you have to believe me. I'm all in." His eyes shimmered with sincerity. "I'm not just saying that out of sheer desperation, although I feel desperate." He smiled ruefully. "But I plan to prove it to you. I plan to show you how much I love you. That you are my first and only choice over and over again. God," he rested his forehead against hers. She could feel his heart slam against hers, and she felt like she could take a full breath again.

"I love you, Solei. I want you to meet my family. I want you to be my family. I want you. Can you please, please, please, give me a second chance? I won't need another. Please forgive me. Allow me to prove how much you mean to me over and over again."

A few students started to pull up in different cars and a couple on bikes and a few more on skateboards.

"Showtime," she murmured.

"Is that a yes?" he asked, still looking worried.

She smiled because her sun once again shone brightly. She leaned up to kiss him, whispering just before her lips met his. "Hard yes."

"OH, WOW," SOLEI breathed as a valet approached their car. Rohan was out in a moment, handing off his keys and opening the door for her. His smile knocked her sideways, and she had to gulp in a breath to try to calm the nerves that buzzed through her like hummingbirds.

He held out his hand to help her out.

"Still not used to that," she murmured—the opening of doors, seating her, helping her out of the car, handing her in.

"Get used to it. I'm seizing any excuse to touch you."

"You didn't say you grew up in a mansion," she said in a low voice.

"That's because I didn't." He slid his arm around her. "My parents and aunt and uncle bought the property about five years ago and built the houses sort of like a compound. It's huge and over the top, but they entertain often, and both sets of grandparents live with us, and when family comes from India, they're here for a month so all the space makes sense."

She nodded. She'd been expecting a graduation party— not something that looked like a celebrity bash at a five-star resort. She could see what looked like over a hundred people on the lush lawn that sprawled out toward the glittering lake. There was a large dock and a stone outdoor patio where people were laughing, talking and drinking. And dozens more on the large deck. The women looked so glamorous in their brightly colored saris and shewar chemizes.

She smoothed her hand down her emerald-green sheath-style dress that had hand-painted ceramic buttons up to mid-thigh on one side. Yup. She'd gone shopping again. She'd left the buttons unbuttoned to her knee.

"You look beautiful," his voice was deep in her ear. "I love your hair up in a twist like that. It makes me think of how it will look later—after the party, flowing down your back and how it will feel against my skin."

Solei tried to swallow, but her throat and mouth felt dry.

"Maybe I shouldn't give her the painting tonight," she said as Rohan opened the trunk. "She'll be so busy and..." Solei trailed off. She'd wanted to bring a hostess gift, and she'd started working on this one their first night back together—not that they'd broken up for that long, but it had felt different. They'd talked until nearly two am at her house. Rohan had caught a couple of hours of sleep before heading back home to the hospital.

At least they wouldn't be two hours apart for much longer.

She'd been worried about his driving and working on so little sleep, but he said he was used to it—residency was like a six-year boot camp. So while she'd worried, she'd started to sketch and then play and then envision artwork unlike anything she'd ever done before.

"Even though you didn't let me have a peek at it yet, I know she'll love it," Rohan assured her, picking up the painting and holding it by the wire that she'd left out of the wrapping paper. There was a card taped on front.

"But this is her night to launch you."

"Think of all the work you've saved her. I launched myself, although I am jelly that she has a B. Solei original before I do."

"You have the whole artist."

He laughed and laced his fingers with hers. "Feel free to glue yourself to my side tonight. These parties can be overwhelming."

"I just might since I don't know anyone else here but Rani."

"You'll be fine. You're more socially adept than I am.

Kiss for good luck." He turned her toward him at the front door.

She searched his eyes. She wasn't really that nervous. She was too happy to be nervous. He kissed her. She didn't care about the party or that she'd worn lipstick and that they were standing at the front door. She melted in the kiss and held on to her man.

The door was flung open wide. "Caught you kissing," Rani sang out. "Thank you, Ring. It's the guest of honor!"

Solei scrambled to peel herself off of Rohan. With her thumb she wiped at a bit of lipstick on his lip. "Do I look ravished?" he whispered in her ear and tugged her inside the house.

And then it was chaos. So many people rushing forward, greeting Rohan, slapping his back, everyone talking at once.

"Hold tight."

MAYBE HE SHOULD have sprung his surprise on Solei earlier when they'd been alone, but he'd wanted to wait until later with all of his family around them. Make another grand gesture, although making him buy another identical garage door because Solei had refused to let him paint over his first mural attempt, had impressed her.

He kept a tight hold of her hand, determined to introduce her properly to his parents and grandparents at least as they entered the house.

"Finally. Your mother has been peering out the windows for the past hour, Rohan," his father greeted him. "Late for your own party." He hugged him. "The whiskey is nearly gone."

Like that would ever happen at his father's or uncle's house.

"Papa, this is Solei Beals."

His father greeted with a namaste.

"Welcome, welcome. Let me get you a drink. Rani has created something she says is epic. Likely she will poison us all. I've reminded the bartenders that I am paying them, not Rani."

"Uncle, I found the recipe online. It's safe. Your guests are safe," Rani said. She hugged Solei. "I love your dress. Prepare to lose it."

"What?"

"You'll see. It's a Kapoor thing. Asha! Shanti! Mom! Dad! Auntie! Solei is here."

"So am I," Rohan drawled, happy to see that Solei had relaxed. Rani was good at breaking any tension. And creating it.

"Rohan, you are late. Sneaking in," His mom excused herself from the group she was chatting with and approached. He held Solei's hand and pulled her a little forward. A fairly massive crowd had gathered around to be introduced. Shanti and Asha looked stunning. His nanima fussed over Solei, exclaiming in Punjabi how pretty she was.

"English, Mama." His mom kissed both his cheeks. "Congratulations, Doctor and Professor," she whispered, and then her gaze fell to Solei.

"Mom, this is Solei." He felt a little out of breath as if he'd done a hard uphill run although he'd only crossed from the foyer into the great room.

"Welcome to our home," his mom said, standing formally next to his father, who'd joined her.

"Thank you. I…ah…made you a painting," Solei said, stepping forward, squaring her shoulders and smiling, her eyes crinkling at the corners, which he always thought made her look so happy and adorable. She took the wrapped painting from his fingers. "I was not sure of the colors of your home, so I chose the colors that Rohan inspires in me. I wanted to thank you both for creating such a wonderful man who lights up my life. He is so kind and giving. He makes me laugh and think and has the heart of an adventurer and the soul of a healer and poet."

Rohan's eyes prickled. Holy hard no was he going to cry in front of his family and people who'd known him his entire life as well as some of his friends and new colleagues at his own frickin' party.

"Oh." His mother teared up, crossing her hands up high on her chest.

"Rohan has been a gift of a son, and I want you to know that I too treasure him," Solei said and handed the wrapped present to his mother.

His mother's hands shook. "You do it." She handed it to her husband. He struggled with the tape, the folds and the string. Rohan brought out the Swiss Army Knife Solei had bought him and handed it to his father, who cut the twine.

His mom eased the paper off of the painting.

People leaned forward to see.

"Solei," he breathed shocked, touched, impressed and embarrassed and so damn proud of her all at the same time.

It was the most unusual and unexpected portrait he could imagine. It was a painting of him, and yet it was built up with some kind of epoxy so that it was three dimensional. There were also items—representing significant aspects of his life—a concert ticket, a tassel from med school, embedded in the portrait almost like it was a treasure map, or a time capsule. A verse from a Hindi prayer scrolled down the side. The picture had a geometric design—pieces making up a whole man. Him.

"You painted this for me?" his mother whispered finally.

Rohan could only stare at it. From a distance, he looked like a portrait, but up close, it was tiny shapes, images, items that made up his life. How the hell had she created such an incredible piece of art? He was utterly humbled. It far outshone his gift to her burning a hole in his pocket. When had she had the time? She'd been wrapping up her classes and classroom. Packing up her house. Looking up rentals online although he was hoping that she'd stay with him until they could find a house to rent or buy together.

He was taking two weeks off before starting his job. The first week they were going to take Frida and hike and camp for a few days along the Appalachian Trail and then they'd booked a beach front house on Kiawah Island for another few days.

"I painted it for both of you," Solei said. "To show you how I see your son."

Rohan tried to look at the painting more closely, but his mom was bent toward the painting, clutching it tightly. From what he could see, it was fairly large. The background was a dark peacock blue shot through with raspberry pink and gold. His head and shoulders were partially painted, and partially created from tiny pictures of him or of things. He could see that he had his hand out, palm up, and words and pictures were in his palm—probably Rani's influence with all of her psychological questions and palm reading one afternoon when Rani had met Solei for an afterwork coffee.

"I googled you," his mother looked up at Solei. "Your work wasn't anything like this. You do huge murals on buildings or city infrastructure."

"I still will. This is new to me. Rohan has inspired me. I feel as if my art will keep evolving with me. And I'm going to be teaching studio arts at a high school in Chapel Hill in the fall."

"Teaching? Why? You make a lot of money from your paintings."

Pink tinged Solei's cheeks. He jumped in quickly before his mom could do more damage. "Because she loves teaching," he said. "And don't ask about money. Are you planning on selling my portrait?"

"No, of course not." His mom couldn't stop staring at the painting. She looked at Solei, and then back to the painting. "A famous artist has painted a portrait of my son, Rohan," she called out, and Rohan wanted to take Solei and run. So typical. "We need to hang the picture. Show everyone. Right now. Rani find nails. We must have some and a…what do you call it…a hammer. That's it."

"Mom, I think it can wait until tomorrow."

But his mom was determined and a debate ensued. Over the fireplace. In the entryway. On the side wall between the windows. The wall going up the stairs. She and his father and a few aunties and uncles walked around the house with purpose. Friends joined in.

"Can I get you a drink?" he asked Solei suddenly. Now? He'd debated timing. Location. Public versus private. What would she prefer? What would make the biggest statement? He hated that he had to think of others when it should be personal, but he wanted Solei to know and his family and community to know that he was all in. She was his. He was hers.

"Sure. We are celebrating you."

But before he could walk her out to the deck where one of the bartenders was set up, his mother was back with Anju

Auntie, Nanima, Mummji, Shanti, Asha and Rani. Both Rani and Shanti held cocktails in both hands.

"Come, come, Solei." His mother put her arm around her. "We need to get you changed for the party."

Solei looked startled.

"Warned you," Rani laughed. "Time to lose the dress. This is an Indian slap down party all in, girl."

"But…" he started to object. She looked delectable.

"Darling, go greet our guests. Circulate." His mom made a gesture like her hand was a paddle on a mixer. "We will take care of Solei."

Rani handed Solei a cocktail. "I asked the bartender to make it extra strong. Cheers!"

Solei looked at him, her eyebrow slightly raised in question.

"He'll still be here when we come down," his mom said drily. "That much is clear." And then his mom, her arm linked with Solei's, headed upstairs to the master suite, and Rohan had a last look at the long, slim, graceful line of Solei's back and the swish of her rounded bottom as she climbed the wide, curved staircase.

"Lucky bastard," Rakesh said, joining him along with Dhruv. Both drank beer and Rohan wished he had one. Rani's strong cocktails were legend, but Rohan needed his wits. The three of them had been friends forever although Dhruv had always kept himself apart from their social circle, but he and Dhruv had often DJed raves and clubs and house parties together in high school. He'd snuck out. Dhruv had sauntered, wearing his rebel and bad boy label along with a motorcycle-style leather jacket with arrogant, aloof pride.

Rohan spotted a server with beer, and he flagged her over.

A lot of people were watching them. Dhruv and his father hadn't been in the same circle, and he'd only recently returned to Charlotte after serving improbably in the army.

"Thanks for coming." Rohan put his arm around his friend.

"Hope your girl's wearing panties. Didn't look like it."

"You shouldn't be looking that closely," Rohan objected. But was she? The dress had been very formfitting. And long. She wouldn't have worried about flashing anyone.

"Just looking out for my brother."

"That's fine as long as you're not checking out Solei's ass."

"Pistols at dawn, boys?" Rakesh drawled.

"Too easy," Dhruv drawled, finishing his beer. He'd been special forces, a sharpshooter. "Rapiers. Bound to be a couple around in this museum."

Rohan laughed. His parents' house did take some getting used to. His mother loved to decorate, and she'd brought in a professional so that the house looked more like a showroom than an actual lived-in house.

"Ready to face your fans? Deep breath." Rakesh nudged him toward where the biggest crowds were—out of the massive lawn and garden area. Both houses had been pressed into service for the party and round tables seating eight had been set up over both lawns. There were two buffets of catered Indian food, and three bars, including a small one down on the patio by the dock.

"I should wait for Solei."

"They'll be hours," Rakesh said. "Besides in that jacket you'll be easy to spot."

"Not that your mom will let her go. She'll probably parade her around and talk about the bank Solei earns for her art. I googled her too. You are a lucky bastard, Rohan. You're the only man who could flip their parental expectations the bird but bring home an artist who easily vaults over six figures in a bad year."

"I definitely should wait for her." Rohan's worry kicked into overdrive. What if Solei changed her mind about him after being swallowed by his family? What if she weren't wearing panties? Maybe he should text Rani to...

"She'll be fine," Rakesh said, swiping his phone. "If she's going to swim with sharks, she's going to have to learn to bite back."

"I knew you were into the kink." Dhruv snagged another bottle of beer as they went out on the deck. "Shanti know that about you?"

"Shanti eats men for lunch," Rohan warned.

"Now that sounds fun," Dhruv laughed. "Ready for the gauntlet? Maybe people will think I'm your bodyguard," he mused.

"Hey," Rohan stopped him. "You're my friend. You've always had my back and I've got yours. Thanks for coming. I know you didn't want to."

It was clear that Dhruv would have preferred to be anywhere else. But he was home now. He was a fireman in Charlotte's metro service. And Rohan wanted him to feel welcome after being in the service for so many deployments.

"Let's do it." Rohan, with his two best friends, stepped out into the crowd, public face on, but his attention was on what was happening to Solei upstairs.

SOLEI TWIRLED IN the mirror looking at the flair of the lime-green and gold lehenga.

"This one is beautiful as well," she said, a little overwhelmed by the choices. Rohan's mom had laid out five and then six and then seven fashion choices—from a sari, Salwar Kameez and now this, a lehenga, which was her personal favorite. She loved long skirts, although she rarely had a chance to dress up, and they weren't practical with her work.

"Definitely the lehenga," Rani said. "You should show off all the hard work you do on your abs."

"Shshsh," both Rani's and Rohan's moms chastised her. Then they laughed. "It's true. You should show off what you have when you have it. Once the children come..." Rani's mom shook her head. "No matter how often you hit the gym it's hard to get your skin to snap back."

Solei did feel a little exposed with the shimmery bra top showing off so much of her pale tummy and bare arms. And she didn't quite have the hang of the long graceful scarf that the other women seemed to effortlessly keep in place, so that when they did gracefully adjust the long, colorful and glitteringly material, it was more of a conversational statement. An attitude. She liked that they talked about her future with Rohan like they accepted it and that it was assured.

"Wear that one," Shanti said, definitively walking a circle around Solei. "You look fantastic, and it's the latest fashion. Plus, the color is dynamite with your eyes. Let's get back to the party."

"Shanti, no rush. She must have jewelry."

Solei felt like royalty as several gold and pearl and gold collar-style necklaces were brought out and displayed along with dangling earrings. She felt overwhelmed by the choices and touched that Rohan's mother would let her wear something so personal.

She ended up choosing chandelier-style pearl and gold filigree earrings and then a simple pearl pendant. She liked the simple chain and had felt too gaudy with so much twenty-two karat gold around her neck. It felt too constraining, like a collar.

"There. Perfect."

One of Rohan's grandmothers stepped forward and took a gold and pearl bangle off her wrist and put it on Solei's. She smiled and blessed her.

"Now you are perfect," she said softly. "Time for the party."

If Solei had thought that she would be reunited with Rohan, she was massively wrong. Rohan's mother introduced her to so many people she had no hope of keeping anyone straight. But she was never alone. Either one of Rohan's cousins or his mother kept her engaged with conversation. And even though she'd been encouraged to eat by many people and the food looked and smelled delicious, Solei never got within a fork's distance of it as there was always someone else to meet and chat with.

No wonder Rohan's cousins and mom and aunt stayed so thin.

The party started to wind down sometime after midnight. Rohan snuck up behind her. "Finally, I can have you back." His breath was warm in her ear.

She turned into him, enjoying his warmth. The night was starting to cool and instead of letting her scarf drape down her back, she'd taken it to wrapping it more like a shawl around her shoulders.

"Did you have a good time?"

"Fantastic. But I would have liked to have spent the time with you."

"Me too, but your family was amazing. So generous,

lending me jewelry and the dress."

"Probably more than a loan, but you'll get used to them."

"I thought there'd be more of a pushback with you bringing me here."

Rohan laid his forehead lightly against hers. She loved when he did that. It was so sweet and intimate, not at all sexual. And she loved the way he held her. She felt such a sense of belonging.

"That's on me," he said softly. "My parents are traditional in some ways even though they've been in the US since college. Their marriage was arranged and so I think they were just reverting to what had worked for them. Plus, I'd never brought anyone home before, so they didn't have any guidance from me. None of this was about them not accepting you. It was more about getting me in their minds safely settled."

He kissed her forehead. "G-rating for now."

She laughed and he led her to the patio by the dock. The lake looked so dark and mysterious whereas earlier there had been a lot of boats out and Rohan's dad and uncle had been giving guests rides around the lake.

"Finally, some quiet and alone time." He dropped down on a swing, pulling Solei onto his lap. She cuddled close and pressed her cheek against his chest. Something dug into her hip.

"Ouch," she shifted and reached for the pocket of his

jacket to move it out of the way. He caught her hand and brought it to his lips. Then he adjusted his clothing so that nothing was poking her.

She spied Rani with a plate of food followed by her two sisters, also carrying plates of food, following her across the lawn.

"There goes our alone and quiet," she said.

He played with her hair. "I knew they'd come. The rest of my family will likely make their way here soon."

He sounded rather smug. She'd thought he wanted to be alone. He'd seemed to want to avoid his family when they'd first started dating. Now he seemed content to full-body immerse. Not that she minded. She loved that he was happy, relaxed.

"If you want to stay here tonight instead of at my place, we can," Solei said. "Your mom showed me the three separate en suite guest rooms and then the downstairs. You were right it's a whole separate house that they built for you. Amazing. I bet that was hard to say no to."

"Not really," he laughed. "Although I didn't seriously consider any jobs that were farther than a two- or three-hour drive home," he admitted. "Are you okay with that? With them?"

"Of course," she sat up a little off of him, but he pulled her back so that she was flush with his body. "They are your family." She looked up at him, playing with his hair a little. She loved its silky texture.

"They are nosy, bossy, interfering."

"Involved. Loving."

"True, but your family's far away. You're not used to having anyone up in your business."

"And now you have us," Rani jumped into the conversation. She handed Solei a plate. "That's to share with Ro if you feel like it." She gracefully sank into a chair opposite them. Shanti and Asha joined them. And within minutes there was quite a collection of Rohan's family, including his grandmother who sat next to them on the swing, smiling at Solei and touching her cheeks and then the bracelet.

"Here goes," Rohan whispered in her ear and kissed her cheek before sliding off the swing and effortlessly picking her up and placing her back down on the swing.

He knelt one knee down in front of her. Solei stared at him, totally confused, and then her breath caught in her throat. No. Way.

"Solei, meeting you was the most unexpected experience of my life. From the first moment I saw you I felt like the sun had come out, and I was finally in the right place at the right time. Every moment that I have known you has only strengthened my feelings for you and my hopes that you will share your life with me—your dreams and goals and triumphs and sorrows. I want to share the same with you and want us to build a life together, be a family together."

She stared down at his beloved face, beautiful eyes shining with love and hope.

"Yes," she whispered.

"Aren't you supposed to have a blingy ring?" Shanti

leaned forward.

"Oh. Yes. That," Rohan laughed. "I jumped the gun."

Everyone laughed, even Solei, although she felt so stunned—not that she doubted her feelings or his for a moment, but Rohan didn't seem the impulsive type at all.

Rohan reached into his pocket and pulled out a light blue box.

"Solei, I very much want to be your husband. Will you please marry me?"

"He's always been a polite boy," his nanima murmured.

"Yes," she said again barely looking at the beautiful solitaire diamond in the platinum setting.

"Is that a yes or a medium yes or a hard yes?" he teased, slipping the ring on her finger.

"Hard yes." She looped her arms around his neck and pulled him back on the couch. She kissed him.

She heard cheers and a couple of pops of champagne corks, but she held on to Rohan, breathed him in.

"I love you so much," she said in a rush. "Marrying you is a very hard and permanent yes."

The End

Don't miss Shanti and Rakesh's story in
Swipe Right for Marriage!

Join Tule Publishing's newsletter for more great reads and weekly deals!

If you enjoyed *A Hard Yes*,
you'll love the next books in the…

Misguided Masala Matchmaker series

Book 1: *A Hard Yes*

Book 2: *Swipe Right for Marriage*
Coming in September 2022

Book 3: *An Unsuitable Boy*
Coming in January 2023

Book 4: *Stealing Mr. Right*
Coming in May 2023

Available now at your favorite online retailer!

More books by Sinclair Jayne

Montana Rodeo Brides series

Book 1: *The Cowboy Says I Do*
Book 2: *The Cowboy's Challenge*
Book 3: *Breaking the Cowboy's Rules*

The Texas Wolf Brothers series

Book 1: *A Son for the Texas Cowboy*
Book 2: *A Bride for the Texas Cowboy*
Book 3: *A Baby for the Texas Cowboy*

The Wilder Brothers series

Book 1: *Seducing the Bachelor*
Book 2: *Want Me, Cowboy*
Book 3: *The Christmas Challenge*
Book 4: *Cowboy Takes All*

Available now at your favorite online retailer!

About the Author

Sinclair Sawhney is a former journalist and middle school teacher who holds a BA in Political Science and K-8 teaching certificate from the University of California, Irvine and a MS in Education with an emphasis in teaching writing from the University of Washington. She has worked as Senior Editor with Tule Publishing for over seven years.

Writing as Sinclair Jayne she's published fifteen short contemporary romances with Tule Publishing with another four books being released in 2021. Married for over twenty-four years, she has two children, and when she isn't writing or editing, she and her husband, Deepak, are hosting wine tastings of their pinot noir and pinot noir rose at their vineyard Roshni, which is a Hindi word for light-filled, located in Oregon's Willamette Valley. Shaandaar!

Thank you for reading

A Hard Yes

If you enjoyed this book, you can find more from all our great authors at TulePublishing.com, or from your favorite online retailer.